Please return / renew this item by the last date shown above
Dychwelwch / Adnewyddwch erbyn y dyddiad olaf y nodir yma

First published in Great Britain in 2020 by Boldwood Books Ltd.

Copyright © Kirsty Ferguson, 2020

Cover Design: Nick Castle Design

Cover Photography: Shutterstock

Every effort has been made to obtain the necessary permissions with reference to copyright material, both illustrative and quoted. We apologise for any omissions in this respect and will be pleased to make the appropriate acknowledgements in any future edition.

A CIP catalogue record for this book is available from the British Library.

Paperback ISBN 978-1-80048-152-7

Large Print ISBN 978-1-83889-878-6

Ebook ISBN 978-1-83889-876-2

Kindle ISBN 978-1-83889-877-9

Audio CD ISBN 978-1-83889-883-0

MP3 CD ISBN 978-1-83889-880-9

Digital audio download ISBN 978-1-83889-875-5

Boldwood Books Ltd
23 Bowerdean Street
London SW6 3TN
www.boldwoodbooks.com

For mum, a survivor

PART I

1

Life wasn't meant to be easy. This was the realization that Vanessa Sawyer had come to. Nothing in her life had turned out the way she had planned, except motherhood, and even then, it had not been an easy road. But she loved her kids, Wren and Ty. They had saved her; they were the reason she woke up in the morning.

She'd married young, just gone eighteen. Mark, her husband, had been in her year at high school and had been dating her best friend Maggie for months. He was nice, charming, popular, and she'd had a crush on him for a while. Looking back, Vanessa could now admit that it was him who had put this whole thing in motion, but she had allowed it by letting herself be swayed by his advances. And she had paid for it.

The high-school dance. An evening of supposedly innocent fun, that ended up staying with Vanessa forever. Maggie left the dance early, saying she didn't feel well. Mark called her parents to ask them to come and get her. Tucking her into the back seat of the car, he kissed her cheek like a good boyfriend. A truly good boyfriend would have driven her home himself, but he didn't want to. That much was obvious. Perhaps Vanessa's entire relationship with Mark would never have happened had he driven Maggie home, but then she would never have fallen pregnant with Wren, her beautiful boy. When Mark strolled back into the hall, his eyes caught hers. He reached for her upper arm and held it firmly. She felt the electricity between them, the thrill of the unexpected and forbidden. He rubbed his thumb along her skin in a way that was entirely too familiar. She tried to pull away.

'Come with me,' he said, just loud enough so only she could hear him. Vanessa saw the heat, the desire in his eyes as he led her out into the cool evening air. Outside, the thumping music was muted, and fractured clouds streamed across the moon, casting dappled light onto their clandestine meeting.

Mark pushed a tendril of hair from Vanessa's face and tucked it behind her ear. Again, she felt the magnetism of his illicit touch. His fingers trailed lightly down her cheek, coming to rest on her shoulder. His other hand slid protectively around her waist as he pulled her close, like a real lover, swaying her gently, slow dancing with her under the privacy of the evening sky. At that moment, she felt like she was the only girl in the world. Nothing bad could ever happen to her. She was pretty, popular, and worthy of being in Mark's arms. Her body begged for his touch, craved it. She wanted to taste him, run her hands over his body, claim what wasn't hers to claim. She knew it was wrong, but she could no more leave the comfort of his arms than the sun could stop its ascent into the breaking morning sky. It was only the two of them, locked in an embrace that threatened to tear their worlds apart. Vanessa molded her body to his. Her heart raced as his hand moved lower, curving over her hip. The universe didn't exist outside of their bubble; a bubble she wasn't going to break.

Small towns had their secrets, and this was just one more to be kept, guarded by some unseen force. Vanessa should have known that nothing ever stayed truly hidden, buried, but in that heady moment, held tenderly in Mark's arms, she couldn't care less. Let the world do its worst. She knew from Maggie's whispered confessions under the cover of darkness that she and Mark had never done *it*. Maggie had stated firmly that she'd never 'fuck' until she was married. Her parents were religious whereas Vanessa's parents trusted her to make good choices, and swaying in Mark's arms as he nuzzled her neck, this felt like a good but dangerous one. Her heart was cleaved down the middle. Which should she choose – loyalty or lust?

'You want this as much as I do, Ness,' he whispered into her ear, sending shivers along her spine. Of course she wanted it.

'What about Maggie?' she countered, pulling back and looking at him, their lustful gazes locked together.

'I haven't been happy in ages; I just didn't know how to tell her. I'm ready to dump her, but it would be better if I had someone else to be with, to go to. It would make it easier. Are you gonna be that girl, Ness?' He brushed her lips with his, just a whisper of a touch, but it was enough. She groaned a little, her defenses crumbling.

'Yes,' she whispered.

'You'll be mine?'

'Yes.'

The night breeze picked up, causing goose bumps to cover Vanessa's arms. Mark suggested that they get into the back of his van and warm up. 'We could... talk some more.'

She nodded and followed him inside. There was an old, narrow pine bench seat bolted to the floor, and a mattress covered in a sheet taking up the rest of the back of the van.

'That seat is a bit hard,' Mark said. He dropped onto the mattress. 'This is much more comfortable. Why don't you come and sit by me?'

He made no attempt to hide the lust on his face; it showed in the way he smiled and how his gaze hovered over her figure before locking with her eyes.

Suddenly a pang of guilt tore through Vanessa.

'I should go.'

Mark saw the indecision on her face. 'I need you. Don't go.' His voice had a vulnerable note to it, and she turned back, staring at him. She could still hear the music, just, and closed her eyes for a moment. She opened them again when she heard soft music coming from inside the van. The song's lyrics spoke of everlasting love and how you, too, could have it. Love everlasting. She swayed with the gentle beat, eyes closed, tucking her legs under as she joined Mark on the mattress.

She opened her eyes when she felt Mark's lips on hers again, insistent this time. Her first real kiss. His tongue explored her mouth, and she gasped. She didn't know that her body would respond this way. Mistaking her shock for pleasure, he pulled her closer, kissing her even deeper. One warm hand slid onto her slightly cool knee, traveling slowly up to her thigh where his fingertip drew lazy circles.

Vanessa pulled back when his finger hooked under her underwear. 'I've never felt like this before, Ness.' She loved hearing her nickname fall from his lips. It rolled off his tongue with such ease and possession. Any lingering doubts disappeared like snow on a warm winter's morning. 'There've been others, but they meant nothing to me.'

He kissed the nape of her neck and God help her if it didn't feel like a little piece of heaven. She tilted her head to the side and let out a small giggle. Mark ran his hand down her long and loose hair, pulling on it affectionately. He turned her gently and laid her down on the mattress. She smiled up at him, and he stared back at her with desire in his eyes.

This was really going to happen.

He removed her underwear, then he spread her legs gently and moved in between them. She could feel how hard he was, and she felt light-headed with desire. She had done that to him. Her body. He settled his weight on her, and she let out a small sigh. She realized that her reservations about loyalty and friendship were almost gone. She was here, with him; it was meant to be.

He used one hand to pull down his pants and boxers. She saw him, really saw him, and had a moment of pure terror before he crushed his lips over hers, tongue battling hers in a fierce dance of desire. She felt him guide his cock inside her. She wasn't sure what she was expecting, but the small, sharp pain was over within a moment or two. She began to buck her hips up to meet his thrusts. She'd never done this before, but instinctively she knew what to do. Some primal need in her made her cry out and claw at his back as he drove himself into her. When he leaned in close, she could smell the lingering scent of his aftershave. He thrust harder and faster, Vanessa meeting him each time, their flesh joining together before being drawn apart. She was keenly aware of each moment he was apart from her. She felt the tension building within Mark, within her, something she'd never felt before. He moved in and out of her as rolling waves of passion pushed all thoughts from her mind, breaking down the walls to her heart. She came. Hard. She bit down on his shoulder as he quickly came too.

No longer a virgin, was her first thought, as the realization of what they'd just done dawned on her. Was she good? With a groan, Mark rolled off her, making the breath leave her body where his weight had flattened her into the mattress. She was a woman now, but what the hell was she going to say to Maggie? She struggled to sit up. Mark was pulling his pants back up, fastening them at his waist. She searched for her underwear, quickly pulling them over her legs.

'Will you tell her?' Vanessa asked Mark.

His eyes caught the moonlight, glinting until he turned away from her. 'Sure, baby. Tomorrow.'

Vanessa was buoyed by the thought. She would lose a friend, a best friend, because of her actions, but she would gain Mark.

* * *

Mark hadn't told Maggie the next day as he'd promised he would. She saw them as they kissed in the hallways, Mark tenderly touching Maggie's face the way he'd touched hers the night before. He refused to look at Vanessa. Ignored her. Acted like she didn't even exist. Maggie, in her love bubble, didn't notice the shift in dynamics between the two of them nor the looks of pain on her best friend's face. Vanessa had given up her virginity in the back of a van to a boy that had lied to her. He had never planned to dump Maggie; he'd just wanted to get laid. *To fuck.* It made her sick to her stomach to think of how easily she had been manipulated.

Soon enough, Vanessa stopped hanging around Maggie altogether. It was too hard to be near the lying sack of shit that was her boyfriend. Mark's cheating weighed heavily on Vanessa's mind and with each passing day, she felt the urge to confess to Maggie. To unburden herself. Yet, despite the way he had lied to her, Vanessa was still a little in love with Mark, and she hated herself for it. He was her first and she would never forget him. When they went their separate ways after graduation, he'd become just one of the many memories, but in the darkest part of the night, she would admit that he was still worth the agony.

Vanessa only realized that she had missed a few periods

during class six months later. Fun fact: learning that you're pregnant during health class is horrific. Her face flushed a deep shade of red, then turned deathly pale as the reality of her situation overwhelmed her. Her stomach churned as she looked at the diagram projected onto the screen. How could she not have known what was going on? *Fuck!*

She groaned and the guy sitting next to her shot his hand into the air. 'Mr Goode? I think Vanessa's about to throw up.' He moved away from her, leaning to the side, just in case.

She didn't throw up; she hadn't, she must have skipped that stage. This explained so much. The tender breasts, the weight gain, turning her slim frame into a curvy one. Vanessa had just thought she was putting on a bit of weight. It hadn't even occurred to her that she might be pregnant.

She was having Mark's baby. What the fuck was she going to do now?

Well, she couldn't put it off any longer. She was starting to show and wearing a thick jumper over her school dress wasn't going to cut it anymore. She had to tell him, now, before someone else did. She'd have to tell—no, she couldn't think of that right now. She didn't even want to think about *that* conversation.

Vanessa waited until the bell clanged, echoing down the hallway, until most of the people had cleared, until Maggie had gone. Vanessa walked up to him nervously, biting on her bottom lip, brushing loose hair from her face impatiently.

'Mark,' she said, urgency coloring her voice.

'Vanessa,' he said sharply. Gone was 'Ness'. He looked around to make sure that no one was watching them speak. It cut her deeply, the lengths he would go to hurt her. She was his dirty little secret. Well not for much longer. Maggie had finally noticed that her best friend wasn't around as much and blamed herself for letting their friendship slide because she was with Mark.

Vanessa, holding back tears, had told her that wasn't it at all, she was just busy getting ready for final exams.

A baby. How weird it was to even think those words let alone say them out loud to him, yet here she was, about to say them to someone else for the first time.

'I have something to tell you,' Vanessa began.

'What? You want another go? I'm with Maggie.'

'Didn't stop you last time.' The retort left her lips before her brain engaged. His murderous look at being challenged made her step back and put some distance between them. It was now or never. 'I'm pregnant,' she blurted out, snapping her mouth shut after the offending words were in the open.

'It's not mine,' he said immediately.

She had expected him to deny it and he hadn't disappointed. *Coward.*

'Well, I was a virgin before I slept with you and I haven't been with anyone else since. Kinda got scared off men. It's yours, Mark. Congratulations, Daddy.' She shouldn't have baited him, but he deserved it.

He slammed his hand into his locker. 'What the fuck, Ness? How could you let this happen?' he demanded, blowing out a frustrated breath.

'How could *I* let this happen? *You* seduced *me*. Told me lies to get me to sleep with you. Don't you dare blame me.'

Anger flared in his eyes. 'Fuck!' he hissed, running a hand through his hand, pulling hard while he sized up the situation.

'I'm keeping it. The baby, I mean. I'll be graduating soon, and so will you,' she pointed out. 'You need to do the right thing. First, you need to tell Maggie, then your parents. Today.'

His face was a mask of anger, something she had never seen before and hadn't thought him capable of. He'd always seemed nice and sweet, if a little cocky.

'Shit no. I'll lose her.'

'You've already lost her. As soon as she finds out, we've both lost her.' Vanessa wiped a hand over her tired eyes. She wasn't getting much sleep these days. 'It's a matter of when, not if, and it's better coming from both of us. Safety in numbers and all that.' She gave a small smile, but it felt wrong. Once Maggie found out, it would be like a bullet that couldn't be unfired.

'OK.'

'OK, we'll tell her together?' She persisted.

'Yes, goddammit.'

'Tonight. Pick me up at six.' Vanessa walked away without giving him a chance to respond. She heard him smash his fist into the locker again and she wondered what she was getting herself into. *Too late now.*

* * *

Vanessa watched the second hand make yet another rotation, clicking loudly in the still, quiet room. She wasn't eager to do this, but it had to be done all the same. Finally, the hands dragged themselves round to six o'clock. She heard a loud rumble outside and pulled the curtain aside. There was his van, and after a few moments it was evident he wasn't coming to the door to get her.

He revved the engine to get her attention and, as she walked toward his van, she wondered how she had ever thought it was romantic. The three of them had spent a lot of time in that van, going camping, road tripping for the day. It held memories, memories that were going to be overshadowed by worse ones in a few minutes. Poor Maggie. Vanessa felt her stomach constrict, and she wondered if she was going to throw up. Her life, Mark's life and Maggie's life were all going to be irrevocably changed.

Mark didn't say a word as she climbed awkwardly into the

van, not even offering her a hand. Nor did he say anything on the short drive over to Maggie's place. She wanted to be the one who told Maggie. She opened her mouth to say so when he barked. 'I'll do the talking.'

Silently fuming, Vanessa slid out of the van and began dragging her feet toward the front door. Mark strode along in front of her. She didn't want to be here, doing this, anything but this but she, they, had no choice. Vanessa reached past Mark to ring the doorbell, but he pushed her arm away and knocked on the door aggressively.

Knock, knock, knock.

Maggie opened the door. Her eyes widened and her face broke out into a huge grin. 'My two favorite people!' She proclaimed, wedging herself awkwardly between them and throwing her arms around them.

Vanessa didn't think she could possibly feel any lower than she did. She was wrong.

'Come in, guys.' She moved aside to let them pass, Vanessa's rounded belly touching Maggie's taunt one. 'So, are you guys here to discuss my eighteenth birthday party? What do you have planned? I promise I'll act surprised.'

Shit! Maggie's birthday was next weekend. *Happy birthday to you.*

Mark cleared his throat, his voice breaking slightly as he spoke. 'Not exactly. We've... we've come to tell you something.' His face was pale, sallow. 'We... uh... sorry Mags, Vanessa and I. We slept together.'

There. It was out now. He'd told her.

'We're... I'm so very sorry,' Vanessa added.

Maggie's eyes swung from one to the other before a flush of rage raced up her neck to settle on her cheeks. 'You're sorry? You're sorry?' she screamed. She took a swing at Mark, who grabbed her hand easily in his. He held it down to her side.

Despite this, Vanessa knew what was coming but did nothing to stop it. She deserved it. The slap from Maggie's other hand caught her across her left eye. Maggie drew back again, ready to deliver another slap when Mark yelled, 'Stop! She's pregnant!'

Maggie slapped her anyway. Vanessa hadn't been expecting that one and her head rocked backward, neck cracking. Panting, Maggie stopped attacking her.

'Shit, Maggie,' Mark said, staring at his now former girlfriend.

'You're really pregnant?' she asked tearfully.

Vanessa wiped her hand across her lips, tasting metallic blood on her tongue. 'Yeah. We didn't mean for this to happen, Maggie. You have to believe me.'

'It was an accident,' Mark added unhelpfully.

'Oh right. So your cock just fell inside her, huh?' The sarcasm was heavy in Maggie's voice. 'Get the fuck outta my house,' she said through gritted teeth.

'Fine then,' Mark spat. 'Just remember that I tried to do the right thing here,' he said unfairly.

But how could Maggie be expected to react any differently? Vanessa stared forlornly at her best friend.

'You heard me, get the fuck out,' she snarled.

Vanessa turned to leave but felt something lodge itself in her hair, close to her scalp, pulling back hard.

'You fucking whore!' screamed Maggie, pulling so hard that Vanessa fell to the floor. Tears fell silently onto Vanessa's cheeks as she stared up at her old friend. 'How could you?' Maggie was crying too. Noisy, angry tears.

It was like she was possessed, kicking out at Vanessa's legs. Mark raced back into the house, grabbing her around the waist, picking Maggie up.

'Get in the van. Now!' he yelled as Vanessa hobbled out of the house and back to the van, hauling herself in.

A few minutes later Mark slammed the front door and ran down the path, throwing himself in the driver's seat and locking the door as if afraid that Maggie would give chase. Maggie would never forgive either one of them, and Vanessa didn't blame her. They had betrayed her trust in the worst possible way. Vanessa felt a sudden rush in her stomach and opened the door just in time to vomit out into the gutter.

'At least she didn't stab me,' he said. Vanessa didn't know if he was joking or not. She didn't care enough to ask.

'As soon as I tell my parents, they'll insist that we get married when I turn eighteen. I can stay at school until then.'

'You know I've always had a bit of a soft spot for you, Vanessa, but this isn't what I want. I don't want to be a dad. You don't want to be a mom either, do you?' He stared her down, the solution in his eyes.

'Yes, I do and it's too late now anyway.' She held his stare.

He hit the steering wheel. The horn giving out a short beep. 'I'm telling my parents tonight. You should do the same,' Vanessa said.

'I guess I'll call you soon.' He was still trying to get out of it.

'You guess? Tomorrow, Mark. After you've spoken to your parents tonight. Call me.'

He frowned at her and pulled out onto the road. She did love him in a way, but she didn't want him like this. Forced into marriage because of a baby. But this is where they were at and they'd have to make the best of it.

* * *

Vanessa didn't say anything as she hopped out of the van once Mark pulled up outside her house. She slammed the door, hearing it echo down the street. She felt sick about what they'd done to Maggie. She couldn't get her look of betrayal out of her mind. Maybe she never would. It made her feel more nauseous, and she hung on to the hanging flower pot to keep her balance as her world tilted violently. The pot moved wildly under the grip, making her feel even worse.

Mark drove off in a hurry. Home to share the good news with his parents that they were going to be grandparents? She didn't exactly want to tell her parents either, as she knew what they'd say: it would be best if she married him, make the best of a bad situation. Vanessa slid the key into the lock, hesitating. She knew that once she said her piece, nothing would even be the same again.

Her parents were in the kitchen when she quietly unlocked the door.

'Ness, that you?' her mother's voice called out.

Gently, Vanessa rubbed her stomach. There was no way she was getting rid of this baby, no matter what anyone said. She resigned herself to marrying Mark.

'Yeah, Mom,' she said wearily, her feet dragging as she headed into the kitchen, 'it's me.' It was a wonder that her mom hadn't noticed her growing frame, the stretched-out school jumper that had seen better days.

'Come on, dinner's ready.' Her mom bustled around the table, putting plates down on the place mats.

Slowly, Vanessa pulled out her chair but hung onto the back of it tightly as her mom sat down. Her parents looked up at her expectantly when they saw she wasn't sitting.

'You OK, Ness?' asked her mom, frown lines creasing her beautiful face. Her mom was her rock. Her best friend in the world, yet Vanessa felt as though she couldn't share this secret with her, that she'd be somehow diminished in her mom's eyes.

'I need to tell you both something and I need to do it while I still have the nerve.' The wooden rail of the chair dug into her palms, and she wondered if she'd have splinters when she broke contact.

'Sounds serious. You OK, honey?' her dad asked, leaning forward in his chair. Where his wife was small and slim, he was a tall and bulky man, physically impressive. Vanessa had always likened him to a tree; strong, roots that ran deep; her mother, the water that nourished him.

She cleared her throat. Once she said the words out loud, there was no going back. 'I... uh... I'm pregnant.' She stammered over the words, seeing the shocked expressions on her parents' faces. Identical.

Her mom placed her knife and fork neatly down on the place. 'What?' she asked, a slightly confused look settled on her features.

She looked toward her dad. 'I'm having a baby.' She tried again.

Her mom opened her mouth to speak, but her dad cut in quickly. 'Whose baby is it?' he asked. He didn't demand; actually, he, they, were taking it pretty well so far.

This was the question she had dreaded. Whose baby was it? She sighed, a sound that was pulled out from deep within her. 'It's Mark's.' *In for a penny, right?*

'Mark as in Maggie's Mark? That Mark?' Her mom's face fell, and it was like a searing knife through Vanessa's heart.

'Yes, Mom, Maggie's Mark. We're in love.' She thought it an easier sell than a one-night stand that resulted in a teen pregnancy. A kindness to them all. A white lie that eased the pain.

'I don't understand,' her mom said, trying to wrap her head

around the bombshells. 'You and Mark are in love? Sweetheart, when did all this happen? I didn't even know they'd broken up.'

'They broke up today. We told her just before, actually. She slapped me and I deserved it.'

Her mom's face darkened. No one hurt her daughter like that, no matter how deserving she was of it. She abhorred physical violence, calling it the lowest form of humanity. Vanessa had once heard snippets of a conversation with her dad where she'd spoken about the abuse in her own home as a child.

'That was uncalled for.'

'No, Mom, it wasn't. I had it coming, and I accept that. I hurt her.'

'And what does your "love" plan to do about this?' interrupted her dad. 'He should marry you. You need to be married. You've almost finished school; give this baby a chance to grow up normally.' Her dad sometimes didn't get her or the situation, but she could see that he was trying to hold his temper in check.

'Knowing Mark's parents, I'm sure they'd say the same.' Vanessa lowered her eyes, unable to take their scrutiny any longer. 'He'll do the right thing, Dad,' she whispered. Yes, she loved Mark, despite the way he'd treated her, and odds were that she'd be married and, of course, a mom in a few short months.

They ate tea in silence, each lost deep in their own thoughts. Later, when the meal was finished, she heard the TV in the lounge click on, the nightly news blaring through the house. She was helping her mom do the dishes, something she always did, when her mom said quietly, 'You don't have to marry him, not if you don't want to. Never marry someone just because you're pregnant.' She said it so emphatically that Vanessa stopped drying the plate.

'Is that what happened to you?' Vanessa asked, shocked.

'I've never told you this but, I was pregnant with you before your dad and I married. We had a brief relationship that wasn't meant to last but I fell pregnant and although it wasn't what I wanted at the time, I was *encouraged* to marry your father.'

Vanessa was shocked. 'Mom, are you not happy?' Her world seemed to roll around her. Was her whole life a lie?

'I wasn't. Not at first. I was in love with someone else, but over time, I grew to love your father deeply – I still do – but I will never forgive my parents for forcing me into marriage just because I was pregnant and might shame them.' Her mind was stuck in the past for a minute and Vanessa stayed quiet, letting her mother drift until she came back to her. 'All I'm saying is, if you don't want to get married, you don't have to.' Her mom raised a hand to cup her daughter's cheek gently. 'We'll support you whatever you choose to do.'

'Mom,' she cried before being enveloped into the comforting arms of her mom. Slim yet strong, gentle yet capable.

* * *

Vanessa woke to the early-morning sun streaming through the chink in her curtains. She had fallen asleep on top of the comforter, too tired and emotionally wrung out to even crawl underneath it. She thought about what her mom had said the night before. She had grown to love her dad, and he must have grown to love her too somewhere along the way. They were happy; why couldn't she and Mark be happy?

Vanessa was keeping the baby and would marry Mark and everything would be OK. She'd make it work. *They'd* make it work. Together.

But what if he didn't want her?

She had to have faith that he'd do the right thing.

* * *

Vanessa was making tea in the kitchen when there was a soft knock at the back door. She moved the lace curtain aside and saw Mark standing there, one hand in his pocket. He wore jeans, a black T-shirt and a jacket to protect against the wind. He looked gorgeous. Her heart stumbled momentarily in her chest; its rhythm upset. She unlocked the door.

'Hi,' she said.

'Hey. Can I come in?'

She moved to let him in, a gust of cool air following him. It would warm up; the sun promised to shine on them soon, warming everything that its beams touched. They stood there awkwardly, staring at each other.

'I told my mom and dad,' he began.

'Yeah, I told mine too.' She waited.

'They think the best thing to do is for us to get married now, not wait any longer. They kinda have this out-of-wedlock thing. They're so pissed at me,' he confided.

'You want to get married now?' she asked, unable to process what he was saying.

'Yeah, they'll give their permission if yours do.'

'I think while my parents are on the same page about getting married, they're gonna want to wait till I turn eighteen and graduate. It's almost that time now. I'll be eighteen when the baby is born, so I won't need their permission. We can wait. Is that OK?' She looked at him imploringly.

'None of this is "OK". I made a mistake – I shouldn't have to pay for it for the rest of my fucking life,' he said angrily.

'Oh, I'm so sorry that this happened to *you*,' she said sarcastically, hands on her hips. 'I can't imagine what that must be like for *you*.'

'Don't be a bitch, Vanessa. I'm just saying I didn't think I'd have to plan my whole life in one night.'

'Well neither did I,' she hissed quietly so she didn't wake her parents. 'We'll get married and have the baby in a couple of months. I think it's a good idea if we both stay away from Maggie, give her the space she needs. Besides, we're a couple now.'

She could have sworn that she saw a shudder run through his body as he turned toward the back door.

'We can make this work, Mark. We can raise this child together, and we can be happy. I promise.'

'Yeah,' he muttered as he closed the door behind him. He didn't sound convinced. Vanessa would have to work extra hard to show him that she and the baby were good for him. Worth loving. She curved her hand around her stomach. She loved this baby fiercely already and would do anything for him or her. Now that it was out in the open and she didn't have to hide, she allowed herself to feel joy at the thought of this tiny human growing inside her. But Vanessa was still in two minds. Part of her was elated that she was marrying Mark, whereas the other part was keenly aware that he was in love with another woman. She'd make him forget about Maggie, and he would love her and only her. Once he saw their child and how wonderful a mom she would be, he'd fall in love with her. She was sure of it.

2

Vanessa hadn't wanted to go to school. By now everyone would know what she and Mark had done to the popular Maggie. They would know that Vanessa was pregnant and call her a slut, but her mom had forced her to get out of bed, brush her teeth and get ready for school.

'You'll have to face it sometime, might as well be today,' her mom said. Steel ran through her mom's body, she was sure of it. Vanessa would have to borrow from her strength to get through the next couple of months.

She walked to her locker and saw the word *whore* spray-painted across it. Well, that answered the question of whether Maggie had shared the news. She looked over toward Mark's locker. Unmarred. *That'd be fucking right.*

People were staring. She felt their eyes, their judgment, hang heavy like it was a weight around her neck. She heard footsteps stop behind her. She prayed it wasn't Maggie. She turned and came face to face with Felicity. A friend, a close one of hers and Maggie's. They'd been friends since elementary school.

'Well, if it isn't the boyfriend-stealing little slut.' Clearly now a former friend.

Vanessa took a stance. 'I'm not talking about this with you, Felicity.'

'Everyone knows what you did, you know. You're *that* girl now. The kind of girl that steals her best friend's boyfriend and then gets pregnant. That's you, Vanessa. Good luck on making friends now, *whore*.' Felicity banged into Vanessa's shoulder forcefully as she walked past, knocking her into her locker. Vanessa breathed deeply. This was going to be a long day.

Vanessa and Mark were married straight after graduating high school. Vanessa was pretty close to having her baby and although she was excited about motherhood, Mark's refusal to even look at her during their vows unnerved her. Only their parents were there to bear witness to their marriage. No friends cheered them on from the bench seats, there was no party afterwards. Nothing. Just a marriage covering up a dirty mistake – that's what they all thought anyway. But not Vanessa. This baby was a gift and would be her hope, her future, her salvation.

They moved into a run-down little house that her parents put down the deposit and first month's rent for as a wedding present. For the first time in her life, Vanessa fell asleep under a roof that was her very own.

While Mark no longer sought Maggie out, Vanessa knew that he still loved her. She felt Maggie's absence from her life keenly, alone and about to have a baby, married to a man whose heart belonged to another. Vanessa and Mark may have slept in the same bed, but he hadn't touched her since that first time. One night during the early hours of the morning, she woke to the bed

jerking slightly, the small bedside lamp was switched on, illumi-
nating the room. Mark sat on the edge of the bed. She carefully
looked over his shoulder and saw that he was masturbating while
holding a Polaroid photo of Maggie, completely naked. Shocked
and disgusted, she lay back down and rolled over to face the wall.
The bed still moved beneath her. She didn't say a word. Not then
anyway.

Vanessa was cold to him over the next few days after the *incident.* He was married, and, for better or worse, she was his wife
now. He wasn't allowed to jack off to his ex-girlfriend's picture. So
she took the picture from his underwear draw and cut it into tiny
pieces, watching Maggie disappear, piece by jagged piece.

He came storming into the kitchen later that night while she
was making dinner. 'Where is it?' he demanded, red cheeks
hinting at the extent of his rage.

Vanessa turned, her bulging stomach making her slow and
awkward. 'Where's what?' she asked, eyes narrowing in anger.

'Don't play dumb, Vanessa. The photo. The photo of Maggie.'

'You mean the photo you jack off to? I cut it up and flushed it
down the toilet. Guess you're going to have to use your imagina-
tion from now on, or shock horror, think about your wife instead.'

His eyes narrowed, and in hindsight she should have stopped
there. 'Why do you even have that? *You* cheated on *her*. *You* threw
her away. Why act all lovesick now that it's too late?'

He snarled. 'Maybe because I'm married to a fucking bitch.'

She was shocked. He'd never spoken to her like that before.

* * *

Two weeks after they moved into their house Mark got a job at a
bar and began staying out later and later, sometimes not even
bothering to call to let her know that he was safe or when he was

coming home. Vanessa had her suspicions but no proof as to what he was really up to. She was about ready to drop the baby, her stomach taunt and uncomfortable, the skin stretched tighter than a drum. She was in a large grocery store in the next town over one day when she heard the rumble of a low voice and the shrill, high-pitched giggle that she'd know anywhere.

Maggie.

Vanessa took in a deep breath. It was bound to happen sooner or later, living where they did. She leaned closer to the shelving, resisting the urge to look through the cereal boxes. Then she heard them kiss and felt physically ill. She had to look. She had to know if it was Mark as she suspected it was. Maybe Maggie had finally moved on with another man, but she knew Mark still loved Maggie and her swollen belly was proof that he could be persuasive when he wanted to be. She moved some cereal out of the way and tried to look through to the aisle, but the boxes on the other side obstructed her view. Holding onto her stomach, she moved to the end of the aisle, intent on catching Maggie and Mark in the act. She had her words all ready. But when she rounded the corner words failed her. The women locked eyes, and Maggie smiled a slow and seductive smile. She slid her hand into his hair, drawing him close for another steamy kiss, all the while staring at Vanessa. She felt like crying, screaming at her to get off him. He was firmly in her grasp, under her spell. Maggie then pulled away from her lover to face Vanessa head-on.

'Oh, hey, Ness.'

The man turned around too. It wasn't Mark at all. It was Vanessa's dad.

'Ness!' He gasped, shocked to see his daughter standing in front of him. 'What are you doing here?'

'What am *I* doing here? What the hell are you doing?'

He had no answer for her. She pushed past him, holding her

stomach as she tried to stride out of the store as quickly as she could. As she waddled to her car, Maggie followed her, screaming.

'How does it feel to be the one cheated on? Huh?' she yelled. 'To have your heart broken?'

Vanessa unlocked the car and pushed her bulk behind the wheel, desperate to get out of there.

'We fucked you know!' Maggie added gleefully.

Vanessa sped out of the car park, seeing her dad in the rearview mirror walk over to Maggie. He appeared to be trying to talk to her, but she walked off.

How could he? What was wrong with him? He'd known Maggie since they were in elementary school. What about her mom? How the hell was she going to tell her what she knew? Should she tell her?

Vanessa managed to make it home in one piece but once inside the comfort of her own home, she let her emotions flood out. Tears on her cheeks, she wailed, the baby moving within her, responding to her distress. Finally, she stopped crying and was blowing her nose just as Mark came charging into the kitchen where she stood by the sink. He was always angry these days. There was little room for compassion and understanding from him. It was like he forgot that she was heavily pregnant with his baby and might need his support.

'What are you crying about?' he demanded, evidently uninterested in her answer. He watched as she dabbed at her eyes before throwing away the soggy tissue.

'Maggie is sleeping with my dad,' she said tearfully, without thinking.

'What did you say?' His voice was low and dangerous and made the hairs on the back of her neck stand up in fear. He glared at her and when she didn't answer quickly enough, he screamed. 'Speak!'

'I saw them at the grocery store, kissing, then she told me what they'd done. It's revenge. I slept with you so she's getting back at me.' She burst into tears again, reaching for another tissue.

Vanessa had her hand around the tissue just as Mark raised his hand and slapped her, throwing her into the table. The tissue fluttered to the floor. She fell along the table awkwardly until she was able to get a proper grip and stand upright.

'You stupid fucking bitch! This is all your fault!' He drew back his arm and punched her in the face, mashing her lip into her teeth. She tasted blood.

'Don't,' she rasped as he wrapped his hands around her throat, cutting off her air supply. Her face began to tingle unpleasantly.

She suddenly felt wetness blooming inside her pants, running down her legs. 'Baby,' she croaked. 'Now.'

Mark looked down at the blossoming stain on her pants and said, 'Fuck me, can't you do anything right?' He dropped her in disgust and she grabbed at her throat, massaging away the pain. 'Well, hurry the fuck up then.'

Vanessa grabbed her overnight bag and followed him to the van, scared of what was to come. A contraction ripped through her body, and she bent over, gasping. She looked up and could see Mark glaring at her from the driver's seat. He looked furious. All she wanted was her mom.

* * *

After six intensive hours in which she'd begged God to let it all be over, Vanessa's mom arrived at the hospital, just in time to see the birth of her first grandchild. Mark had finally given in and called her. He hadn't held Vanessa's hand or come near her while she sweated and grunted to bring their child into the world. Her mom had glared at him when she bustled in, the nurses giving the surly young man a wide berth.

'Mom, it's a boy,' Vanessa whispered, looking down at his tiny screwed-up face. 'A boy,' she breathed, leaning down to plant a feather-light kiss on his forehead. Vanessa looked up at Mark, who barely even glanced at his son or at his wife.

'I'm calling you Wren,' she whispered to the baby.

'What a bloody pussy name,' Mark commented loudly, making the little one stir.

Everyone in the room gave him a look of disbelief. Why would he choose this moment of all moments to ruin? Vanessa could see her mom gearing up to say something, so she placed a calming hand on her arm. 'Not now,' she muttered.

'Mark, a wren is a songbird with the most beautiful call. His name is Wren,' Vanessa said, claiming something as her own. She refused to look at him.

'I think it's lovely, honey.' Her mother smiled.

'Thanks, Mom.' She handed over her precious bundle to her mom, knowing that Mark would not want to hold him. Nothing would ever change with him; he would always blame her, hate her. She only hoped that his attitude wouldn't extend to his son. She didn't allow herself to think of the slap, the punch, the choking. It wouldn't do her any good.

* * *

Life fell into a predictable rhythm. Mark continued to spend late nights at the bar where he worked, and from the smell of him, had a few drinks himself. He stayed out late and while she worried, she tried not to care. Wren took up all of her time, caring for him, loving him and above all else, ensuring his safety. She needed to protect him from his disinterested and still violent father. Mark slapped her for any perceived infractions, and she was still sure that he was having an affair, maybe not with Maggie but with someone.

One night, three weeks after she had caught her dad with Maggie, she had just put Wren down for a nap after a feed when there was a knock at the door. She glanced at the hall clock. It was after nine in the evening.

'C'mon, Ness. Let me in, I want to explain.' It was her father. He was drunk, standing on her doorstep, yelling at her through the window to let him in. She opened the wooden front door but left the screen door bolted.

'I don't want anything to do with you, Dad. Leave me alone.'

He tried to open the door until he realized that it was locked. 'She came on to me!'

'Like that makes it OK. You've known her since she was five, what the hell is wrong with you? What about Mom? Have you told her yet?'

'I'm sorry.'

'You're apologizing to the wrong person.' She hardened her heart against him. Two liars in her life was two more liars that she could handle.

'I can't tell her, she'll leave me,' he wailed.

'Well, you should have thought about that before you fucked Maggie, shouldn't you? I won't forgive you until you tell Mom. Did you know she did it for revenge? Or are you so deluded that you thought she actually liked you?'

He shook his head.

'Get out of here, Dad, I don't want to see you again. I have enough shit without adding yours to the pile.' Vanessa closed the door on him. He called her name a couple of times but she stayed strong. When it went quiet, she peered through the side window, watching as he sloped off to his house three streets away.

Mark would be home soon. She needed to clean her face. She'd been crying again. Wren was a wonderful baby and so easy to care for, but she was exhausted and cried all the time when Mark wasn't around.

Who knew what kind of mood Mark would be in when he came home? She could usually tell by the way he pulled up and walked into the house. Sometimes he was cordial to her, treating her like a stranger that he had to be polite to, and other days, he was into her the moment he walked through the door. They lived in a small, two-bedroom home with a huge backyard. Vanessa loved taking Wren into the backyard to feel the sun on his face, drooling on her while she read a book, or tried to. These treasured moments with Wren were all that kept her sane. She had no friends, save her mom, and keenly missed having a chat to someone without having to watch and evaluate every word that came out of her mouth. In those first few months of motherhood, she grew up fast. She matured beyond her years. Her mom visited her every couple of days bringing nappies, formula and food for the pantry. While Mark had a good-paying full-time job, he often drank away the extra money, leaving them short on bills. Her mom helped, occasionally slipping money into her bag. Vanessa would cry when she found it, but she couldn't afford to return it. Would they ever get out from under their mediocre lives?

* * *

Mark's van skidded down the driveway. He pulled up just short of hitting the garage and slammed the door, a sure sign that all hell was about to break loose. Vanessa was in the kitchen when he came barreling inside. She heard the clink of glass and immediately knew he had bottles of beer with him, jostling against each other in a box. He must have taken them from work again.

There was an electricity bill on the fridge, it had been there for a month and she had brought it up with him once, but he'd shut her down. It sat under a magnet of Wren's tiny handprint, a present from her mom. It was past due and although she didn't want to mention it to Mark again, especially when he was in this mood, she had to, or they'd be cut off. Again.

Mark took a beer from the small box, popped the cap and took a long pull. His eyes watched her and she felt small and afraid. He put down the beer on the table, no coaster underneath. There would be a ring on the surface now. He scowled at her. Now was not the time, but she went in anyway. 'Mark...' she began tentatively.

'Don't start with me, Vanessa, I'm not in the mood.'

She swallowed the apprehensive lump in her throat and pressed on regardless. 'It's just that the electricity bill is overdue, and I need money to pay for it.'

She'd expected the backhand but was still unable to move away fast enough. She fell against the table, which stuttered sideways with her weight. She rubbed her cheek where his slap had landed. It would bruise later; it always did.

'Don't speak to me!' He roared at her, spit flying from his mouth. 'All of this is because of you!'

She didn't dare point out that he'd come on to her, seduced her, cheated with her all those months ago. It wasn't worth the black eye. She could hear Wren screaming from his cot in the bedroom. She tried to run to him, to put herself out of Mark's reach but as she bolted past him, he reached out and grabbed the end of her ponytail. She was able to pull free, tears springing into the corners of her eyes with the pain. She got to Wren's room and slammed the door closed, bolting the lock that she'd installed using Mark's own tools.

Vanessa hurriedly picked up the screaming, swaddled baby. She opened the large bedroom window, shushing Wren, and climbed through it. She took off at a fast walk to her parents' house. She could still hear Mark screaming, the eerily silent night broken only by his yells.

Vanessa knocked on the door, which was opened by her mom after checking who was there through the peephole. It was night-time after all. She took one look at her daughter with her grandson strapped to her body and threw the door open wide. 'Come inside, quickly.' She ushered Vanessa in before sticking her head back out and looking up and down the street. Her mom showed her and the softly mewling Wren into the kitchen where she made a calming cup of tea. Vanessa placed her sweet baby boy into the portable cot her mom had set up in the spare room. She watched him for a few minutes as he went back to sleep, delaying the time until she had to explain why she was on her parents' doorstep in the middle of the night.

'What happened, Ness?' asked her mom quietly, when Vanessa walked into the kitchen a few minutes later.

'Nothing.'

'Vanessa,' she warned, 'don't lie to me.'

'I asked Mark for money to pay the electricity bill.'

'Does he hit you?' She asked, her hand waving in the direction of her face. She tried to hold Vanessa's gaze, but Vanessa looked away.

'When he can catch me,' Vanessa said sadly. 'I deserve this. It's my trade-off for what I did. For having Wren.'

Her mom reached out and touched her daughter's hand. 'Darl, if you want to come home, just say so. We'd love to have you.'

'No,' Vanessa said quickly. She couldn't live under the same roof as her dad again, not until her mom knew the truth. 'It's OK, I can deal with Mark. I just needed to give him some time to cool off.'

'Well why don't you and Wren stay tonight at least?'

Vanessa looked at the clock over the sink. 'I'd better be getting home. I just needed a breather, that's all. Thanks for the tea, Mom.'

'Do you want me to give you the money for the electricity bill?'

Vanessa hadn't felt this low in a long time. Her mom had given more than enough already, money that she herself couldn't afford, but Vanessa was stuck. 'Yes please,' she whispered, ashamed but also grateful. She hugged her mom and then fetched Wren from the spare room. She hadn't seen her dad and she didn't want to. He would have heard her arrive and was deliberately staying out of her way.

* * *

He came home, out of the blue, during the middle of his shift. Vanessa had put Wren down for a sleep and was making potato salad for dinner when the front door banged open, rebounding off the wall. Startled, she didn't register the look on his face until he grabbed her by the arm and dragged her to the bedroom.

They hadn't had sex since the night that Wren had been conceived. He couldn't stand her, and she couldn't stomach the thought of him touching her. She had become so disillusioned with her husband; the only time he laid hands on her was when he hit her.

He didn't ask, just threw her onto the bed, grabbing at her singlet strap, ripping it free so her bra was visible.

'Show me what you got, Ness,' he said, eyes bulging, mouth snarling. He was like some rabid dog intent on claiming his kill.

She rolled over on the bed, reached for the lamp, pulled it free from the wall and held it in front of her like a weapon. 'Come near me and I'll bash your fucking brains in.'

She thought it would be enough to frighten him, but he lunged at her. She swung the lamp toward him. It connected with his arm, not his head as she had planned. China rained down on them both as the lamp base shattered. He slapped her face then put a hand over her mouth, cutting off her cry for help. He fumbled one-handed with his pants while she tried to struggle free.

She kept fighting, so he punched her in the stomach, the air whooshing from her lungs, leaving her breathless and gagging. Her head was throbbing from the slap, her lungs gasping for air. She felt him moving inside her. It hurt as he thrust into her, his hand over her mouth. The attack seemed to stretch on and on, but eventually he was done. He stood, pulled up his pants and without saying a word, left the room. Vanessa was too stunned to cry. She didn't move for the longest time. Not until she heard Wren fussing in the next room. Finally, she rolled off the bed and changed her clothes.

* * *

Two months later, Vanessa discovered she was pregnant.

It was a bittersweet moment. She was ecstatic to be having another baby as she loved motherhood, but at the same time, she was petrified. She wondered how the hell she was going to protect two kids from Mark. One was hard enough.

When she told her mom she was pregnant again, she cried,

hot tears sprinkling her face. Her mom dried her tears and asked the question that Vanessa had been asking herself.

'Are you going to keep it?'

Was she? Could she?

'I'm just saying. Two is... much harder than one,' her mom said diplomatically. 'Then there's... Mark.'

Vanessa knew what she meant. Her mom had borne witness to the late-night visits, the cuts and bruises that she had stopped trying to explain. It was a small town, hard to hide secrets; she wore makeup, but people knew. She was sure of it. They treated her differently, like she was damaged goods.

Wasn't she? Hadn't she always been?

Vanessa was basically dead inside, except when she was with Wren. A smile from him could make her day. A laugh like golden sunshine warming her face. What if her mom was right? What if it was better to fix the problem before Mark even knew about it?

In the end, Vanessa decided that she couldn't just get rid of it, so she told Mark.

'What the fuck do you mean you're pregnant? How did this happen?' Conveniently forgetting his part in her pregnancies seemed to be his go-to.

'You should know. You asked me the same thing when I fell pregnant with Wren. You know exactly how it happened.'

'You did this deliberately,' he accused, his fists bunched at his sides.

She couldn't believe that he was blaming her again. He'd forced himself on her. What did he think might happen?

'You think I want another child with you?' she said quietly, her voice pitched low, almost talking to herself.

He backhanded her.

'Christ, Mark! Just stop it!'

He grabbed her by the front of her top, yanking her close to him, so close that his beer breath flowed over her face. 'Don't you tell me what to do. Ever.'

She thought he was going to hit her again, but instead he pushed her away and stormed out the back door and into the shed where she heard him banging around.

Two babies. She sighed and gently touched her stomach, making a promise to this baby that she'd protect him or her as much as she could, including against their dad.

* * *

Vanessa was at the grocery store with Wren when someone spoke behind her.

'So, this is the little bastard.'

Vanessa turned, an unhappy and squirming one-year-old Wren draped over her shoulder and a red plastic basket looped over the other arm. Maggie was standing in front of her looking perfectly made up and tanned next to Vanessa's scraggly, unkept and pale appearance. Vanessa hadn't bothered to cover up the dark rings around her haunted eyes and the fading bruise visible across one cheek. She was wearing yesterday's clothes.

'Maggie,' she said softly, taking her in. 'You look good.' And she really meant it.

'Yeah, well, you look like shit.' Maggie had always been honest with her.

'Thanks,' she whispered, a ghost of a smile on her face. She hefted Wren in her arms, juggling the basket, one corner poking in painfully under her breast. He thrashed his head around until his eyes eventually settled on Maggie. 'I made my bed, Maggie. I hurt you and I'm taking responsibility for that, but you don't get to call my son names.' There was steel in her voice as she defended her baby.

'I'm sorry. He just looks like you both... you and Mark.' Maggie inspected Vanessa's face carefully. It was clear she had noted the bruise. 'Are you OK?'

Vanessa moved her hair over her cheek. 'Why do you care?'

'I don't, I guess. I've just heard rumors, and it looks like they might be true.'

'Yeah, well, I walked into a cupboard door, nothing more.'

They both knew it was a lie that dropped from her lips. It hung in the air.

'You hate me,' Vanessa blurted out, not sure why she even talking to Maggie.

Maggie considered her next words. 'Yeah, I guess a little, but I'll always worry about you.'

'I'm pregnant.' Vanessa had no idea why she told her; there was no reason to.

Maggie's eyes narrowed. 'You always did know how to hurt me,' she choked out before turning and walking off. Vanessa wanted to call out after her. To apologize. To tell her what happened. But what was the point? It was over with Maggie. She was lost to her. Again.

Vanessa stared after her for a long time, lost in the past. Eventually she came back to the present, Wren wriggling in her arms. She popped him down on his feet and hung onto his little hand. He looked up at her, trusting, a wide grin on his face. She stared at him. Yes, he did look like Mark, but as he grew older, he favored her a little more. A year of beatings, no apologies on his part and silence on hers. People knew what went on inside their home, yet nobody did anything. Mark had always been popular, charming everyone with his good looks and quick tongue. Working at the bar, he got to know the locals even more. He was one of them; she was just a slut who got what she deserved. Small towns had long memories. Her mom pushed her gently to leave him and come home without actually coming out and saying it. She was supportive, and the offer was tempting, but Vanessa felt like this was her punishment for what she did to Maggie. The only bright spot in her life was Wren, and, soon, this new baby.

* * *

The night their second child was born, Mark was at work, pulling the late shift. Typically, on nights like those, he finished around two in the morning. But no matter what time he came home, he was always drunk and angry. Vanessa went into labor while she was feeding Wren. He was happily munching on his tea when she felt a contraction and the warm rush of her water breaking.

'Shit.' She went to get the mop and cleaned the floor before changing and ringing her mom to let her know. Her dad answered. 'Is Mom there?' she asked coldly, no *hello*, no *how are you*. She was sticking to her guns, even under these circumstances. It had been a year since she had spoken to him properly. She could admit that she missed him, missed being close with him, but she wouldn't back down.

'Ness. Are you OK?' He must have heard the fear in her voice and the concern in his was almost her undoing.

She stayed silent. Eventually he sighed. 'I'll go get her.'

'Is it time?' Her mom asked breathlessly as she came to the phone.

'Yeah. I'm scared, Mom.'

'I'll be right there.' Vanessa hung up the phone and hobbled to get her hospital bag, putting it by the front door, fighting another contraction as she did. She pulled Wren from his highchair and cleaned him up, another contraction rocking her body. She couldn't help but cry out. Wren, in her arms, turned at the sound. He stared at her, then laid one little chubby hand against her cheek. She was touched by the kindness of her son's innocent gesture.

'Thanks, my beautiful boy,' she whispered, kissing his forehead before putting him down. She rang the bar and Mark answered.

'Mark, it's me.'

'Vanessa?'

Who else would 'me' be?

'Yeah, it's Vanessa. I've just gone into labor so I'll meet you at the hospital. I'm leaving in about five minutes when Mom gets here.' She felt another contraction building and gripped the phone, trying to breathe through it.

'Can't leave, gotta close up,' he said casually, as if he wasn't about to become a dad again.

She couldn't think. 'I'm having a bloody baby, Mark. You need to be there.'

'And not one of these guys paying my wages gives a shit that you're having a fucking baby,' he hissed into the phone. 'They only care where their next drink is coming from and that's me.' He hung up on her. He fucking hung up on her!

'Mommy?' She turned, bending down to her little boy

'Wren, honey, Mommy is going to hospital now. Remember how I told you that you're going to be a big brother?' He nodded, not understanding at all. She smiled anyway and was scooping him up in her arms for a hug when her mom knocked on the door. 'I'll be bringing your baby brother or sister home in a few days.'

But she was worried. She hadn't felt the baby kick in the past few days. Wren hadn't let up the closer they'd got to his birth, but this time, there was nothing. She had been so scared that she couldn't even bring herself to go to the doctor to get herself checked out.

She let her mom in, who gave both her and Wren a big hug before taking her grandson from her daughter's arms. Her mom rang an ambulance and as they waited Vanessa said, 'I don't want to do this by myself.' She was scared.

'He'll come,' her mom said optimistically, 'and if he doesn't, well, then fuck him.'

Vanessa stifled a small laugh. She knew within her heart that he wouldn't come. There was always something more important than his family. Than Wren. He was no father to him at all.

So she wasn't surprised that he wasn't at the hospital waiting for her. Nor was he there when the doctor told her gently that there was no heartbeat and that her baby had died in the womb, the umbilical cord wrapped around her tiny neck. Her baby girl would be born dead.

Vanessa lay on the bed in shock, her whole body shaking. Her teeth chattered and she couldn't seem to get warm no matter how many blankets they put on her. She was numb. Having to deliver her dead child was the most horrific thing she had ever done. Worse than anything Mark had inflicted upon her.

The nurse called her mom and soon after, she came striding through the door, her gaze immediately falling on Vanessa who burst into tears. Her mom sat on the edge of the bed and gathered Vanessa into her arms. 'I know, baby. I know.' The nurses caring for her gave the mother and daughter their privacy, and they stayed locked in an embrace for a long time. Vanessa's eyes were puffy and red, her heart was broken.

'I lost her, Mom. I did this.'

'It's not your fault, Ness. I know it doesn't feel like it now, but it's not.'

'Where's Mark?' Vanessa asked, her voice hoarse from crying. Her throat felt ripped raw, like her heart, torn into tatters.

'We can't get ahold of him.'

'But the bar must be closed by now. Did you try his cellphone?'

'Yes, darl. He's not answering.' Her mom bit her bottom lip, clearly wanting to say more about the absentee Mark, but she held her tongue.

Vanessa rolled over on the bed. 'I lost his child and he can't even be bothered to show up.' She didn't know why she had expected anything else of him. Was he at home purposefully ignoring the hospital and her mom's calls? Was he that callous? She thought of his hands on her throughout her pregnancy. Yes, he was.

Her mom rubbed her back until she finally fell into an uneasy sleep plagued with nightmares. She stayed in hospital for two more days, her mom taking care of Wren at her parents' home. She had explained to Wren that Mommy wouldn't be bringing a baby home with her because the baby had gone to heaven. Mark never came to see her. He didn't even ring to check on her or to see how Wren was, or even find out where he was.

She came home without her daughter, a piece of her heart having died with her. When the taxi dropped her off at the curb, she stood there, wanting desperately to flee. To grab Wren and run and just keep running until she felt safe and happy again. She knew it was just a dream, that she'd never actually get away and start afresh.

Mark's car was in the driveway, and she steeled herself for seeing him. She wished he were at work so she could just have some alone time for a little while before the inevitable confrontation. She unlocked the front door, pushing it open as quietly as she could. The longer she didn't interact with him, the better. She was so damn angry with him.

She shuffled down the hallway to the room they shared. She looked at the bed where he had attacked her and made a baby.

The thought of sharing it with him now was repulsive. He had battered her love for him right from her body and there was nothing left. She lowered herself carefully onto the bed and lay curled up on her side, the large tears rolling down her face to drip off her nose. She had sworn to protect her baby, but she hadn't. Was she being punished still? Hadn't she suffered enough living with Mark every day?

She heard heavy footfalls coming down the carpeted hallway. She stopped crying, swallowing her tears with difficulty. She couldn't be hurt by anything he did anymore, surely? Her tear-filled gaze met his as he lounged in the doorway.

'So, it died, huh?'

Her breath stilled. OK, he could still hurt her with his callousness. 'Is that all you have to say? Your daughter just died!' She began to cry again. 'You weren't even there for me.'

'I had other shit to do, Vanessa. The world doesn't revolve around you.'

'No, just you.'

'What the fuck did you just say?' he demanded, walking two steps into the room. Her body tensed up, waiting for the punch. It didn't come.

'I didn't want another baby with you anyway,' he growled.

'Then you shouldn't have raped me.' Truth only.

He slammed his fist into the wall, his hand going through the plasterboard. *Good*. She hoped it hurt. At least it wasn't her face.

'Don't talk to me like that again, Vanessa,' he warned.

'Or what? You'll do it again? Been there, done that. No fucking way. You touch me again and I'll kill you in your sleep.' She meant it.

He backed off, maybe seeing the truth and conviction in her eyes. She would never let him violate her again. He thumped the wall again and turned, walking back down the hallway. Vanessa let out a shaky breath.

'Wren's fine, thanks for asking!' She couldn't resist the parting shot, she just didn't care anymore.

'Don't give a shit,' came the faint reply.

He may not have cared about Wren, but she sure as shit did. She couldn't wait another night to see him, she needed to hold him in her arms and smell the sweetness of his hair. She rang her mom and asked her to bring him back home to her.

Not even ten minutes later she was opening the front door to an excited Wren. The instant she saw her little man she felt like bursting into tears again, hoping the hot flow would burn the pain from her heart. Instead, she grabbed Wren and hugged him to her chest, smoothing down his fine hair and kissing him.

'I won't stay,' her mom said, and Vanessa knew that she wanted to say something to Mark but didn't want to make it worse for Vanessa. 'Sure you don't want me to have him for one more night?'

'Yes, but thanks, Mom. I need him home.' She kissed her mom's papery cheek and closed the door, holding Wren tightly in her arms.

'I missed you, sweetheart. I love you so much.'

'Mommy!' he said as he snuggled into her neck, placing a slobbery kiss on her shoulder. It was just what she needed. She just had to focus on Wren now. Make sure she could protect him.

3

And that's what happened for the next eight years. Vanessa had adjusted and finally accepted her lot in life. It was difficult, and she fought it for so long but in the end, it was just the way it was. She was *that girl* after all. Mark was who he was, and he was never going to change his attitude toward her or Wren. He resented her for tying him down with a child, reminding her of that fact every chance he could. He could have had a real life, he could have been happy with Maggie, on and on he'd go. She let it go in one ear and out the other. His words couldn't hurt her anymore.

'Vanessa!' bellowed Mark. She had been folding and putting away Wren's school uniform. He was in his room helping her. He was always helping her. They had such a close bond. They shared a glance. It was a voice that meant trouble.

'Stay in your room, Wren. I mean it.' Her voice was stern, but her face softened as she kissed him on the forehead. 'Love you, sweet boy.'

She walked down the hallway quickly, knowing how impatient Mark was. 'Are you after some lunch, Mark?' she asked politely.

'No, you dumb slut, I don't want anything to eat, Jesus! I want my goddamn black pants. Where are they?'

Vanessa wracked her brain. She had already done the wash, and she knew for certain that there had been no black pants in there. 'They weren't in the wash, Mark,' she said cautiously, aware that he was on the verge of rage. Over a pair of pants, of all things. The slightest thing set him off these days and Vanessa was amazed that his words and his fists still managed to hurt her.

'What do you mean?' His eyes narrowed to slits, and she took half a step backward.

'You were wearing gray tracksuit pants when you came home last night. Not your work pants.' She had thought it odd but didn't say anything. 'I have no clue where your pants are.' She tried keeping her voice neutral, but his fist shot out anyway, punching her, breaking her nose. Not for the first time. She was gushing blood, trying to catch it in her hands for some reason, as if she could stuff it back in and it all would be OK. She felt the familiar flare of pain followed by the dull throbbing. She must have cried out because she heard little footsteps running down the hallway behind her. *Wren!* She tried to turn, to scream at him to stop, to run away. But Mark attacked her again, slapping her about the head, connecting with her nose more than once. The pain was excruciating; she cried out again. She couldn't help it. She saw Wren out of the corner of her eye just as Mark pushed her back onto the table, leaning over her, slipping his hand around her neck. She clawed at his hand, trying to break the hold he had on her. She saw spots in front of her vision but willed herself not to pass out – who knows what he'd do to Wren. She let go of Mark's hand and flailed her hands behind her back, trying to shoo Wren away to safety.

Suddenly Mark gave a yell of pain, and his hand dropped from her throat. 'You little fuckhead! Wait till I catch you!' She looked down. The remains of a wooden statue given to her by her parents as a wedding present lay broken at Mark's feet, the head snapped off. He was rubbing his temple, a black bruise beginning to appear under the skin.

Wren had hit Mark and run. She heard the front door open and slam close, and she knew that he would be running to his nannie's house. Vanessa struggled to pull herself together so she could follow Wren, make sure that he was OK. Mark's hand circled her wrist, grinding the bones together painfully. Tendons stood out in his neck; his eyes bulged from their sockets. He tightened his grip, then threw her across the table. She skidded across the top, landing painfully on her side on the floor. It had all happened so fast. She had kicked one of the chairs and it was now laying on its side. She had the insane desire to tuck it back neatly under the table. Her nose throbbed, the blood pulsing in her head in time with her labored breathing. From her vantage point on the kitchen floor, she saw a small pair of feet just peeking out from the hallway.

Shit! Wren had only pretended to run. What if Mark saw him?

Terrified, she motioned for him to go, to run away. She had to keep Mark's focus on her so he wouldn't see Wren. So he wouldn't kill him.

'You're such a fucking loser,' she taunted, standing up slowly, blood still dripping from her ruined nose, staining her top and dripping onto the floor. *I just cleaned that damn thing.*

'*I'm* the fucking loser?'

'Just let me go, Mark. Let *us* go.'

'Let you go? I'll let you go when I'm good and ready. You ruined my life.'

'This again?' She smiled through the blood that coated her teeth. 'Your life was going nowhere anyway. You had the chance to be happy with us, to be a dad, but you chose something else.'

The little feet had disappeared. Hopefully hiding in the wardrobe in his bedroom like they'd practiced.

Mark grabbed Vanessa, throwing her face down over the table. She fought, and she fought hard. He pulled her head back by her hair, smashing her face down into the table. She screamed, her nose shrieking in unison. She knew what was coming; she heard him undoing his belt. He grabbed hold of her pants, pulling them down roughly. He forced himself inside her with one violent thrust. He put his hands around her waist and fucked her hard. She bit her lip, but her eyes still leaked tears. She would not let him know how much she was hurting; it would only serve to heighten his pleasure.

'You always were a slut,' he said as he pulled out.

'And you were always a fucking asshole.' She couldn't help herself.

She heard the belt whistle through the air before it hit her, slapping her back, buckle end raking through the fabric of her thin T-shirt, shredding it and the skin beneath. She stuffed her fist into her mouth to stop from screaming out. It would bring Wren running. Mark might kill him; she hadn't seen him this angry in years. Over a pair of fucking pants.

Mark quickly tired himself out. He wasn't as fit as he used to be, the beer drinking catching up to him. Breathing heavily, she heard him put his belt back on. 'You'd better go get that little shit stain from your mom's, but I don't want to see him. Understood?'

She nodded. Her back was on fire, but she didn't dare move until she heard the front door slam shut. She throbbed all over. She straightened up with difficulty. Rather than go to the doctor's, she put her hands on either side of her nose and clicked it back into place with a horrific crunch and a burst of white hot pain that for a moment surpassed the pain of her back. She hobbled down the hallway looking for Wren, whispering his name, terrified that Mark hadn't actually left and that he was waiting for her. She kept looking over her shoulder.

She finally found her son in her wardrobe, cleverly hiding in her hanging dressing gown. 'Oh, sweetheart, come here. Are you OK?' she asked, smoothing down his sweat-slickened hair.

His eyes were filled with tears. 'Why does he hurt you, Mom?'

Vanessa could have said a lot of things, none of it for little nine-year-old ears though. She wanted to tell Wren that his dad loved him, that it had nothing to do with him, but she couldn't lie to him like that. Mark hated Vanessa and by extension, Wren. Why didn't he just leave them? The only reasons she could think of was that he liked tormenting her, them. She couldn't leave because he'd threatened to kill Wren, just to get her back. She believed him. He was psycho, and she never knew how he was going to act in any given situation. She thought back to his missing black pants. They definitely hadn't been in the wash. It was possible that he'd left them at his girlfriend's house. It was something that she'd hoped for before, thinking him being happier would mean less pain for her and Wren. But if he was with another woman, it wasn't helping them at all.

'Mom, are you OK?'

'Just a sore back. Do you think you could put some cream on it for me?' He nodded and he went into the kitchen while she went into the bathroom and grabbed the tube of antiseptic cream that she kept for such occasions. It wasn't the first time and it wouldn't be the last. She went and sat in the chair, pulling her top off to hang around her neck. She leaned forward to expose her back. It must have been as intense at it felt because Wren sucked in a deep breath. 'Mom,' he said, a waver in his voice. She knew that she was covered in blood and how frightened he must be, but he hid it well. This wasn't the first time he'd seen something like this. The cream was cold but soothing. It stung at first, but it seemed to help. He'd used the belt on her before but never with such ferocity.

As Wren coated her back gently and lovingly, she thought of the easy friendship that she used to have with Maggie and how she'd give anything to get it back, but it was gone forever; too much had happened for them to ever be friends again. She thought about her mom, knowing what she did about her dad and Maggie. It was time, she knew. She'd given her dad years to come clean, but he obviously wasn't going to, so she felt that she had no choice. It was time to be honest. Starting with herself. Shit had to change. Wren... he could be next. He finished applying the cream and she rolled down her T-shirt.

'Thank you, sweetheart. I'm sorry—' She couldn't finish her sentence. She took a deep breath. 'Sorry that you had to see that.'

He touched either side of her face with his warm hands. 'I love you, Mom, but I hate him,' Wren whispered. She couldn't argue with that.

* * *

It took Vanessa another two months to work up the nerve to tell her. Vanessa knocked on the door, Wren's hand gripped in hers, giving her courage. This was going to be one of the hardest conversations she'd ever had, especially with someone that she loved with her whole heart. Her mom was the person she trusted most, besides Wren. She had been there for everything, and now she was going to cause her entire world to implode.

'Hey, honey, what a nice surprise. Come in,' her mom said.

'Wren, sweetheart, go play with your toys, I need to talk to Nannie for a bit.' She didn't want Wren in the room.

She watched as he walked away. 'Everything OK?' her mom asked. The tension coiled within Vanessa.

'No, not really. I have something that I want to tell you. Is Dad here?'

'No, he's at the grocery store. Why?'

Vanessa sat, then stood, then sat down again. 'Mom, I'm guessing you've pieced together what happened with Mark, myself and Maggie over the years. I was seduced, allowing myself to betray my best friend. I'm still paying for it now, but it seemed that Maggie wanted to even the score. Mom, she said she and Dad slept together,' she confessed hurriedly. There, she'd finally come clean. She felt like a weight had been lifted from her shoulders and unfortunately placed on her mom's. 'I believe her, and Dad confirmed it. I gave him the opportunity to tell you or I told him I would, but he hasn't done it, so I'm keeping my word. That's why we grew apart. I couldn't trust him until he confessed to you.' She looked at her mom, who sat in silence, staring at the wall above Vanessa's head. 'Say something, Mom.'

'How long have you known, Ness?' she asked calmly, her eyes connecting with her daughter's.

'I was pregnant with Wren when I found out.' She hung her head. How could she have let this stand for all these years? She was so caught up in her own dramas that she had forgotten to do what was right for her mom.

'You've kept this from me for all these years? How could you?'

Vanessa let out a pent-up breath of frustration. 'I didn't know how to tell you and I kept thinking that Dad would tell you, but he never did. Then the longer it dragged on, the harder it became to find the right time. I felt that I'd missed my window or something.'

'Why now?'

'Why? Because I've decided that I need to be more honest with the people in my life; I need to improve myself, for me but mainly for Wren. He deserves the best mom he can possibly have. I hope you forgive me for keeping this from you.'

Vanessa stood and called to Wren that they were leaving. The boy received a wooden hug and kiss goodbye from his nannie. She was clearly in shock, but she needed to be alone to process this information. Vanessa had dropped the bombshell that she had come to deliver; it was up to her mom and dad now to work through what next.

* * *

Vanessa also needed to make things right with Maggie but had no idea how to approach that particular landmine. In the end, she decided to use the same approach as she had with her mom. Knock on the door and drop the truth. She left Wren with the next-door neighbors. They'd babysat Wren before when she'd been in a pinch. She knew that they'd heard the arguments but, like everyone else, hadn't intervened. She didn't blame them; they were elderly and Mark was batshit crazy. He'd probably kill them if they interfered.

Vanessa reached out a shaky hand and pressed the doorbell. She looked around at the neatly kept lawn, the weeded garden. After waiting for a couple of minutes, she decided that Maggie wasn't home and turned to leave.

'What are you doing here?' her old friend's voice demanded. Vanessa turned back around to face Maggie, who had appeared in the doorway. She looked unhappy but curiosity had obviously got the better of her.

'Hi, Maggie. I came... to talk to you.'

'What can we possibly have to talk about?'

This wasn't going to be easy. 'Can I come in?'

She looked behind her as if checking that she could admit

Vanessa into her beautiful home. Maggie walked back into the house and waited for Vanessa to walk inside before she closed the front door to keep the air-conditioning in. She led her to the kitchen where a small table adorned an otherwise plain room.

'You wanted to talk, so talk.'

'Can we at least sit down?'

Reluctantly Maggie dropped into one of the chairs.

'I've been working up the courage for this conversation,' Vanessa began.

'For nine years?' interrupted Maggie.

'I know, better late than never I suppose.' She tried to smile, but it felt forced, so she pinched her mouth shut for a moment. She took a deep breath. 'I need to get a few things off my chest. I'm trying to make amends to the people that I hurt. And I hurt you the most. I want to say that I'm sorry. For every single damn thing that I did to you. It was unacceptable, wrong and a shitty thing to do to a friend. You were my best friend and I hurt you so badly. Betrayed you. I can understand if you never forgive me, but I'm asking anyway.' She sucked in a breath.

'You pounced on my boyfriend the moment my back was turned.'

Vanessa didn't point out that he'd hit on her. It wasn't the time. She had come to apologize. Besides, who knew what story he'd told her; she'd never had the chance to defend herself, never getting near enough to Maggie.

'Forgiveness is not that easy, Vanessa. You can't just come in here and ask. It's not fair.'

'I lost everything that night. You, the rest of my friends, my self-respect and my reputation. I've suffered and now I ask you. Forgive me.' Vanessa hung her head. 'I know you're sleeping with him.' It had been a shot in the dark but one that felt right. He'd never got over Maggie, his first love.

'You know about that?' she asked, picking at her fingernails.

'Yeah, but I don't care, I just want to warn you that he's not the kid you knew in school. He's changed.'

'Warn me? Away from Mark? The man you stole from me? We're adults, we can do what we want.'

'I'm not worried about him; I'm worried about you. He... he... hits me.' It was the first time she'd said it out loud, and she'd only done it to protect her friend. 'He hurts me. He raped me, got me pregnant, then my beautiful baby girl died. He didn't even bother showing up to the hospital or the funeral. That's the sort of man he's turned into. I'm worried for Wren's safety. He's petrified of his dad. We never know which Mark we're getting when he comes home. Then there's you. He'll eventually do the same to you.'

'This is a huge lie to get me to stop seeing him,' declared Maggie, angrily standing up. 'I think you should leave now. Even if it is true, did you ever think you might deserve it?'

'Every damn day.'

She stormed down the hallway, flinging open the front door for Vanessa to follow. 'Vanessa?' Maggie fumed when Vanessa was outside.

Vanessa turned back.

'Don't ever come back here again.'

Vanessa nodded and trudged down the rough-patterned brick path.

4

With a heavy heart, Vanessa unlocked and opened the door, pulling Wren through with her. He was dragging his feet as much as she was, neither of them wanting to go inside. Mark's car was out the front, which meant he was inside waiting for them, like a venomous black spider waiting for its prey. She felt like running, but she had nowhere to go and no money. No choice.

She bent down and whispered in his ear, 'If things go badly tonight, you need to go to Nannie's straight away, out the bedroom window. No staying to protect me. I'll be OK, understood?' Although he was young, he knew what to do.

He nodded. She felt terrible that she was putting so much on his little shoulders, but he seemed to be coping well. He was her little dude, her beautiful boy. She never wanted him to change from the empathetic and loving kid that he was. Wren's safety was her number-one priority. His happiness a close second.

Mark was sitting at the kitchen table dunking a biscuit into his coffee. He had a crumb clinging to his upper lip until his tongue snaked out and grabbed it, pulling it back into his mouth. He repulsed her. She felt like confronting him about his affair with Maggie but decided that she'd wait and see how this conversation went.

'Mark.'

He grunted at her, slurping his coffee noisily. 'You're not happy,' she began. She waited for him to confirm what she already knew, but he stayed stubbornly silent. 'I'm not happy either. I haven't ever been happy with you, and I suspect you feel the exact same way. So why don't we just call it a day and go our separate ways?' Vanessa said in a rush, stumbling over her words in her haste to get them out before he cut her off. But he didn't. He didn't even speak. He simply picked up his nearly full cup and flicked his hand, and suddenly she was covered in near scalding-hot coffee. It was soaking through her top, burning her. Pulling it quickly over her head, she threw it onto the ground. Her hair dripped, and coffee covered her face. Trying to wipe down her chest, already feeling the searing pain of the burn, she knew she needed to get cream on it straightaway in case it blistered. She went to leave.

'Don't.' His voice was low, and she risked a quick look at his face. His brows were lowered and knitted together.

She froze.

'Know why I don't leave your worthless ass? It's because I live for moments like these. Moments where I can make you feel miserable, hurt, alone. Moments like this when I can make you feel like the disgusting slut that you are. No one will ever want you if I leave you. Everyone remembers what you did. Seduced me, then deliberately got pregnant.'

She wanted to remind him that he was the only man that she'd ever slept with so how could she be a slut, but now didn't seem like the right time to point that out.

'Besides, I'd never skip out on my wife and child. I have a

reputation to protect.' She wasn't sure what reputation he was trying to protect, but, whatever.

'Just leave us, Mark. You can finally go and be with Maggie. A real couple. Just like you used to be.'

'You know about Maggie?'

'Yeah, I saw her today and she confirmed it.'

'Good, I hope it hurts.'

'The only thing that hurts me around here is you. I'll take the kids and leave you. I'll go back home if I have to.'

'You said "kids".' His eyes narrowed.

Her face paled. 'No I didn't, I said "kid". Wren. I meant Wren.'

'You pregnant again?' His eyes went to her belly and her mind flicked back to being thrown over this very table. Yes, she was pregnant again. She lowered her head, admitting the truth. She had only just confirmed it yesterday at the doctor's surgery. She had put it off and put it off, but she had to know. She was nearly three months pregnant. She had panicked, determined not to blurt it out to Mark, and here she was, doing just that.

'Now we really can't leave each other.' He smirked.

She lowered her head in defeat. Trapped by her own body, his actions, yet again. She couldn't see any way out of this black hole of a marriage.

'Don't get any ideas. I'll hunt you down. I'll hurt Wren. You know that I will. Then your parents. So don't even think about it.' Mark's face always took on this intense look whenever he was about to hurt her. It was almost like he checked out mentally then slammed back into focus. He had that look on his face now. He got up and left, and she took her soiled and stained top to the laundry. She didn't know why she was bleaching it – it was ruined – she should just throw it away, yet she scrubbed and scrubbed away at it, hiding her real fear. She was terrified that this baby would be born dead too. She began to cry until a small skinny arm encircled her waist. 'I love you, Mom.'

'I love you too, sweetheart. So very much.' She dropped a kiss on the top of his head, then held on to him tightly, never wanting to let go.

* * *

Six months later and Vanessa was in a hospital bed, petrified that they wouldn't be able to find a heartbeat. She had felt the baby kick just this morning and rationalized that he or she would be fine. She didn't have it in her to survive another child's death, she just didn't. Mark was a no-show yet again. She'd called him and he'd flat-out refused to come this time. She didn't beg, she couldn't stand the thought. He had barely spoken to her since the whole Maggie affair thing and she had been enjoying the relative quiet, but she didn't want to give birth alone. Wren wanted to come. In fact, he demanded it. He didn't want to stay next door.

'I'm coming with you,' he'd said in his best authoritarian voice, and because she hadn't had the will to argue, she'd said yes. He was ten now, old enough. He'd been so sincere and serious; she'd known he'd meant it. What could she have said but yes?

She briefly wondered if Mark was with Maggie right now. If Maggie knew that she had gone into labor. Then she realized that she didn't much care what either one of them thought. The most important person in her life, the one she loved the most and who loved her the most, was going to be there for her, holding her hand every step of the way.

Wren sat by her as she asked for the tenth time. 'Is the baby alive?'

The nurse who smiled down at her with empathy in her eyes confirmed again that there was indeed a heartbeat. The hospital knew her history so they understood her constantly sought reassurance and were more than willing to accommodate her. She still hadn't got over her baby daughter passing away before she even had a chance to meet her, and she knew she never would. But now was the time to think about the new baby that was about to be born.

She lay on the bed, holding Wren's hand tightly as another contraction shot through her body like a cannon blast.

'Breathe, Mom. Just breathe,' Wren said loudly over her moan of pain. She looked over at him, inhaling deeply, and her heart filled with pride. She copied him and he gave her a smile. So grown up for ten years of age.

Finally, at precisely 3.32 p.m., after laboring for nine hours, her second little baby boy was born. And he was perfect.

Wren stared at the naked baby lying on her chest. 'Mom,' he said in wonder, 'that's my baby brother.' The look of pure joy on his face as he grinned at her was priceless. She was so glad she had let him come; he'd encouraged her and fed her ice chips the whole time. Who could have asked for a better labor partner?

'Yes, he is. And now that you're a big brother, it's also your responsibility to protect him always. You need to be there for him and love him.'

'He's just beautiful,' came a soft voice from the doorway.

'Mom?' Vanessa was shocked to see her. Her mom hadn't spoken to her since she'd told her about her dad's affair with Maggie. 'How did you know we were here?'

'Well, I went to your house to talk to you and your neighbor Verna said that you and Wren had gone to the hospital. Looks like I'm a little late, though.'

'Nannie, I have a baby brother. I'm going to love and protect him.' For a moment, they were all thinking the same thing. *From Mark.*

'I know, darling, isn't it wonderful?' she said as she opened her arms up for a hug. He slid off the bed carefully so as to not disturb the baby and hugged his nannie.

Vanessa looked at her mom as Wren settled back on the bed. 'I kicked him out,' her mom stated.

'Oh, Mom, I'm sorry. I didn't want you to be unhappy, I just had to tell you.'

'Let's not speak of that right now,' she said, 'not when we have a new addition to the family. What's his name?'

'Well, since Mark won't care, I'm naming him Tyson, Ty for short.'

Wren smiled and her mom peered down at the baby now swaddled on her daughter's chest. 'Hey, Ty, welcome to the world. You are so loved.'

Vanessa swallowed the lump in her throat and looked over at her eldest son. 'I couldn't have done it without you, Wren. Thank you, honey.'

Vanessa knew that her mom wanted to ask where Mark was and why he wasn't here, so she answered before she could. 'He didn't want to come. With Maggie, I suppose.'

'I had heard the rumors. They're true, I take it?'

'They are.'

'And she had the cheek to call you the S-word,' she said over Wren's head. Vanessa gave a quiet chuckle at her mom's comment.

Her mom took a reluctant Wren home with her for the next few days, although they came up and visited Vanessa and Ty for a few hours a day. Vanessa used the time to think. By the day she returned home, she'd created a plan, but she needed her mom's help to carry it out.

She had to leave. The safety of her children was paramount. She didn't care about his threats anymore.

Vanessa had just started packing Wren's suitcase when she heard a knock at the front door. She stuffed the suitcase into the back of the wardrobe and walked to the door. She moved aside the curtain and paused for a moment.

She opened the door. 'Maggie. What are you doing here?' she asked in a flat voice. She didn't have time for this.

'Can I come in?' Maggie said, looking around her as if paranoid someone would catch the two of them talking.

If Maggie wanted to talk, then Vanessa didn't have much choice, but she needed to make it quick. 'Come in, but I really only have five minutes – I have to go and pick Wren up. What's wrong?' she asked, getting to the heart of the matter.

'It's cozy,' Maggie commented, looking around the room.

'Yeah, it's a real palace,' Vanessa said sarcastically. 'Maggie, why are you here?'

'I wasn't very nice to you when you came to see me.'

'That's fine, Maggie.' If all she wanted was absolution, then Vanessa was happy to give it to her, but she needed for her to go.

'I guess I didn't want to hear, want to believe the things you were saying about Mark. I guess I wanted him to be the guy that I remembered. But he's not. I know that now. For a while we were happy, well, at least he said he was happy to be finally back with me. I was flattered that he chased me for so long and fought so hard to get me.'

That was news to Vanessa.

'But he began to put me down, little snide comments at first. How the women in his life had him by the balls, stuff like that. Then he started talking about you and the baby that was coming and about Wren and he got really angry.' She hiccupped, on the verge of tears. 'I wanted the man he used to be, not this ball of anger that he's become. He said that you had ruined his life and broken him, and I think that he may be right. Not the part about you, but the part about him being broken.' She paused for breath. Vanessa didn't say anything, she knew Maggie would get to the point soon, well she hoped she would. 'He hurt me, Ness. I said that maybe you weren't to blame for everything and that at some point he had to take responsibility for his own actions.'

Vanessa sucked in a breath. That wasn't good. 'What did he say?'

'He didn't say anything.' She pulled up her top. On one side she had a huge black and purple bruise, she probably even had a cracked or broken rib. It was brutal, ugly.

'Oh, Maggie, I'm sorry.'

'I really didn't want to believe you, but you were right.' She dissolved into tears and Vanessa gave her the hug she so desperately wanted, needed. Only Vanessa would understand. Maggie was rigid in her arms for a moment before molding her body to Vanessa's.

'I'm not sure what you want from me, Maggie.'

'I want... actually... I didn't think much past coming over here and clearing the air. I've seen your bruises, everyone has. Why do you stay?'

She wanted to tell Maggie that she was about to leave but decided to keep that information to herself. 'Honestly? Some days I don't know. I think I stay out of guilt. For what I did to you.'

'Ness, you don't need to pay with your life. I forgive you.'

The words Vanessa had longed to hear for so many years and here Maggie was, saying them. She forgot her time crunch and hugged Maggie. 'What are you going to do, Maggie?'

'I've loved him since school and in a way, I still do... or did, but I have to protect myself somehow.'

Vanessa understood the allure of love and of Mark; she too had paid the price. In school, she had thought he was the one, but after they'd married, she'd seen the real Mark. The man who was a powder keg waiting to explode.

'I'd better go. I don't want him to find me here.' She looked around her as if expecting him to catch her in the act at any second.

'Maggie, I'm glad you came. Maybe we can get past this and be friends again.'

'I'd like that. I've missed you, Ness.' Vanessa touched her on the arm briefly, saw her to the door and watched her drive away. She empathized with her, she really did, but she had her own worries, namely protecting Wren and three-day-old Ty. She would ensure that they were safe from their dad. Forever.

5

Vanessa was walking down the street on her way to the grocery store, so intent on finding her cellphone in the depths of her bag that she didn't see the man in front of her until she collided with something unyielding. Gasping in shock, she took a step back and looked up. At first there was no recognition there until he said in a surprised tone, 'Vanessa?'

She took a good look at the large man whose bulk blocked the sun from her view. 'Oh my God, Billy! Hi, how are you?'

'I'm great.' She noted his eyes as they ran over her, taking in her long, scruffy, tangled hair, the blue-black tinge under her eye and the yellowing bruise that marred the side of her face. Suddenly she was self-conscious and tried to flatten down her hair into some semblance of order.

'You look good,' she said, and he did. Billy had been a friend from school. They hadn't exactly travelled in the same circles, but he was one of the few people who had been nice to her after everything with Mark and Maggie back in school.

He gave her the signature smile that she remembered: lopsided and sincere. She felt her stomach do a lazy turn and was taken aback by it. She hadn't showed an interest in anyone, so gun-shy she was with men. Mark may have played the field and slept around, but she had been faithful to a man that would have cared if she had cheated but only because it would have reflected badly on him. She was his, he'd told her often enough.

Ignoring the feeling in her stomach, she asked Billy what he was doing in town. Last she'd heard, he had been living in the city.

'My mom passed away recently and I'm here to sort out her house so I can sell it.'

'Oh, Billy, I'm so sorry, I didn't even know she was sick.'

'Heart attack. She'd had a good innings.' Vanessa remembered that Billy's mom had had him later in life, so she had been older than all of his friends' parents.

'I'm sorry if this is forward, but are you OK?' Billy asked. 'I can't help but notice the fading bruises on your face and the finger marks on your wrist.' Vanessa glanced at her wrist, pulling her sleeve down to the middle of her hand. 'Vanessa, are you in some kind of trouble? Is it Mark?'

It was public knowledge that she had married Mark right out of school when she was pregnant.

Vanessa looked around, as if afraid that Mark would come running down the street to hurt her. She had spent so long in hiding, hiding her bruises, hiding her broken bones, hiding who she was, that it was difficult for her to open up to anyone, yet she felt a calm settle over her, the uneasy feeling lifting. There was something about Billy, there always had been. 'I... I... uh. I don't know what to say.' She looked down at her bitten-down fingernails – a stress-related thing.

'Tell me the truth,' he encouraged gently.

'The truth? I've not told many people the truth, only one person actually. Mark... he... he hits me sometimes.' *There!* She'd said it out loud to Billy, and she felt like a weight had lifted from her shoulders. 'Sometimes' was an understatement.

He reached out and drew her into a gentle hug, before wrapping his long arms firmly around her. She was aware that they were near the bar and Mark could catch them at any moment, but she felt so comforted wrapped in Billy's embrace that she began to cry softly. He rubbed her back, soothing her, much like what she did with Wren when he was upset. It worked. Her soft sobs tapered off. She stepped out of his embrace.

'God, how embarrassing. I'm so sorry, Billy. I'm mortified.' Vanessa rubbed the remainder of the tears from her eyes, wishing she could rub the shame from them too.

'Don't be. Let me ask another question. Would you leave him if you had somewhere to go?'

She didn't even need to think about it. It had come to the point where she just *had* to leave. She didn't mention the already packed suitcases hidden away at home for the day she built the nerve. She needed to protect both her children: they were the most important thing to her.

She nodded slowly. 'I think he's going to kill me one day,' she whispered.

'Well that solves it then. I'm helping you move out. Tonight.'

'What?'

'I own an investment property on the other side of town that I was going to move into while I sorted Mom's house, but why don't I stay at Mom's and you take the other house? You've got a little one, right?'

'I've two. Wren and Tyson, Wren is ten and Ty, he's only a baby.'

'Oh, well, I guess congratulations are in order. The house is empty, but you can take furniture from Mom's house.' He smiled again.

'I'm worried for their safety, but are you sure about the house?'

'Definitely. It's time to go. Head back home, pack up some things, a few bags, boxes of stuff you can't live without and I'll bring my pickup and trailer round and take you and your boys over. How's that sound?'

Vanessa couldn't verbalize her thoughts, so she merely nodded, smiling like an idiot at him. She gave him her address and her phone number, and he put them in his phone straight away. 'What time shall I come over?' Billy asked.

'Mark has a split shift tonight, so he'll be gone by eight o'clock. So maybe eight-thirty? We'll be packed and ready to go. I don't have any money to repay you or for rent, though.' She was stricken and embarrassed. She couldn't rely on more generosity, not when Billy was already being so generous. 'I don't work, what with Wren and now Ty...' Her voice trailed off. They only had Mark's wage coming in, and that was spent as soon as she got her meager portion.

'Don't worry for now. I won't charge the deposit and we can talk about rent when you're on your feet again.'

She felt like crying. 'Why are you helping me?' she asked bluntly.

'Why? Because I'm a nice guy and you're a nice girl. I remember when I was new to the school, you were kind to me.'

Vanessa had thought that he had a little crush on her in school, but she couldn't read people anymore. Maybe he was just being helpful. 'Thanks, Billy.' She put her hand on his arm, and he looked down at it. She felt a blush creep up her neck. She couldn't have an attraction toward her new landlord, that wouldn't work. She had to focus on her children.

'OK, I'd better get over to the other house and open the

windows – give it a good airing out for you. It's probably a bit musty.'

'I honestly don't care, Billy. I'd sleep in a tent to get away right now.' He laughed, but then he saw that she was serious. She could see a flash of pity in his eyes and she had to swallow her pride.

'See you tonight,' she said turning to go before realizing that she'd been heading the other way. She turned back and walked toward him. He let out a throaty laugh as she passed him. She threw him a smile in return.

* * *

Vanessa was throwing clothes and toys into a box ready to add to the suitcases she'd already packed when she heard the front door open. She quickly stuffed the box she was filling back into the wardrobe, safe, hidden.

'Vanessa!' He screamed. 'Where's my dinner? I've got to be back at work in an hour.' She knew he'd be pissed that he had to do a split shift – the shift he hated the most – and he was usually a complete bastard to her and Wren for the hour in between. She already had his dinner cooked and was keeping it warm in the oven. She quickly walked down the hallway, spotting Wren in his room. She stopped in the doorway and put her finger to her lips in a shushing motion. Ty was with her mom, a deliberate act on her part – not that Mark would ask where his son was anyway. He showed about as much interest in Ty as he did in Wren.

He was popping the cap off a beer bottle when she walked into the kitchen. He glared at her but didn't say anything as she donned some oven mitts and slid his dinner from the tray to the table in front of him.

'Be careful, it's hot,' she warned.

'Not a fucking idiot,' he mumbled under his breath, loud enough that she heard it. He ate quickly, all but licking the plate. For all that he complained about her cooking, it never stopped him from eating it all.

Vanessa flicked a quick glance at the clock, seeing that he would be leaving for work in ten minutes. She would finish packing their bags and then she would be leaving this house, and Mark, forever. She thought about Billy, the almost familiar pull of attraction making her feel guilty. She had done nothing wrong, yet she felt she had. He was just being nice. Helping out an old friend, that's all.

Mark burped, signaling the end of his beer. He drank a lot these days. At work, at home, in the car on the way to and from work. She was surprised that he'd never been caught drink driving.

'I'm leaving,' he announced. He didn't say goodbye, and she didn't care. She waited until she watched his car reach halfway down the street. She had half an hour before Billy arrived with his trailer.

She strode down the hallway, entered Wren's room and grabbed his bag from under the bed. She handed it to him as he sat on the floor playing with Lego.

'What's going on?' he asked in surprise, seeing her flushed and excited face.

'We're leaving, that's what's going on. Pack some of your toys, maybe a favorite book or two. Whatever we can't take, we'll buy later. I'll going to get mine and Ty's bag. We have to be ready in twenty minutes.'

Vanessa watched as what was happening dawned on Wren's face. 'We're leaving home?'

She nodded.

'We're leaving Dad?'

She nodded again, watching his face light up. She should have done this years ago. 'A friend of mine is helping us move and lending us a house.'

Wren stood, crushing himself against her chest. 'Mom,' he said excitedly. 'I can't believe it.'

'Believe it, honey. Now quickly pack a bag – Billy will be here in twenty minutes to pick us up, and we absolutely must be gone before your dad gets home.'

A shadow passed over his face at the mention of his dad. 'I'll be ready,' he said, a serious look on his face.

What had she put this poor child through? The horrors that he had seen and heard. The attacks he'd witnessed and the many times he'd had to patch her up. Once, he'd even applied her makeup when Mark had left her with a broken wrist and a face full of bruises. She'd asked so much of him over the years, but now was the time to take him away from all the horrible things he'd faced. They were going to make new, happy memories. Vanessa, Wren and Ty. Just the three of them.

She had the bags and boxes by the front door and was ready to go with ten minutes to spare. There was some furniture that she was taking since Billy was bringing a trailer. There was a knock at the door, and she peered out the window. She saw it was Billy and opened the door. She smiled. 'Thanks so much for doing this, Billy, you have no idea how much this means to us and how it's going to change our lives.' She couldn't express in words the debt she felt toward him, the level of gratitude.

'Happy to help, Ness,' he said, using her childhood nickname. She liked it. It sounded good rolling off his tongue. Suddenly, she felt shy around him and was saved by Wren coming up behind her.

'Billy, I'd like you to meet my eldest son, Wren. Wren, this is an old friend of Mommy's, Billy. We went to school together.'

Wren reached out to shake hands with Billy. The older man grasped the young boy's small hand in his large one and shook it solemnly. 'Nice to meet you, Wren. Would you like to help me load the pickup and trailer?' Wren nodded, a proud look on his face at being asked to be involved in such an important grown-up job. The whole thing was surreal; they were leaving for good. She kept expecting Mark to come storming into the house and make them stay by force but, of course, he was at work.

Billy and Wren began loading bags and boxes into the pickup and the trailer. Wren was straining to help move some of the lighter furniture, but he did it. Billy clapped him on the back once they had everything loaded. 'Want to ride with me or your mom?' he asked.

'You please,' said Wren politely. Billy smiled over the top of his head while looking Vanessa in the eyes.

'OK, I'll follow you there.' She grabbed her keys, took one last look around the somewhat barren-looking house that she had lived in for so many years. She felt nothing, no ties and no regrets. She locked the door from the inside and pulled it closed after her. She was finally leaving the man who'd hurt her, who'd beaten her, degraded her and made her a shell of who she used to be. After making sure that Wren was safely strapped into the front of Billy's car, she hopped into her own car and turned the ignition. She was filled with a sense of peace and happiness. She looked in the rear-view mirror at the dwindling house, wondering what Mark would think when he came home and found they were gone. He would pitch a fit, that's for sure.

Ten minutes later, Billy reversed into the driveway of an old Victorian-style house. She parked out the front and as she got out of the car, she admired the front of the house. It was beautiful. The porch light was on, casting a small warm halo of light. Billy must have put it on when he was airing out the house this afternoon.

As they met up at the front door, Billy slid the key into the lock and said, 'Welcome to your new home.' Wren ran ahead, followed by Vanessa. The house had charm and character.

'Billy,' she breathed, 'it's perfect, just what we need.' She pulled him into a hug, standing up on her tippy toes to throw her arms around his neck. Suddenly she realized how intimate it was and stepped back. She saw the look of longing on his face. Wren was standing in the corner of the room and without a doubt, he would have seen her hug Billy, but she didn't think he'd mind. She was happy, throwing her son a smile that he returned quickly.

'Can I choose my own room, Mom?' he asked.

'My love, you can have any room that you want.'

'There's a room that's blue!' he screamed after running down the hallway. 'I'd like that one.' Blue was his favorite color – could this house be any more perfect? She smiled over her shoulder to Billy before he left to unpack the rest of the pickup.

Before long, Billy came back into the house. 'That's the last of it, Ness. Where do you want this box?'

'In the corner, please. I'll unpack once Wren has gone to sleep. I'm picking up Ty in the morning from my mom's house, but did you want to come round for coffee so I can say thank you for all you've done? It's not much—'

'It sounds perfect,' he said, cutting her off. 'Say eleven?'

She nodded her head. She could tell he wanted to hug her again, but he settled for dropping a chaste kiss on her cheek. She could feel the blush settle on her cheeks. She was burning up.

'Don't forget to lock up after me.' Billy smiled.

She nodded again. He'd given her his number in case she

needed help. Holding another man's phone number in her hand after so many years felt surreal.

She couldn't believe it. She'd done it. She'd left Mark. He would never hurt them again. Wren and Ty were safe. She just hoped that Mark had done no lasting damage to Wren. He seemed OK, empathetic and the perfect son, but although he usually talked to her about everything, she didn't know what was going on inside his head. He was her best friend, and she loved him so much.

Wren came back inside from exploring the backyard in the light of the spotlight attached to the corner of the house. She hugged him close to her.

'Can you believe it?' she said. 'We're finally free. We can start again, just the three of us.' He hugged her tightly, and she noticed how tall he was getting. He was going to tower over her soon.

Mark would be getting home from work in an hour. She felt a hot ball of fear settle in her stomach. He thought of them as his property, and if he found out where she lived, he'd come to bring her home. Forcibly if necessary. That couldn't happen.

Her mom had given her money, enough to fill the pantry and pay the bills until she worked out what she was going to do. For the first time ever she would be in control of her own fate. It was an exhilarating feeling, and she smiled to herself. There was no bed that night for her or Wren, so she had put Wren on the couch for the night. Billy said he'd bring beds as soon as he could from his mom's house. She moved comforters and blankets to the floor in the large bedroom. Sometime during the night, Wren had snuck into her bedroom, and now shared the space with her. She hugged him to her, molding around his curved body. She smiled into his hair, inhaling the scent of shampoo.

She would be getting Ty in the morning from her mom's house, then their home would be complete. Her mom had been so supportive, offering to babysit Ty while Vanessa sorted things out with Billy and the new house. Her mom had known the old lady who had lived there before Billy brought the house, she'd been moved into a nursing home by her children. Vanessa had brought the cot and nearly all of Ty's stuff with them as baby stuff was expensive to replace and obviously Mark wouldn't be needing it. There was no way that he'd be getting to see her children. He could take her court if he wanted to, but he wouldn't win.

The ring of her cellphone startled her, and she quickly silenced it. Wren mumbled in his sleep but didn't stir. One guess as to who it was. *Mark.* A jolt of electricity coursed through her. She was afraid, imaging that he was outside, waiting in his car. She knew that was silly; there's no way he knew where they were already. He would never connect Billy to her, he probably didn't even know that Billy was back in town. The ringer stopped, and she put the phone on the floor. It rang again almost immediately, and she ignored it again. It stopped, and she sighed before it rang again. He continued to ring her nearly every ten minutes, so she put it on the kitchen bench and went back to bed, dreaming of her boys playing in the backyard.

They were free.

6

By nine the next morning, Vanessa and Wren had unpacked the kitchen boxes, had breakfast, dressed and brushed their teeth. Vanessa had been up since dawn, unpacking boxes in the lounge, making muffins, checking her phone and worrying that Mark would bang on their door at any moment.

'How about we start unpacking your room until we have to go and pick up Ty?' Vanessa suggested to Wren. He came and hugged her. She was getting more hugs and kisses from him than ever before, but she would take every touch she could get. Once the house was set up, it would feel more like a home, although she already felt at ease here.

There was a knock at the door at about ten o'clock and both Vanessa and Wren froze in fear. It was a quiet knock, not the bang of someone whose family had run away and been found.

'Who is it?' she asked timidly through the wooden door, not daring to look through the glass panel at the side.

'It's just us, honey,' said her mom, and Vanessa opened the door.

'I thought I was coming to you,' Vanessa said, confused.

'You did, but I wanted to see the new house. Wow, it's lovely.'

'Right?' Vanessa smiled as she took Ty so her mom could take a look around. Nannie gave Wren a hug and kiss, then he took her on a tour of the house. Vanessa kissed Ty on his plump little cheek, cradling him to her breast. She couldn't breastfeed so he was already on formula.

Her mom came back into the lounge. 'It's just perfect,' she exclaimed. 'And Wren's room is so blue. It's spectacular.'

Wren giggled and hugged into his nannie. He was so affectionate, it was wonderful. 'I like it here, Mom – it's our house now that Ty is home.' He walked over to Ty and grasped his little brother's hand in his. Ty curled his fingers around Wren's, and he laughed, something she couldn't get enough of. Things were going to get better; she just knew it.

'It has all worked out perfectly. It was meant to be. Besides, we're due for some good luck.' She laughed, the sound foreign to her ears, and she cut it off abruptly.

'It's OK to be happy, Ness, darling. So... what happens when Mark finds out where you are? You know he came round last night.' her mother said directly, staring into Vanessa's eyes.

'Shit. I'm sorry Mom. I gather it's going to be soon – it's a small town after all. People will find out that I've left him, they'll talk, and he'll find us. It's inevitable. I'll just call the police or Billy every time he shows up. Billy is basically around the corner and has already volunteered to come around whenever we need him. He's been so sweet.' She felt the beat of desire again and was embarrassed. She must have blushed again because her mom said, 'Ness, it's OK to like someone else. You know I'd love to see you happy and if Billy is the one to do it, then I'm ecstatic for you. In the meantime, is there anything that I can do for you, honey? You know, to help out?'

Vanessa had been wondering how to bring this particular

topic up, so her mom bringing the question up eased Vanessa's burden. 'Actually, yes. I'm going to try to get a part-time job so it'd be a huge help if you could watch Ty and Wren after school. Would that be OK?' She looked at her mom with apprehension, saying her words quickly out of habit before she was cut off.

'I would love that!' her mother said immediately, and Vanessa felt another huge weight lift from her shoulders. Soon she would float away if not anchored to the ground.

Eventually, she had to come back down to Earth, but not today. 'I've got Billy coming over at eleven for a thank-you coffee and choc-mint muffins. The oven works great.' She was trying to bury the hint, but her mom picked it up quickly.

'Oh, I see. Well, I guess I'd better get going so you can get ready for your date,' she said with a cheeky grin.

'Mom! It's not a date, just a thank you.' But she was still blushing, heat flaming her face.

'Just remember, it's not cheating – you've left him.'

'He's just a friend from school.' Even to her the lie sounded wrong. Her priority for the past ten years had been Wren; she was not used to looking forward to something for herself. It was an unfamiliar feeling, and she felt a pang of longing.

'OK, I'm heading off now, have fun and say hi for me.' Vanessa's mother gave her daughter a wink before showing herself out the door.

Vanessa set out the muffins on a plate and boiled the kettle, ready for the coffee that she had promised Billy. Her phone vibrated on the kitchen bench where she had left it last night.

'Is that Dad?' Wren asked, seeming to hold Ty tighter in his arms as he sat on the worn wooden chair at the kitchen table.

'Yes, baby, it is your dad. He called lots last night too.' In fact, when she had checked her phone this morning there were twenty-five missed calls, all from Mark. As if she'd pick up. She was no longer his slave. She was a free woman to do as she pleased.

'I'm just going to ignore his calls. I have nothing to say to him anyway.'

'That's a good idea, Mom,' Wren said, sounding wise beyond his ten years.

Vanessa looked at Ty in his brother's arms and thought, *Mark is never going to hurt you like he hurt Wren.* It was her vow to her youngest child.

There was another knock at the door, and Vanessa cautioned Wren to always ask who it was as he passed his little brother to his mother.

'It's Billy. May I come in?'

With a huge grin on his face, he opened the door. 'Hi, Billy,' he said, now all shy.

'Hey, Wren,' he said as he put a hand on the boy's shoulder.

Billy came toward Vanessa in the kitchen, and her heart beat out of time. 'Hey,' she said as he kissed her on the cheek.

'Hey yourself. This must be Ty,' Billy said, looking at the newborn in his mother's arms. 'He looks like you, Wren.' Wren seemed to stand up even straighter with the compliment. Vanessa put Ty into the travel cot that was set up in the lounge. 'Something smells good.'

'Mint choc chip muffins, and I'll make you that coffee.' She bustled round the kitchen, aware of his eyes on her.

She placed a steaming cup of coffee in front of him and then gave him a muffin on a small side plate. She was nervous, she realized with a start, like she was back in school and he was her first crush.

'Is there anything I can do for you? Build furniture? Move boxes? Something like that?' He was sincere in his offer to help and took a big gulp of coffee, which burned his throat, making him cough. He was nervous too. She got him a water, and he drained it quickly. 'Thanks,' he managed to choke out.

'Well, I guess I do need a bed at some stage. I slept on the floor last night, but it was the best sleep I've had in a long while until Mark started calling and didn't stop all night. I ended up putting the phone on silent and in the kitchen. He must be so pissed at me.'

'You aren't afraid?'

'There's nothing that he can do to me that he hasn't already done.'

'Oh, Ness,' Billy covered her hand with his. 'I'll go and grab the bed from Mom's house. I reckon any furniture you take is good for me – she was kind of a hoarder. I think I'll be living there sorting for about a year at this rate.' He bit into a muffin. 'God, this is good,' he said through his mouthful. 'I haven't had home-cooked anything in a long time.'

Being appreciated wasn't something that she was used to, and she blushed again. She had never blushed so much in her life. What could she say? Billy brought the girl out in her.

Wren came back into the room. 'Want a muffin, honey?' Vanessa asked.

Wren said yes and grabbed a muffin off a proffered plate, taking a small bite. 'Billy is taking us round to his mom's place to pick out some furniture. Do you want to come, or do you want me to drop you off with Ty at Nannie's?'

'I want to come too,' Wren said eagerly. It was obvious that he liked Billy a lot. He was bonding with him quickly. It was nice to see him look up to someone. Vanessa hadn't realized how much Wren was craving a role model, a man who showed interest in him. It was lovely to see.

'Are you sure this is OK, Billy?' she asked again.

'I'd do anything for a... friend.'

He was flirting with her, but she couldn't remember how to flirt back. It had been so long since a man had shown any interest in her. She was used to cutting words and brutal fists, nothing more.

After tidying away the plates, they set off, Vanessa dropping Ty at her mother's house before meeting Wren and Billy at his place. They were already inside when Vanessa arrived, Wren taking a tour of the house.

Vanessa couldn't shake an anxious feeling as she kept expecting to see Mark around every corner, but when she looked, he was never there. There was so much that she needed, and here was Billy offering to give her anything she could want. She was so grateful. And she kept saying it.

'Vanessa, you don't need to keep thanking me – I'm happy to help.' He put his hands on her shoulders. 'Truly.'

An hour later, Billy started loading the trailer with Wren's help. When everything was packed up, they drove back to their home and started unloading.

'Billy? Want a cold drink?' Vanessa called from the house.

'Yeah, that'd be great, thanks.' He came over sat down on the porch next to Vanessa, and she slid the cold water in front of him. 'It's so nice to see Mom's furniture in your house. She always had a soft spot for you and Maggie.'

At the mention of Maggie's name, Vanessa's stomach twisted.

Billy saw the look on her face. 'You two still not talking?'

'She's sleeping with Mark. He's been hitting her. I feel for her, but I can't get involved. I have enough on my plate. Especially where Mark is concerned.'

'I'm sorry, Ness, you didn't have much of a choice with Mark, but Maggie has a choice, she's not married to him.'

'It's not as easy as that. You get trapped in this cycle. You're made to feel worthless, afraid, always told that no one will ever love you because you're this, you're that. It's... hard. I think she feels trapped, just like I was. Until you came along.' She gave him a shy smile. 'Mom told me that Mark went round to her house last night. Probably hoping that she'd lead him to me, but she never left the house. She didn't want to call the police and inflame the situation.'

'Do you want me to talk to him?' Billy asked. He was a large man, physically impressive, taller than Mark and hadn't let himself run to fat like Mark had.

'No! That's a terrible idea. Sorry, but that would make things so much worse. He would kill me.'

'OK, don't panic, I won't say anything. But if he ever comes here, *ever*, I need you to call me, all right? I'll come right over and take care of it, day or night.'

'I appreciate that, Billy, I really do. He'll come for me eventually, but for now he'll be licking his wounds. Besides, he doesn't even want the boys, and he only made me stay because I screwed up his life and he thinks I should pay with mine forever. I have to move forward; I refuse to stay stuck in the past.'

'Jesus.' Billy rubbed a hand over his day-old beard. He reached out his hand and lightly touched hers, rubbing her fingers gently. She could hear Wren coming and pulled her hand back. She wasn't sure what was going on here, and Wren didn't need any more upheaval and uncertainty. He needed stability, and she was going to provide it.

Billy stood up. 'I'd better get going. I'm really glad you could use Mom's stuff. Call me anytime, Ness. OK? Anytime.' Vanessa saw him to the door.

When she came back into the kitchen, Wren was waiting. 'I like him, Mom. I think he's going to be a great friend. To you and me and Ty.' Approval delivered, he ran down the hallway to his blue room.

7

The next six months seemed to go by quickly. Vanessa couldn't have been happier with the house, her boys and her freedom, but she kept waiting for the other shoe to drop. For Mark to drag her kicking and screaming back to their old house. There was just no way he was going to let them go without a fight. She knew he'd want revenge.

Wren was happier than he had ever been. He stopped jumping at loud noises and she hoped eventually the haunted look would leave his eyes. He would go around every morning and every night to check the doors and the window locks. He was vigilant about safety and protecting his family. But Vanessa knew that if Mark wanted in, then Mark would get in. She kept her cellphone in her pocket at all times and had a landline installed, with a second handset in the baby's room, which also had a lock on the door – a good one – installed by Billy. Alongside this, Vanessa had put an old milk crate outside the window, resting on the ground, so Wren could get out of the window if need be. The screen popped off easily and noiselessly. She also kept a baby carrier hanging in the wardrobe in case her boys had to leave in a hurry and run to Billy's. He hid a spare key for Wren in case of an emergency and they'd drilled what to do. You could never be too careful. It was sad that she had to do all of this, but she would protect her children at all costs.

* * *

It was still dark outside when Vanessa woke up. She lay on her side and tried to listen for any sounds in the old house. Vanessa wasn't sure what woke her. It wasn't Ty – the baby monitor by her bed was silent. Wren? Possibly. She should get up and check. She looked at her phone; it was two-thirty in the morning, what would Wren be doing up? Then she heard a noise, small and almost inaudible, but it was there. She was sure she wasn't imagining it. Quietly she rolled out of bed, gripping her phone, and made her way through the darkness of the now familiar house, touching furniture as she went. She checked on Wren, asleep in his bed, and Ty, flat on his back and snoring slightly, his face slack. She went to the front door and ensured it was locked, then repeated it for the back door. The same. She headed back to the front door in the darkness and moved the curtain a little to peek out. Mark's car sat outside her house. Quickly she let the curtain drop, fear making her head swim. Vanessa backed up a couple of steps before turning and running into the kitchen where she grabbed the first knife she laid her hands on from the knife block. She backed herself into a corner, knife by her side. Then she remembered the phone in her hand. She wasn't too proud to ask for help. She rang Billy. It had been ages since she'd heard from Mark, but she'd had a feeling that everything wasn't OK.

He answered on the third ring.

'His car is out the front. I can't tell if he's in it or not. I'm scared.' She bit her bottom lip, the knife wavering by her side as she wondered if she could actually use it on another human being.

'Get somewhere safe, lock yourself in Ty's room. I'm coming right now.' She could hear the determination in his voice, the desire to protect her and the boys.

She put the phone in her pocket and, holding the knife out in front of her, ran to Wren's bedroom. She put a hand over his mouth, and he woke up with a start. He knew the drill. Stay silent. Don't make a sound. She motioned for him to go next door to Ty's room. She followed him in and spun around, throwing the bolt in the lock. 'Billy's coming,' she whispered, devastated by the frightened look on her son's face. Just when he was beginning to live a less scared life, here they were again. His mouth was slack, and his eyes were dark pits in the shadowed room, illuminated by a small night-light.

When someone knocked on the bedroom door, she let out a squeal of fright and Wren grabbed her hand tightly.

'It's me, Ness, open up.' Relief flooded through her at the sound of Billy's voice, and she quickly unlocked the door. 'You OK?' he whispered so as not to wake Ty.

'Yes, we're OK.'

Billy squatted down so he was looking up at Wren. 'You all right, little man?' At those words, Wren threw himself into Billy's arms, who almost lost his balance. He hugged him back before letting go of the boy and standing up. 'He wasn't in his car. Maybe he was just trying to scare you. I'm surprised you made it this long without him finding out where you were living, but I'll go and check the rest of the house, all right? Lock the door behind me again.' He left the room, and she did as he said. She pulled Wren to her side and wrapped one arm around him. He slid his arms around her.

'Why won't Dad leave us alone?' he asked, looking up at his

mom. 'He doesn't even like us.' He sounded way too old for a ten-year-old. Having a dad like Mark, going through what he had, had given him a perspective that other kids his age couldn't even imagine.

'I don't know, honey. I don't know what your dad is thinking.' She left it at that. She had much more to say on the subject, but Wren was not the right audience.

Billy knocked on the door again, announcing himself. 'He's not here. I didn't see any evidence that he was inside either.'

'But I heard noises, like someone was moving around but it was sneaky like. I don't know, maybe I imagined it after all. I was half asleep.' As they spoke, they heard a car peel down the street. Vanessa looked out her bedroom window. 'He's gone. If he wasn't in the car and he wasn't inside, then where the hell was he?'

'I don't know,' Billy said, 'but he's gone now and that's all that matters.'

'Thanks for coming to check it out. I'm sorry I called you in the middle of the night.'

He gave her a gentle smile that curved up the edges of his lips and she couldn't help but smile back, her previous fears almost forgotten. 'Call me later?' he said in a low voice.

She didn't trust herself to speak, so she just nodded. She heard him lock the front door on his way out.

'All right, Wren, let's get you back into bed.' She glanced at Ty, then rested her hand on his tiny chest, feeling the rise and fall of his breathing. God, she loved her kids. One final look at his relaxed face and she ushered Wren back into his room. She was sure that he was asleep before his head even connected with his pillow. It took Vanessa a lot longer to drop off. The first tendrils of dawn were already licking at her windows when she finally fell asleep.

* * *

Vanessa woke, trying to wipe the gritty feeling from her eyes. She'd better have a shower before the boys woke up. Checking her phone, she saw she'd only been asleep for an hour and a bit. Not nearly long enough. After her shower, she went to the kitchen to organize breakfast for Wren, but he had beaten her to it.

'Morning, Mom,' he said cheerily, pouring milk onto his cereal. He looked well rested despite being woken up in the middle of the night.

'Morning, honey. You're making your own breakfast? I'm impressed.'

'Dad used to tell me that making food was women's work, but I don't believe that.'

Smiling, she walked over and gave Wren a noisy kiss on top of his head. 'Love you, kiddo.' She watched as he finished making, then eating his breakfast. Wren had come so far in these last few months. Imagine how he'd be in a few years. *Stability,* she thought again.

Ty started to cry, signaling that he too was awake. 'I'll go get him up and ready to take you to school.' School had always been a safe haven for Wren; he could fall into one of his books and forget about the darkness in the world around him.

Vanessa walked into Ty's room and looked at the fussy baby. 'Good morning, my darling boy. How are you today?' He gave her a smile of sorts and gurgled; his earlier cries forgotten. She picked him up out of his cot, changed his nappy and took off his pajamas, put him in fresh clothes and took him into the kitchen where she sat down and gave him his breakfast. Wren packed his lunch, which he'd also made himself, and put it into his bag. Ty let out a whopping burp, which had Wren dissolving into giggles. Vanessa smiled too.

'Alright, let's get a wriggle on.' They all moved out to the car and Wren climbed into the back seat and buckled his seatbelt while Vanessa strapped Ty's harness into the capsule. Now that they were both safe, she backed out of the driveway, checking both ways, looking for Mark's car more than anything. Once they pulled up at the school, she blew a kiss to Wren. This year he was walking to class alone, wanting to be a big boy, but now and then she was allowed to walk with him. Not this morning, though.

She looked down at the gas gauge and realized that she needed fuel. There was only one place in town to fill up, a sad-looking café attached to a garage that had been owned by old man Phillips since she could remember. He'd been working on cars forever, his wife running the café. It had been a little neglected – OK, a lot neglected – for a while now.

From the exterior, it looked abandoned; weeds grew through the gaps in the concrete yard, the sign was faded and peeling, and the interior... she didn't even know where to start. She normally just ignored it, taking Ty in with her, paying for her gas, then leaving again. It smelled like old fried food and it hadn't seen a lick of paint in a while. The food in the heated cabinets was deep fried, shriveled and entirely unappetizing.

She had filled up her bomb of a car – brought for her by her parents when she graduated high school. Her dad had taught her to drive it. She missed her dad terribly, but she still wasn't ready to speak to him. She readjusted Ty in her arms, as she walked in to pay for her petrol.

She skimmed the bulletin board while she was waiting.

Staff member needed. Start ASAP. No experience necessary. Part time. Enquire at register.

Well, she did need a job and it couldn't hurt to ask what it was.

'Vanessa? Is that you?' She turned around and saw a familiar face.

'Toby!' She gave him an awkward hug as she had Ty attached to her. Vanessa had also gone to school with Toby, old man Phillips' son. They'd been close until he had moved away just after graduation.

'You had another baby, I see. What's his name?'

'Tyson, Ty for short. He's such a little gem.'

'So how is Wren? And Mark?' he asked casually. He must have already caught up on the gossip to know Wren's name.

'Actually, between you and me, I've left Mark. I moved out; things are actually beginning to look up.' She smiled at him, a genuine, happy smile.

'I saw you looking at dad's bulletin board. I put a few things up this morning. Anything catch your attention?'

'Yeah. You're looking for someone. To do what?'

Toby leaned against the counter, standing exactly where his mom used to stand when she served them snacks after school. 'What do you think of this café?'

'What do I think?' She shifted Ty to the other arm, absent-mindedly jiggling him up and down. 'Well, I think there's potential for it to be a really nice café that people can come in, sit down and have a nice lunch or snack in. But what do I see? Neglect. Sadness. A waste.'

Toby was silent.

'Oh God! I've offended you, haven't I?'

'No, not at all. Mom passed away and the place has kind of gone to ruin. Dad has tried to keep up, but he was never good at this kind of stuff.'

'Oh Toby, I'm so sorry to hear about your mom's passing. I

always remembered her as a lovely lady who made a mean apple crumble.'

'Thanks Ness, I appreciate that. She'd been sick for a while. Tell me,' he said after a moment's pause, 'what would you do differently?' Toby asked.

Without missing a beat, Vanessa said, 'Well, I'd start by putting up a new sign at the front with "Under New Management" on it. Repaint the concrete tiles in an appealing terracotta color. I'd like to see some outdoor tables and chairs, maybe with umbrellas for hot days. I'd redo the floor inside, polished concrete – it's hard wearing and looks great. I'd overhaul the menu, if you can call it that, and lastly, I'd add fresh food and muffins to the menu. I think that's about it.'

He just stared at her. 'What? You asked,' she said defensively, changing the increasingly heavy Ty to the other arm again.

Toby smiled. 'All right then.'

'All right then what?'

'You have yourself a job. Can you start tomorrow?'

He took in her open mouth and wide eyes and began laughing. 'You should see your face right now. Dad needs help, we're losing money on this side of the business and you clearly have an eye for improvements and details.'

Surely, he didn't just offer her a job. Did he?

'So, can you start tomorrow? There's no one to train you, but I'm sure you can work most of it out. I need to go back to the city; I can't spend any more time here, and Dad's been a bit... stuck since Mom died. He needs a woman's touch around the place. Here's my card, contact me to talk about budgets and staffing. You can hire another part-timer to cover you as I know you've got a family and you're a single mom now.'

'I just can't believe this. You're seriously offering me a job?'

'I'm seriously *giving* you a job, and I'm really hoping you're going to take it.' He put his hand out.

She reached out her free hand to shake his. 'You have yourself a deal.' She gave him a smile and he briefly touched Ty's soft cheek as he said goodbye.

She had a job!

As soon as she got home and put Ty down for a nap, she rang her mom. 'Hey Mom, it's me. Can you come over? I've just put Ty down and I have news.' she said excitedly. She was dying to tell her mom what had happened with... everything.

Within ten minutes her mom was sitting across from her, drinking a cup of tea. 'So,' she said. 'You look like you're going to burst. What has made you so happy?'

'Actually, I have two things to tell you. One good, one not so good.'

'I prefer good news first.'

'OK, remember Toby from school?'

'Little Toby Phillips?'

'Yeah, except he's all grown up now.'

'Is that the good news? That you ran into an old friend?'

'No, but something good *did* happen. He offered me a job running the café next to the gas station in town.'

'Oh, Ness! That's wonderful. I'm so proud of you. You'll do an awesome job.'

'Do you think you could watch the kids when I'm at work?' She held her breath; her taking the job depended on her mom helping her out.

'Of course I will, I'd love to have more time with my grand-children.'

Vanessa breathed a sigh of relief, then touched her mom's hand, covering it with her own. She could feel the bones in her hand, thinner than she remembered, delicate, bird-like. 'Thanks, Mom.'

'Now,' she said, 'what else did you want to tell me? What is the bad news? Do I even want to know?'

'Probably not.' Vanessa toyed with the cup of tea in front of her, turning it round and round.

'Ness. What happened? You're beginning to worry me.'

'Mark was here last night. He was outside, and I had to call Billy. I thought I heard something in the house, I thought it was Mark, but there was no sign of him inside. Then his car took off down the street. It scared me, and Wren was awake as well. I just want this all to be over, for Wren to have a normal life. He's just starting to laugh again, to loosen up, I want that to keep going, not have him regress because of fucking Mark.'

'I agree. He can't be afraid all the time. He's scarred by his father; it's not right.' Her mother paused before continuing. 'I have to ask. You and Billy, is there anything going on there? I mean, seriously, no one would blame you. He's a good guy and you deserve so much more than Mark.' She almost spat his name in disgust. 'Billy's a keeper you know.'

Vanessa blushed. 'There's nothing going on.'

'OK, OK, I won't pressure you about it, but remember you know you can come to me anytime, with anything. Speaking of exes, I saw your dad the other day.'

'What? Why? You're not getting back with him, are you?' Vanessa was worried for her mom, her dad had done the wrong thing by her and kept it a secret for all those years. Her mom was still vulnerable from spending thirty years with the man.

'No, I'm not taking him back, I have no intention of it, but he's having money troubles, so he's asked if he can move into the guesthouse out the back for a while. I said yes.' She sipped her tea. 'Thoughts?'

'Mom, you can't. This is just a ploy to get closer to you and you've let him come back halfway already by letting him stay on your property. Before you know it, he'll be back at home. Tell me you've thought this through?' Vanessa was worried, very worried. Her mom was fragile, and she never could say no to her dad.

'Oh honey, I have. I'm not getting back together with him, I'm just helping him out till he's on his feet again. He made a terrible mistake and I believe he's sorry, but it's over. He wants to see the boys every now and then. He misses Wren and he'd love to meet Ty. Would that be OK?'

Vanessa looked at the doorway as if expecting her children to magically appear, conjured by her memory.

'That's a serious ask. You may have forgiven him, but I haven't. Not yet.' She ran a hand through her hair, mussing it up.

Her mom stood up, rinsing her cup and putting it on the draining rack. 'Have a think about it, and I'll see you and the boys tomorrow.'

'OK, Mom, thanks, I'll drop Ty off first thing in the morning, take Wren to school then go check out the cafe.' She kissed her mom goodbye at the door and watched her drive off. There was something a little off about her mom, but she put it down to her dad coming back into her life. The nerve of him to ask her for help after what he did.

8

Vanessa was wiping down the already spotless counter when she saw Toby standing outside the café, taking in the freshly painted exterior. 'Vanessa! The place looks great, well done,' he said as he entered. 'You've done such an amazing job – there are even people sitting outside eating something that I hope there is still a slice of because it smells so good!' She was so pleased that he liked everything that she had changed. She had put hours and hours of thought into how to make the café shine. Old man Phillips and her had clashed on some of the changes, but after a phone call to his son, who had chastised his father, he had come around. Especially when he saw the finished product. She included him where she could, but he seemed to be happy now to leave it all up to her.

She enjoyed working and earning her own money; there was a sense of pride attached to being able to support her children. She didn't rely on her mom now for anything except babysitting. As the months passed, she met new people and began to form friendships with the regulars. People from all over town came to the café, not just for petrol or repairs anymore but to taste her cooking, the cakes, muffins and fresh sandwiches. She had done that, herself.

Toby touched base with her less and less as time progressed. He could see that the café's numbers showed promise so he was very happy with her. She had hired a part-timer, Leanne, a girl in her twenties who was able to take the shifts that Vanessa couldn't. Quite often, Vanessa's mom would pop down with the boys if she were working the late shift. Wren, now eleven, would come behind the counter and help her serve people, telling them to have a good day, or help her cook out the back. He was such great company, and those times together only served to highlight just how delightful he was. Her mom would sit out the back with Ty, who Vanessa cuddled whenever she could. He was growing up so fast, and her heart swelled with love every time she thought about her children.

She still thought about Mark often. He knew where she worked, the town was only so big, yet he'd made no effort to harass her. It unnerved her more than she cared to think. What was he playing at? She had seen him standing across the road staring at the café a couple of times. It was only a matter of time, she was sure of it. She tried not to worry, but subtlety was not one of Mark's strong points, so of course she was wary. It made her uncomfortable knowing that he could come for her at any time.

Vanessa still worried about protecting her boys. She worried that she'd put too much weight on Wren's small shoulders. After all he'd seen, to be growing up into such a wonderful young man was a credit to his personality. He was also a great big brother and would make a great role model when Ty was older.

* * *

Another few months passed without her seeing Mark at all. He stopped standing across the road, staring at the café. With her fingers crossed, it seemed like he was finally going to let her and the boys go. She had expected, well, she didn't know what she expected, but silence from him wasn't it. Over a year of silence.

She hadn't seen Billy for a few days. He had decided to set up a new business since he was going to be in town for the foreseeable future, landscaping, like he'd been doing since he'd left high school. He loved working with his hands, designing gardens for clients. Although he'd used the excuse that sorting his mother's house was taking longer than anticipated, Vanessa knew that his future depended on her; he was just too polite or scared to say so. With his landscaping business he sometimes had Wren help him do easy jobs like weeding. Wren got a kick out of driving around in the pickup, sitting up front, being treated like a man by Billy and earning some pocket money.

Vanessa didn't know how she felt about Billy's absence. Was he backing off from their friendship? Or was he giving her time to get herself together? She wasn't sure, and she didn't know what it meant for her or for them.

She was sweeping the floor in the café one morning after dropping Wren off to school. Her was hair falling out of its loose bun, jeans clinging to her curvy shape, which was complemented by a slouchy gray top that hung from one shoulder. She was staring intently at a stubborn piece of dirt on the floor that just wouldn't move when she felt someone's stare and for a terrifying moment, she thought it was Mark. She turned slowly, the hairs on the back of her neck rising. But it was Billy, standing there, grinning at her with his slightly lopsided smile that she found endearing.

'Billy, you scared me!' Her hand immediately went to her hair, smoothing it down. Suddenly she felt self-conscious about her choice of clothing.

'You look busy,' he said, indicating the broom. 'Want some help?'

'How are you at swinging a mop?'

He saluted her playfully before going into the back room and returning with a mop and bucket of soapy water. He began to clean the floor, starting in the far corner. They worked in silence for a few moments before Vanessa moved to the walk-in fridge to sort out some stock. She heard him speak but the whirring of the cooling systems meant she didn't hear him.

'Pardon?' she said as she came back out on to the main café floor.

'I said that the place is looking really good. You've really turned it around. Toby must be happy. How's old man Phillips taking all the changes now?'

Vanessa laughed. 'Well, as you know, at first he wasn't happy, and we had a few clashes about... well... everything really, but he's come round, and he loves the boys, always finding a reason to come in when they're here. Not everyone copes well with change, but I think he's doing a wonderful job.'

'Except you,' he said, finishing off the mopping.

'Except me what?'

'You cope well with change.'

'What does that mean?' she asked, surprise on her face.

'Only that you've had so much thrown at you – you left your husband, became a single mother, started a new job – but you look amazing, and happy.' He looked away, as if embarrassed by his words.

'Thanks, Billy,' she said softly, blushing at his kind comment. She didn't know what else to say, but she did know how it made her feel, like a teenager again.

* * *

While putting on the sausages to cook, Vanessa said to Wren, 'Hun, how 'bout you go run a bath for Ty and I'll get dinner ready for you?' Wren nodded and took Ty from her arms. She watched as he left the room, talking to his little brother, hearing Ty's garbled and cheerful responses. She could hear the pair of them giggling from the kitchen, it was a lovely sound to hear. It made her heart swell with love. Wren was so attentive to Ty. Always playing with him and taking care of him. She couldn't be more proud of him. Vanessa walked down the hallway and stopped at the bathroom door, peering around the corner. Wren was leaning over the bath pouring water over Ty's head who giggled underneath the waterfall of warm water.

'Honey?'

He looked up. 'Yeah, Mom?'

'I just wanted to tell you how much I appreciate your help. Love you.' She went back to the kitchen to check on dinner then made her way down the hallway to her room.

She was intending to get changed after a hard day at the café. She pushed open her bedroom door and stopped in stunned shock. All of her clothes were strewn across her bed and floor, every drawer opened and empty, her cosmetics in the bathroom were carelessly thrown across the floor. Her bed had been slashed, the knife marks going through to the stuffing of the mattress. From her vantage point, she could see the bathroom mirror. In red lipstick were the words: *You're next.*

Stifling a scream, she backed out of the bedroom and closed the door. She ran into Ty's bedroom where Wren was getting him dressed after his bath. She took him from her son's hands, finished dressing him and grabbed the nappy bag.

'We're going to Nannie's house. I've barely seen her all week. So, c'mon, let's go. Chop, chop.' She turned off the stove and ushered them quickly to the car.

Wren gave her a quizzical look, and she knew what he was going to ask. 'What's wrong, Mom?'

'Nothing, sweetheart, I just changed my mind about eating at home. And I miss Nannie,' she finished lamely.

He could see right through her. 'He did something, didn't he?'

She looked at him in the rear-view mirror; his fists were clenched by his sides in anger.

She chose not to answer, just kept driving. He was looking out the window the next time she glanced at him, fists still clenched. 'Maybe we'll even stay the night,' Vanessa said cheerfully. 'We haven't done that in a while either. Nannie won't mind – she loves having us over.' She was being overly bright and happy, but Wren would know something was up. He knew her better than that.

'Mom,' he said, his tone so stern that she felt like a schoolgirl in the principal's office about to get a rap on the knuckles.

Vanessa sighed, glancing in the mirror at him again. 'Your dad might have been in the house.'

'What?'

'I don't know for sure so we're going to Nannie's so I can call the police to check it out. It'll be fine, Wren, OK? Don't worry, honey.' She wanted to shield him, but she also wanted to be honest with him. He was her best friend, someone who had been through the wars with her and lived to tell the tale.

Her mom was surprised to see them this late but didn't ask any questions even when she saw the strained expression on Vanessa's face, but once they had settled the children, she had pounced on her daughter.

'What is going on and why do you look so scared? What happened? Is it Mark?' She looked as worried as Vanessa felt.

'Someone broke into my house,' she said, twisting a piece of hair around her finger, almost mirroring her mom who was playing with her fringe. 'I suspect it was Mark,' Vanessa continued. 'My room was trashed but the rest of the house was OK.'

'Well, are you going to call the police?' Vanessa thought about it. Should she call the police? What would they even do? Give him a talking to? What would that achieve? There was no way to prove it was even him.

'Yeah, I think I might. Even if they can't prove it's Mark, at least there'll be a record of the break-in.' She pulled out her cellphone, scrolled through until she found the local police station's number.

Officer Emily Beck knocked on her mom's door later that night. Vanessa and Emily had shared some of the same classes at high school.

'Officer Beck. Did you go to my house?' Vanessa was almost scared of the answer.

'Evening, Vanessa. May I come in?'

Vanessa opened up the door and Emily strolled inside. She saw Vanessa's mom and headed toward the kitchen to say hi. Everyone knew everyone here. But Vanessa couldn't wait for them to finish their small talk. 'Did you find Mark?'

'Yes, at the bar.' Beck regarded her with cool, blue eyes.

'Well, did you question him about the break-in? Where he was, things like that?' It felt like she was pulling teeth trying to get information out of her.

Beck raised her eyebrows and Vanessa felt like a chastised child. 'Yes, I questioned him. He said he'd been at the bar during the day and after work he was with his girlfriend, who vouched for him. I believe you know Maggie?' Twisting the knife. Beck had sided with Maggie when the shit had hit the fan.

'You know I do, Emily. Are you trying to say that he didn't trash my bedroom? Who else would do that? I was targeted, I'm sure of it.' She blew out a frustrated breath, her voice had been getting steadily higher as she spoke.

'We've taken fingerprints and photos from the scene. It could have been a crime of opportunity.'

'Emily, he wrote "You're next" on my mirror – feels pretty bloody specific to me.'

'It could still be someone trying to scare you.'

'Yeah, my husband.' She was adamant that it was Mark behind it, but that Maggie was covering for him.

'Did you speak to Maggie? Alone, I mean? She might have a different story to tell.'

'No, I spoke to them both. Nothing was stolen as you pointed out, no locks were forced, and no real damage was done. I'll file a report, but it's not high on our list of priorities.'

'Great, thanks, Emily,' she said, trying to keep the sarcasm out of her voice. She saw the police officer out and returned to the kitchen.

'Well, that wasn't much use. Might as well not have bothered calling them,' her mom said to Vanessa, turning from the bench and offering her daughter a cup of tea.

To say Vanessa was disappointed was an understatement. What did they expect Maggie to say when Mark was standing right there?

'Are you going home, honey, or do you want to stay here?'

'I was going to stay but now I want to go home. He's not chasing me away from my home again, besides, I need to clean up and Wren has school tomorrow.'

Twenty minutes later, they were back at home with Wren and Ty settled into their beds. Vanessa was just about to tidy up the mess from the break-in when there was a quiet knock at the front door, close to her bedroom. She looked out the window before opening the door.

'Billy! What are you doing here?' It was late.

'Your mom called me, wanted me to come over and keep an eye on you, maybe help you out.' He came inside, then pushed open her bedroom door. 'Shit. What a mess.'

Vanessa sighed. Billy looked up in response. 'I'm not annoyed at you, but my mom shouldn't have bothered you. I'm sure you were busy.'

'Nope, free as a bird, happy to help. Sure nothing was stolen?'

'No, I've been around the house and checked, anything of value is still here. Your mom's bed has been slashed. It's ruined, I'm so sorry.' Vanessa became teary. This loving and gentle man had given her something important to him, and it had been destroyed on her watch.

'It doesn't matter. It's just a bed. Do you want me to stay the night? I can sleep on the couch.'

She thought about it, about her hard-fought independence. She'd called upon him so many times already. She only wanted to do it in emergencies. 'No, it's OK, but thanks.'

'All right, I'll help clean up then I'll be on my way.'

With two of them working, her room was returned to rights shortly after they started. When they finished, he grasped her by the shoulders and kissed her gently on the cheek, lingering. If she'd just moved her head toward him a little, he'd be kissing her lips. But she wasn't sure that she was ready for that, and she had to be ready... and sure. He pulled back, looking disappointed, but then understanding flooded his eyes.

'I really appreciate you coming to help me, yet again. I'll call if I need you tonight, otherwise I'll call you tomorrow. Maybe we can catch up...'

It was gloomy in the hallway, but she still saw him smile. He left, and she touched her cheek where he had kissed her. She made sure the door was locked – she wasn't taking any chances.

'Fuck, I thought he'd never leave,' a voice growled behind her.

Vanessa gasped, but a meaty hand was clapped over her mouth, cutting off any noise. It was Mark. He let go but dragged her to the ground by her hair. He knew for certain that she wouldn't make a noise now, in case she woke the boys. They both knew that she'd never subject them to him. She tried to huddle into a ball, knowing what was coming next, but still her breath was stolen when he kicked her with his boot. She felt an excruciating pain in her side as a rib snapped. She looked up, locking eyes with him. 'Please,' she whispered.

'You filthy slut. Bad enough that you ran, but to be fucking Billy while you're married to me? No fucking way.' He kicked her again and a small noise escaped through her pursed lips. She was trying so hard to keep from screaming, but the pain was building with every second. Soon she wouldn't be able to stop herself.

He pulled her up by the front of her shirt, the material ripping, the sound of her breath coming hard.

'I'm not yours,' she hissed at him, spitting in his face. How dare he come into *her* house and attack her.

He released and wiped the spittle off with his sleeve. 'Finally, some spirit. I wondered where the real Vanessa had gone, not this fucking insipid, mousy woman that I lived with day in and day out.'

'Then why didn't you leave if I was so boring?' She taunted, feigning to the left to get past him. He countered her, blocking her path to freedom.

'I told you, you fucked up my life, so it's my job to fuck up yours.' He grinned maniacally at her.

'Oh yeah? And what were you going to do with your life? Go somewhere? Be somebody? I don't think so – once a loser, always a loser.' She said, as she had done before. She was provoking him, but she didn't care. It felt good to say those things. Felt good to stand up for herself, even though she was going to pay for it.

He smacked her across the face, catching her high up on the cheekbone. Vanessa bit her lip so hard that it began to bleed, the copper taste leaching from her lip and into her mouth.

'I could have been with Maggie. Got out of this fucked-up town. You ruined my chance.'

'Well you're free now. I'll divorce you and you can marry Maggie and live happily ever after.'

She began to cough as he grasped his hand around her throat, slowly cutting off her air supply. 'Think you're so smart, hey bitch?' He let go of her throat, and she dropped to the carpet with a thump. She prayed that Wren hadn't heard it or their furious whispering. He slapped her again, putting all of his strength behind it. The same side as before. She could already feel the swelling, the blood rushing to her face, the throbbing filling her body, her rage building.

She managed to scramble to her feet, push past him while he was unsteady and shoot down the hallway. She turned back to see him following her. She ran into the kitchen and grabbed a knife from the knife block again. It all seemed so familiar, except this time she knew for certain that he was in the house.

'You're going to stab me?' he asked, laughing. 'Can you even do it, Ness? Stab a man in cold blood? Watch him bleed out in the same place where your kids eat their Cheerios? Is that any way to treat your husband?' he said in a mock loving voice.

'You're not my husband, you're just some guy who knocked me up.'

He reached out, grabbing her wrist and grinding her bones together so hard that she dropped the knife with a sharp yelp. He pushed her back onto the bench, her back connecting painfully with it. He lurched forward, yanking her chin to keep her still, then forced his tongue into her mouth. She gagged and he covered her nose, until she couldn't breathe and began to struggle against him. He pulled back, her mouth popping open. He tried to shove his whole fist inside her mouth, he'd done this before, and it never failed to make her panic. She couldn't breathe around his fist and reached up, trying to claw at his hand. Then she did something she'd never done before. She bit down as hard as she could, her hands still wrapped around his, forcing his fist to stay partially inside her mouth. She could feel metallic blood sliding down the back of her throat, this time his. He yelled and finally pulled his fist out, only after delivering a punch to Vanessa's ear with his other hand that left her head ringing, a woozy feeling enveloping her. She couldn't pass out. God knows what would happen to her children if she did.

'You bitch!' he hissed, cradling his damaged hand. She could see the rivulets of blood trickling from his injury, running down his wrist, and she smiled with satisfaction. Her grin wide, her bared teeth covered in his blood.

'Wren!' he screamed suddenly.

Vanessa looked at him in terror before she bolted from the kitchen down the hallway, trying to reach her son before Mark could. She got so close to his door, just past Ty's, when Mark tackled her from behind. She turned, landing awkwardly on the threadbare carpet on her back. She tried to get up, but his weight suddenly pinned her down, air leaving her body for a long moment until her lungs adjusted to the extra weight. The door to Wren's room stayed firmly shut. He must have still been asleep, having not heard his dad's yell. *Small mercies.*

Mark yanked down her pants then her underwear and Vanessa, knowing where this was headed, tried to buck him off her. She gnashed her teeth near his face, but he reared back out of her reach. She grunted in pain as he thrust two fingers inside her. He was too strong for her to fight, and there was nothing nearby that she could use as a weapon. He kept pushing his fingers in and out, hurting her. He knew he was hurting her; she saw the look of victory in his eyes. *Sadistic fuck*. Well, she wouldn't give him the satisfaction of crying. There would be no tears from her. She bit her lip in agony, and her blood mingled with Mark's.

'I knew you loved it like this,' he chuckled. 'Hard and rough, just like a slut does. And Ness? You always were hot for me.'

Suddenly Ty's bedroom door flew open and there Wren stood, in his Star Wars pajamas, his lamp with its thick base held aloft in his hands. Before Mark could even turn his head to comprehend what was going on, Wren smashed the lamp down on his dad's head. Mark slumped to the ground with a soft moan.

Vanessa watched him for a moment to make sure he was really out cold and only became aware of her state of undress when Wren said, 'Mommy, are you OK?'

The use of the word *Mommy* brought her back immediately. Wren was nearly twelve and hadn't called her that in a long time. He was scared. She quickly pulled her top down while she scrambled to find her dignity by pulling her underwear and pants back up.

'Wren, sweetheart, why did you come out of the room? And why were you in Ty's room anyway?'

'I was in Ty's room 'cos I couldn't sleep by myself. I heard him yell my name. I recognized his voice and when I heard you both coming down the hall, I knew I had to do something.'

'You're such a brave boy,' she whispered, pulling him in for a hug.

They both looked down at Mark, lying on the floor. They should ring... someone. Vanessa was wracked with indecisiveness.

'Mom?'

'Yeah,' she whispered, aware that she might be in shock, just a little.

'We should call Billy. He'll know what to do.'

'Sure,' she said. Wren took her by the hand and led her into Ty's room. He locked the door once she was inside. He led her to the rocking chair in the corner and pushed her into it. She looked at him blankly. Wren then pressed number one on the landline handset – the speed-dial number for Billy – and switched it to loudspeaker. The phone connected after only a few rings.

'What is it, Ness?' came the concerned reply.

'It's Wren,' he said softly, urgently.

'Wren! What's wrong? Where's your mom? Is she OK?'

From across the room, Vanessa heard the questions Billy fired at Wren in panic.

'Dad was here, he hurt Mom. I think he's still here, but I hit him with a lamp.' She could hear the fear in Wren's voice, and she felt like a shit mom for bringing this down upon him yet again. His whole little body shook, his eyes wide and disbelieving. Slowly she pushed herself, with a little difficulty, out of the chair and moved to the door.

'I'm coming right now!'

Reaching out, she touched the bolt on the lock. It was cold.

'Don't go out there, Mom. He might still be there. Wait for Billy,' Wren pleaded. Billy would be on his way in a matter of seconds, but Vanessa had to know now, was he still there?

'I'm just going to stick my head out there, OK?' Slowly she slid the bolt to the side and opened the door wide enough for her to see that Mark was gone. Shocked, she opened the door fully and looked down both sides of the hallway. There was no sign of Mark at all. Not even any blood to prove that he was here. Vanessa heard the key in the front door and ran down the hallway to meet Billy. She fell into his arms, her vision blurry with tears of relief. He wiped them from her cheeks. 'Ness! What are you doing out here? Get back in the bedroom with the boys and I'll check the house.'

It was a familiar scene, locking herself in to keep someone else out. Vanessa anxiously watched over her boys, caressing Ty who was screaming, his face red with rage at being woken from his slumber. Then she put her arms out for a hug from Wren. She knew how hard standing up to his father had been. She knew it had taken guts.

'You're so brave, Wren. And I'm so proud of you. I worry so much about you and your brother, I just want to keep you both safe and I feel like I'm failing in that.' She was honest with him. They had that kind of relationship, young as he was; they'd been through so much together, this was just another chapter in their story, one that was far from over.

Billy knocked gently. 'He's gone, Ness. Why don't you pack up the boys and come and stay at my place for the night? Plenty of room and it'd make me feel better.'

Vanessa looked at him, so sincere, so caring, then at Wren, whose eyes had a faraway look to them, glazed over. Vanessa was worried about him. Maybe Billy was just what he needed tonight. 'OK.' She began to get some stuff together for Ty, enough for a day or two, just in case. As she turned, she saw Billy holding Wren off the ground in a bear hug.

'You OK, buddy?'

Wren studied his face for a few moments before mumbling, 'Yes.'

Thank God for Billy.

Billy put Wren down and hustled them all into his car, pulling into his driveway a few minutes later. Once the boys were settled in the spare room, he made Vanessa a tea and slid it across the table. 'Do you want to call the police?' he asked quietly.

'What's the point? There's no evidence that he was ever there. Just like last time. They'll think I'm making it up.' She held her head in her hands and sighed deeply.

'What did he do to you?' he asked, but still, the question hit home.

'Nothing I'm not used to.'

'Fuck!' Billy hissed. 'Let me go over there and sort him out. I'll make it so he never comes near you again.' His face had darkened, and his eyes shadowed with rage. She knew that he meant it.

'Don't do anything. Please, Billy. I just want to get on with my life, not make it about Mark and what he does or doesn't do to me anymore. I have to focus on Wren and Ty. They need me and I need them. But I appreciate the offer,' Vanessa said, steepling her fingers underneath her chin.

They shared a hug and then Billy bent his head, his lips touching her nose lightly as he kissed her. When she didn't pull away, he pressed his lips against hers, tentatively at first, then with more pressure. Vanessa parted her lips and his tongue slid inside her mouth slowly. Vanessa had never been kissed like this before and she felt a feeling come over her, one that she thought she'd never feel again, desire. As he wrapped his strong arms around her, his hands exploring every inch of her back, she felt like this was fate. Ever since she'd met Billy on the street, they had just clicked. Breathless, she pulled back.

'Um—' she stuttered, not knowing what to do now. Billy smiled at her, kissed her on the cheek, then took her by the hand and walked her to the bedroom. He grabbed a blanket and pillow from the wardrobe; he was taking the couch, giving Vanessa his bed for the night.

Vanessa appreciated his tolerance of the situation. She knew that he wanted to do something, anything, to help her out, make her difficult life easier, but talking to Mark wouldn't help. She knew that better than anyone. She had been expecting something like this to happen, so it hadn't come as a major surprise. Vanessa drifted off to sleep, her arms wrapped around Billy's pillow, wishing it were him, the taste of his kiss on her lips.

* * *

If the bubble of happiness surrounding her new life had not burst with Mark's attack, it had one month later. All the light in her world descended into darkness with a phone call in the middle of the night one Thursday.

Vanessa patted her side table, grabbing at her phone groggily. The screen blinded her as she looked at the time. It was after four in the morning and Toby was calling her. She didn't think it was to discuss the budget.

'Toby, what's wrong?' she said, instantly awake.

There was silence, long enough that she repeated his name.

'Sorry, Vanessa, I'm just... trying to make sense of it all.'

'What's happened?' She felt a seed of apprehensiveness grow within her.

'The alarm in the café was tripped in the early hours this morning, so Dad went down to the shop to check it out. It had been trashed. The guy was still there. Ness, he beat Dad pretty badly – he's in the hospital.' The seed blossomed.

'Oh God, is he OK?' She couldn't believe this, who attacks an old man? *A coward, that's who.*

'He should be OK, but he's got some broken bones and a concussion.'

'I'll come right over.' He said no, but the way he said it told her so much more. He was scared. She called her mom and asked her to watch the boys while she went to the hospital.

'Ness! I told you not to come,' Toby said as Vanessa rushed in to the hospital ward.

'I had to come. Your dad and I have become close – he's a friend as well as my boss and the kids love him.' She slid her arms around Toby and felt him shudder. Then he stepped back.

'When I got the call, I was terrified that they were going to tell me that my dad was dead. I couldn't have dealt with that. But this is bad enough – he's covered in bruises and scratches, a broken arm, broken wrist. Whoever did this is an animal.'

She looked at Toby's drawn face. 'Look, he's a tough old man, he's going to be fine.' She tried to reassure him.

Toby nodded. 'He'll be in hospital for a while, then recovery. He's already told me to find someone to hire to work in the garage, "And be smart about it, boy,"' he said in a fair imitation of his dad.

* * *

The cleanup of the café took longer than expected, nearly two weeks. Whoever had broken in – their identity was still yet to be revealed – had done a real number on the place. Every corner had been trashed, food and appliances destroyed. Old man Phillips didn't seem to be recovering as fast as Toby had hoped he would. The bruises faded, the cuts healed, the broken bones began to knit back together, but he just wasn't the same. Vanessa went up to visit him every day, sometimes taking the boys with her. Finally, he was released and cleared to go home. Toby hired a nurse to help him out and a cleaner to do the housework so that he was well looked after.

One day when she went to visit old man Phillips, he confided in her. 'I don't think I want to do this anymore,' he said it in a voice that sounded devoid of hope. The voice of a man who had lost everything.

'You want to die?' She was shocked.

'What? No, woman, I don't think I want to work in the garage anymore. I'm not sure I can go back.'

Vanessa breathed a deep sigh of relief. He wasn't talking about dying, just retiring. She reached out and grasped his hand. 'It's nothing to be ashamed of. Something traumatic happened to you there – it's natural to be nervous or frightened to go back to work. You don't have to – the guy that Toby hired is working out all right so I'm sure he'd be happy to stay on full time. Do you want me to talk to Toby for you?'

'I really should do it myself, but thanks, Vanessa.' He gripped her hand back, giving her a gentle smile. Patting his hand one last time, she stood up and drove home, wondering what kind of man would beat up a defenseless old-timer. A thought crossed her mind, which she dismissed, but in the late hours of the morning she revisited it. Someone had broken into the café with the intention of completely destroying it. Maybe, just maybe, someone angry, out for revenge, trashed it and old man Phillips just happened to be there. He was certainly capable. *Mark.*

9

It had been nearly three months since the attack in her own home, but every time Vanessa walked down the hallway she relived the moment that he had thrown her to the threadbare carpet and done what he did. She couldn't get the look of determination in Wren's eyes as he smashed the lamp on his dad's head out of her head. He would do anything to protect her, at all costs. Allies, confidants and friends as well as a mother and son. Theirs was a relationship that could not be broken. Billy had once said to Wren that he was the man of the house and that it was his responsibility to protect his mom and baby brother. So far, Vanessa couldn't fault him.

But then again, Billy was shouldering much of the burden of protecting her family too. He was such a sweet and caring man, very protective of the three of them, like they were his family. She figured that since he didn't have his own, perhaps they were. It felt nice to belong to something special. She knew that she was a lucky woman, having a man like him in her – their – lives. At school, their friend groups had overlapped; he was more friends with Mark, but they had got to know each other, bumping into each other frequently at parties that she would go to with Mark and Maggie. He had always been nice to her, and he was one of the few people that had still talked to her or stood up for her after the whole pregnancy thing. She had never forgotten the time he'd even stood up to Maggie.

Maggie had been calling her a slut, egged on by her friends. They had Vanessa cornered while Maggie went to town on her, unleashing her rage on her in the most vicious and public way. Vanessa had been on the verge of tears but hadn't wanted to give them the satisfaction, so she'd forced a mask of indifference over her features.

'Enough!' roared a voice. Maggie, stunned, had stopped her tirade.

The crowd that had gathered to watch the drama unfold parted for Billy, heads above the rest as he'd shouldered his way through them.

'That's enough, Maggie,' he'd said in a stern voice that brooked no argument. 'What's done is done. No more.' He'd grabbed Vanessa by the hand and pulled her along, leaving the crowd behind them.

'Don't look back,' he'd warned. 'It shows weakness.' Once they had turned the corner, he dropped her hand. 'Are you all right? That was brutal. Why didn't you say anything?' he'd asked.

'Because everything she was saying was true. I deserve what's happening to me. The pregnancy, the basically forced marriage.'

'You could say no to the marriage, Vanessa, you know that right?'

'Our parents are pushing for it and I don't want my baby to grow up without a dad, even if it is Mark.'

Vanessa smiled at the memory. Billy had been so nice to her that day and continued to protect her at school after that. As her stomach had expanded, the bullying had got worse. Then they'd graduated and Billy had moved away, not even knowing if she had a boy or girl. It was a shame, and she had missed him and his caring ways.

Now, years later, here he was, back in her life and still playing the role of protector. It was a good look on him. She so appreciated him and the way he cared for Wren and Ty. Wren loved him, she was sure of it, and she knew that the feeling was mutual. They spent a lot of time together, Billy teaching him how to be a good man, just like he was. Wren already had a good sense of what was right and wrong, but Billy helped him hone it. And Ty, well Ty was loved by them all. He was an amazing kid and she lavished love on him. He too loved Billy. Billy played endless games using the trucks and piles of sand in the sandpit out the back. He would sit, squashed in the corner of the small sandpit with Ty until dinner was ready. Yes, Billy was family. Now she just had to work up a way to tell him. They hadn't yet worked out how to act on their growing attraction to each other, and she was holding things up, not knowing how to move forward. She knew Billy was a good man, but she was still hesitant after her experiences with Mark. Would she ever get over what he'd done to her?

Vanessa was finally beginning to think that Mark's campaign of terror had run its course. He was happy with Maggie, or so she assumed. She's heard that they had recently had a baby together. Vanessa hadn't even known she was pregnant but wished her well. After the night that Maggie had turned up at the door, they were closer to mending bridges but they still weren't friends. Vanessa hoped that one day they could bury the past, but she thought that was up to Maggie to decide if and when. Their baby's name was Charlotte, after Maggie's grandmother, with whom she was very close too. Maggie's mom was a widower who had never got over the death of her husband, so her grandmother had moved into their home to help care for Maggie, who was just eight at the time. She didn't remember her dad very much and it bothered her. Her mom had put away all the photos of her dad, furthering Maggie's fuzzy memories of him.

Baby Charlotte was nearly three months old now and Vanessa thought that she should make the effort to go over to Maggie's and take a peace offering, congratulating her on the baby, but she'd have to pick a time when she knew that Mark was at work. The gossip was that Maggie wasn't coping too well, and Vanessa promised herself that she would visit in the next few days. Depression after a baby was far too common, but if Vanessa could help, she would. She had suffered from it too, although she had so much else going on at the time.

* * *

A couple of days later, Vanessa's cellphone vibrated in her pocket as she left work, giving final instructions to Leanne. Running the café had been her salvation and she couldn't thank Toby enough for taking a chance on a woman that had never had a job, ever. Except being a mother, that is. That came with its own set of challenges, which Vanessa thought made her a stronger candidate for the job, even though Toby had decided to hire her on the spot, regardless. Independence suited her. She could provide for her family, finally. She had great kids, a job she loved, and she had never been so happy.

'Hi, Mom. Good timing, I just left work.' Her mind was still buzzing with her happy thoughts.

It had been a while since Vanessa had had a long conversation with her mom, it was usually hurried as she picked up the boys and took them home ready for tea and a bath. Actually, when she thought about it, Vanessa hadn't sat down and spoken to her mom for a good few weeks so when she called, she was happy to hear from her. 'Hi, Ness. Do you have time to pop round before you go and get Ty?' Vanessa pulled her phone away from her ear and checked the time – she had five hours before she picked up Ty. Once a week she gave her mom a day off and left him with one of the girls from work, Lucy, who was a single mom, needing extra money. It was working well for all of them and Ty most of all. He was such a happy, well-adjusted little boy. Luckily, he didn't know Mark nor remember anything about that period. She just wished that Wren could have the same blank slate – and her for that matter too.

'Sure, Mom, be there in about ten minutes.' Putting the phone down, Vanessa thought that her mother had sounded a bit... funny. Frazzled, maybe. Vanessa wondered what could be so important that it couldn't wait until tomorrow when she dropped Ty off before work. A knot of worry began to grow in her stomach. What could it be? She wondered if maybe she'd done something to offend her mom and that's what she wanted to talk to her about, but it was no good guessing.

'Mom?' she called as she used her key to unlock the front door.

'In the lounge, honey.'

She walked into the lounge and saw her mom sitting on one end of the couch, her dad on the other. She frowned. 'What's he doing here?' Vanessa asked, striving and failing for neutrality.

Her mom sighed as if she'd rather be having any other conversation. 'I invited him.'

'So what, he's back in your life now, just like that?'

'It's not like that, Ness, and even if it was, it's none of your business.'

Vanessa was taken aback by her mom's stinging words but had none of her own with which to retort.

'I'm sorry, honey, it's just, I'm going through something and your dad has been helping me through it. Actually, he's been a huge help and support to me, but now it's got to the point where I need to tell you.'

'Tell me what?' she whispered, her heart hammering in her chest. 'Mom, you're scaring me.'

Her mom looked at her dad, who covered her hand with his own. That gesture alone filled her with fear. 'Mom?'

'I... I... have breast cancer. Stage four. They've given me six months.' She stopped talking, giving Vanessa a minute to process the information her mother had just dropped on her like a ton of bricks. Her mom had breast cancer? How, when did this happen? Her eyes filled with tears that sped down her cheeks, coating them in glistening droplets in a matter of seconds.

'Six months till what?'

Her mom sighed. 'To live.'

Vanessa was stunned into silence for a long time. 'How long have you known?' she finally asked, her tearful eyes meeting her mom's calm and accepting ones.

'Two months.'

'Oh, Mom, isn't there anything they can do for you?' She hiccupped back her tears, covering her mouth.

'No, they caught it too late and I'm not spending what little time I have left in a hospital being poked and prodded. I'd rather be at home with my family.'

'Mom! You've been looking after the boys this whole time!' she said in dismay. 'Why didn't you tell me earlier? I would have found someone else to take them.'

'That's exactly what I didn't want. I want to spend as much

time with my family as I possibly can. Your dad is moving back into the house to care for me until...'

Vanessa launched herself from the chair, kneeled down on the floor in front of her mom and gently hugged her. She could feel her bones through her top. How could she not of noticed this before? She hugged her mom every time she picked up the boys. She hadn't noticed because she was too busy. The realization hit her quickly and made her cry out.

'It's OK, honey, let it out. I did. It took me weeks to come to grips with this. With dying.'

Vanessa couldn't believe they were even talking about this, let alone that it was actually going to happen. She stood up and looked down at her dad. His eyes were glistening with unshed tears. 'Daddy,' she said. He stood and stretched out his arms so Vanessa could step into them. He wrapped his strong and familiar arms around her. Oh, how she'd missed this. He looked as distraught as she felt and she realized that he'd aged too, no doubt since his wife's diagnosis. Her mom was her best friend, besides Wren. What was she, her daughter, going to do without her? What was her husband of thirty-odd years going to do? He must be so lost, but he hid it well. For her mom's benefit, no doubt.

* * *

Her mom, Claire Elliott, died nearly six months later to the day, on a Thursday, at home, surrounded by those she loved and cared for the most. She slipped away peacefully in the bed that she shared with her husband Alex while holding onto her husband's and Vanessa's hands. Wren was crying, Ty looked confused and even Billy, stoic Billy, had tears in his eyes. Vanessa shed many tears that day. Every time she thought of a memory, surrounded by her things, she thought of her mom. She was in or the cause of so many of the good things in Vanessa's life. She had whispered, 'I love you' before she had passed, for she did love each and every one of them and they all knew it. Vanessa had smoothed back her hair, kissing her mother's forehead. 'I love you too, Mom.' She had embraced her dad, the ferocity of his hug telling her how much he was hurting.

* * *

Vanessa didn't know what to do with herself, so she rearranged the flowers on the front hall table for what felt like the hundredth time.

'Ness,' said her dad, nearly making her jump through the roof with stress. 'Come and sit down, the flowers are perfect – she would have loved them.' He led her to a vacant seat.

Six short months ago her mom had been alive, now she was lying in a mahogany box at some funeral home waiting to be cremated. One night when she couldn't sleep, Vanessa had researched cremation. After they'd been cremated, the thigh bones often didn't burn through completely, so they smashed them up with what amounted to a hammer of sorts. Surely that was a fake website and they really didn't do that? After that disturbing discovery, she had closed the browser and deleted her history lest one of the boys opened her laptop and looked at what she was searching for.

The front door opened, and Vanessa was up like a shot, a dazed look in her eyes, yet ready to play host as her mom would have wanted. It was Billy, with a bunch of roses, and she dropped back into her chair, suddenly exhausted before the wake had even begun. Billy came over to her.

Vanessa and Billy's connection had been deepening for a long time now but since her mom had passed, Vanessa was beginning to see Billy. Really see him. 'How are you holding up?' he asked. She knew that he was worried about her, about the boys who had lost someone so close to them, someone that they spent time with just about every day. Wren and Ty came into the room, a faraway look in Wren's eyes. He was going to miss his nannie just as much as Vanessa was. She wanted to hold them, both of them, take their hands, comfort them and tell them that everything was going to be OK. But she couldn't move. She was stuck in one place, staring in the direction of her children. When Vanessa didn't get up to comfort her children, Billy did, wrapping his arms around Wren first, kissing him on the forehead then doing the same to Ty. He threw Vanessa a look, but she was helpless to go to them.

There was a knock at the door, and she jumped up so fast that she felt dizzy. 'Steady on there, Vanessa,' her dad cautioned. She smoothed her hair down and went to answer. She took a deep, steadying breath before opening the door.

Her mom had lived in the town her whole life, so many people had attended her funeral and were soon crowding into the house and backyard, eating food and sharing stories. Vanessa looked at the trestle tables laden down with food and wondered if she had organized enough to go around. Her mom would never forgive her if people went hungry. Never *have* forgiven her. She stifled back a sob, then felt a hand on her arm.

'Ness, have you eaten yet?' asked Billy. She shook her head slowly and he fixed her a plate of two sandwiches and a small cup of lemonade. He guided her toward an empty chair, then watched over her as she nibbled on the corner of a sandwich.

In the corner of the room, she noticed Ty sitting alone. His eyes were red-rimmed and he was clutching a tissue tightly in his little hand. She handed Billy her plate and drink, gave him a small kiss on the cheek, then walked over to her youngest son. She squatted down in front of him and gripped the hand that wasn't holding the tissue.

'You alright, my darling?'

He shook his head. He was too young to know the pain of death and he had loved his nannie, being with her nearly every day since Vanessa had gone back to work.

'Come here, poppet,' she said as she wrapped her arms around Ty, drawing him closer for a hug. In her arms, he broke down, his small body quivering, his tears soaking into her top. 'It's going to be OK, Ty. I love you. Poppa, Wren and Billy love you too, but you know what?' He looked up at her. 'You're going to have to help me take care of Poppa. He's extra sad. Do you think you can do that?'

'Yes, Mommy,' he whispered. He pulled out of her hug and went over to his poppy, who was talking to another neighbor. Vanessa watched as Ty hugged her dad. He stopped talking and bent down, hugging Ty tightly in his arms. Vanessa felt her eyes well up, threatening to spill tears down her face. She was trying so hard to stay strong for her family. If she fell apart, well... she didn't know what would happen.

The wake was mercifully short. Vanessa couldn't handle much more of the hugging and the platitudes, the compliments about her mom and people telling her she was in a better place. No, her place was here, with her family. Slowly the guests left, hugging everyone, right down to Ty who was no longer clutching his tissue. He was being so brave, Vanessa's heart went out to him. When the last of them had gone, Wren came up to Vanessa and slung his arms around her. 'How are you, Mom?'

The strain of the day finally caught up with her, and that simple question was her undoing.

She began to cry, not small sobs but an anguished cry that

wracked her body with shudders. If Wren hadn't been holding her tightly to him she would have slipped to the floor. 'Mom!' She felt the world tilt wildly, saw Billy come striding over as he and Wren helped her into the bedroom, forcing her to lie down.

A while later there was a knock at the door.

'Mom? Can I come in?' Wren asked. She nodded, then realized that he couldn't see her nod. 'Come in,' she said weakly. Wren walked in and sat gingerly on the edge of the bed.

'Billy sent me in to ask you if you felt up to going home. He thinks you'd be more comfortable in your own bed.'

Vanessa sat up and looked around her. She was in her parents' room. She touched the bedspread on the other side, her mom's side. She began to cry softly.

'I'm going to miss her too, Mom.' He moved closer. 'What shall I tell Billy?'

'Tell him I'll be out in a minute.'

Once Wren had left the room, she took another moment in her mom's room then slowly stood up, aware that she had fainted. She walked out into the lounge. Billy was holding hands with Ty, wiping the tears from his small face.

'Ness, you OK?' Concern was written all over his face, his brows knitted, his lips smashed together.

'I'm OK.' She turned to her dad. 'Are you OK, Dad?'

He choked back his tears as he nodded. 'I just want to be alone now. Stressful day.'

'Sure thing, Dad, call if you need anything. I mean it.' She kissed him goodbye, followed by a handshake and a touch on the shoulder from Billy, and a hug from the boys. She grabbed Ty's hand and walked out the door, never wanting to see that house again.

10

It took some months for Vanessa to be able to think about her mom without breaking down entirely. She now understood that she should be thinking about her mother's life and the things she did, rather than her death, which was painful and distressing. She chose to block that part out, focus on her life. She missed her. The boys, now twelve and two and a half, were suffering in their grief, just the same as she was, but Vanessa didn't know how to handle their emotions, let alone process her own.

Since her mom had passed, Billy had spent every night over at her house, making sure she took care of herself and the kids. During the couple of weeks where her grief was at its strongest, he'd realized that she wasn't taking care of herself and she was forgetting about her kids, which was out of character for her.

She cared deeply for him but he'd taken a hard stance with her. 'Vanessa,' he'd said sternly, arms crossed over his chest as he stood at the end of the bed. 'I know you miss your mom, but the boys need you, especially Ty. He doesn't understand what's going on.'

'Can't you just tell him?' she'd asked.

'No. He doesn't understand. You're his mother, it's time you began acting like it.'

'My mom just died, Billy.'

'Yes, and I know exactly how you feel, but you don't have the luxury of feeling sorry for yourself and staying in bed all day, are you listening?'

Chastised, eyes welling with tears, she'd nodded.

'Right, let's get you up and into the shower – I know it's been a while.'

The talking-to had helped her put everything in perspective, and at first, he was staying there to take care of the boys while she grieved, but his dinners turned into nights staying over. They never mentioned it, or talked about it, but gradually Billy was there all the time, something that Vanessa felt was just right. They had moved into a sort of dating, where the other knew that there were very real feelings there. They had shared that beautiful first kiss and many more since.

Vanessa had gone back to work a few weeks after her mom's death. She'd needed the distraction and to get back to her normal routine. A huge bunch of flowers from Toby had arrived at the café the day she started working again. She had been touched. Then again, he'd lost his mom too and knew what it felt like, the devastation it could cause.

* * *

Vanessa was mopping the floor at the end of the night, three months following her mom's death. She had forgotten to lock the door, which was unlike her, but she was looking forward to getting home. She realized with a start that she was looking forward to seeing Billy, and she knew then that her attraction to him couldn't be denied anymore. She wanted him, and she intended on telling him when she got home. What was the point in waiting any longer? Life was too short, and she knew there was a risk of being hurt again, but she was willing to take that chance.

The bell on the door jangled and without looking up, she said, 'Sorry, we're closed.'

'Good, that makes this easier.'

She spun around quickly.

'Mark,' she breathed.

'In the flesh,' he said, smiling a wide grin.

'What do you want?' she asked, her eyes wide, panicking.

'What do you think I want? I miss you.'

'You don't miss me; you miss the control you had over me.'

'Whatever,' he said as he launched himself at her.

She completely forgot that she had the mop, a weapon, in her hand. She shoved the bucket at him, hoping it would fall and cause him to slip so she could duck out the back. But it didn't work. Her keys lay in full view on the counter. She made a grab for them, her hand just grazing them before she was pulled back by her hair. She screamed in pain. No one would hear her because the café was surrounded by now empty buildings, but she screamed anyway. He smashed her face into the counter, breaking her nose once again, blood gushing down her chin and pattering onto the bench, startling in its color contrast to the cream laminate. Then he pulled her back and let go of her hair. Suddenly free from his hold but off balance, she collapsed to her knees. He punched her, landing across her eye before she fell to the ground and he laid into her with his boots, breaking at least one rib, the familiar pain stabbing her. She was certain it was the same damn one as last time. She curled up in a ball, trying to make herself a smaller target, all the while screaming.

Suddenly the kicking stopped, and she dared to look up. There was an arm around Mark's throat, and he was being hauled backward through the small gap that led from behind the counter into the café. Gingerly she stood up, holding her side, and saw Billy grappling with Mark.

'Let's see you go for me, hey?' Billy taunted, letting Mark go, pushing the smaller man from him.

Mark, enraged, charged at Billy who punched him in the throat. Mark went down, gasping and spluttering, lying on the floor. He looked up at Vanessa as she came and stood next to Billy, laying a hand on Billy's forearm. 'That's enough.' She turned and practically spat at Mark. 'I'm not scared of you anymore, don't come around here otherwise I might not ask Billy to stop next time.'

Mark scrambled to his feet and took off out of the café, coughing, holding his throat.

'How did you know I needed you?' she asked in wonder.

'Wren just had this feeling that I should come and pick you up. That boy is so in tune with you.'

'Where *are* the boys?' she said, panicking.

'They're with your dad, we can go pick them up now.'

As she stood wrapped in Billy's arms, she whispered, 'Move in with us. I want you around all the time. We've been heading in this direction for a long time, but I've been scared to trust, to love, but I've come to realize that you're not Mark, you're worth loving, you're worth it Billy.'

'OK, but what about us, Ness?

'I think it's time we told the kids that we're seeing each other. We have been for a while now, we just never noticed.' She smiled at his words and he hugged her hard. She released a small groan of pain. He looked at her face. 'Let's clean you up.' He went and got some napkins, wetting them out the back then gently wiping her nose. 'Can't have you going home like that. Do you need to see a doctor?'

'No need.' She grabbed either side of her nose and pushed it back into place.

'Shit! That must hurt,' he said as the cartilage crunched home.

'Used to it, I guess.'

Billy frowned but didn't say anything.

11

Vanessa made up her mind to finally do what she'd been meaning and wanting to do for some time. She needed to go round and check on Maggie, and after last night, it felt much more urgent. She had intended on doing it but then she had found out about her mom's diagnosis and everything had been about her. The grief had taken its toll on Vanessa, but she felt strong enough now to go and see her. She worried for Maggie's safety. Mark had been put down and embarrassed by Billy, so who was he going to take it out on?

Vanessa rang the doorbell and waited until she heard slow footsteps inside the house.

'Who is it?' Maggie's voice called out wearily.

'It's Vanessa. Let me in, Maggie.'

She heard the lock disengage and the door swung open. She was thin, wearing old clothes, her hair hung over one eye and she refused to raise her head properly.

'Let me guess, your black eye matches this one,' she said pointing to her own eye as Maggie finally looked up, her lank hair falling away from her bruised face. 'Oh, Maggie. I'm so sorry.'

'What happened last night?' Maggie asked.

Vanessa sighed. 'He ambushed me, attacked me at work, broke my nose and probably another rib, but Billy came in, got him off me and hurt him. I guess he came home and hurt you. I'm so sorry.' And she *was* genuinely sorry. Ducking and covering wasn't an option with Mark. The storm followed you until it eventually broke.

'Why are you here?'

'I realized that I haven't met Charlotte yet, I've been a bad friend, but with Mom...'

'I was really sorry to hear about your mom, but I didn't know what to say, given what I'd done to her. Didn't think your family would want to hear from me.'

'I appreciate that. I... I also wanted to tell you first that I've decided to divorce Mark.'

There was stunned silence for a moment before Maggie exploded. 'What? You can't do that! He'll kill me. I'm as good as dead if you divorce him. Please don't.'

Vanessa felt for her, she really did, but Mark was her past, Billy was her future and she wanted a clean slate. She didn't want to tell Billy yet. She wanted it to be a surprise once she worked out what to do, and Maggie was part of that plan.

Maggie began to sob. 'You can't do this – he will actually kill me. Please, Ness, help me. In the beginning, he was the boy I remembered, loving, caring, attentive, but he changed, just like you said he would. He doesn't spend any time with Charlotte, just like he didn't with Wren and Ty. I should have believed you, even after he started hitting me, I still thought I could make him change, but I can't.'

Vanessa reached out and touched her on the shoulder. 'Get out, Maggie, while you still can.'

'I have nowhere to go.'

'Hang on, let me make a phone call. I'll be right back.' Vanessa walked back to her car at the curb and made a quick and pleading call. She needn't have begged; the answer was yes straightaway, then she followed it up with another quick call. She returned to Maggie, wiping her eyes on the bottom of her dirty top.

'I have a solution if you're serious about wanting to leave.'

'I am, I can't stay here anymore. Any day he's going to start on Charlotte. I can't have that.'

'Here's the deal. I'm going to help you leave him, OK?'

She looked up at her tearfully, hope in her dull, blue eyes. 'How are you going to do that?' she whispered.

'My dad has a guesthouse out the back of his house and he's willing to let you and Charlotte stay there until you get on your feet, however long that may take. Billy will come round now and take whatever stuff you need. You can be gone in two hours, but you have to do it now. What do you say?' Vanessa waited. Maggie was silent and at first Vanessa thought she was going to reject her offer out of fear, but then her old friend threw her arms around her.

'Yes! A thousand times, yes! Oh God, Ness, I can't believe you'd do this for me.'

'I've been where you are, and somebody helped me too. I'm just helping a friend – we all are. Let's go inside and start packing. Billy will be here soon with his trailer. The bungalow has everything you'll need so just pack clothes, toys, baby stuff, that kind of thing. I'll go and stock your pantry later, OK?'

Maggie was dazed. Vanessa remembered the feeling well; the one where someone finally gave you permission to leave but also hands you the keys to your new life. It was empowering but also overwhelming, so Vanessa tried to keep it upbeat and fun while they packed, holding Charlotte, giving her kisses, missing the days when Wren and Ty were little ones.

Just under two hours later Maggie and Charlotte were in the guesthouse checking out their new home. 'It's lovely, Ness. And thanks, Alex, I appreciate you putting the past behind us and letting us move in. I know it hasn't been easy since Claire.'

Her dad bowed his head at the mention of Vanessa's mom. She knew that her dad missed her terribly. Maybe having someone else around would help his grief and loneliness.

'Just promise me one thing, Maggie,' he said. 'Don't go back.'

She nodded. 'I promise.'

* * *

When Vanessa followed Billy back to the house that night, she decided it was time to have the talk.

'Billy?' she asked before they went inside.

'Yeah? How's the nose and ribs feeling, and the eye?' he said, ticking off the things that Mark had hurt.

'Uh, fine I guess, a little sore.' She had a sheepish look on her face.

'What's wrong?' he asked, looking a little worried.

'Nothing, I just wanted to ask you question.' She looked down at her hands, picking her nails for a second before looking up into his eyes. She was so afraid of rejection, of what Mark had always said. *No one will ever love you.*

'Can we make this, us, official?'

Suddenly, he heaved in his breath and started to laugh.

'What's so funny?' she demanded, startled at his reaction.

'I thought you were going to tell me to move back home. This is so much better!' He picked her up and spun her around. 'Hell yes, let's make it official! You and me. I've been waiting so long to hear those words from you. It should have happened in high school Ness.' She giggled, a tinkling sound that filled the room almost as much as his laugh.

'Ness, we are going to be perfect together.'

'We already are.' She beamed. She had dared to dream, and it was paying off.

They made love that night for the first time. Boyfriend and girlfriend, partners, equals, soulmates. She had never been with anyone but Mark and only one of those times was consensual. This was so different. Billy was gentle with her, he took his time and loved her like a man should. She wasn't ashamed to admit that she cried. Afterwards, they lay in each other's arms, Vanessa listening to the thud of his heart as she lay her head on his chest. She had it all now and she had never, in her entire life, been this happy. Vanessa thought back to the day years ago that she'd met Billy on the street and this whole new life had been put into motion. She smiled; things were working out just as they should.

* * *

Vanessa made sure that Maggie and Charlotte were safely tucked away and settled at her dad's house, then, two days later, served divorce papers on Mark while he was at work. Wren knew what was happening as Vanessa had discussed it with him days ago.

'Mom! You're finally doing this, I can't say I'm not happy. Dad is an asshole.'

Vanessa wanted to tell him not to swear, but she agreed with the sentiment, so why correct him at all? He wanted to skip school to be there with her, afraid that Mark would come for her.

'I'll be OK, darling. He won't come around here, and if he does, I'll call the police. Now get ready for school, honey.' Wren left with a backward glance.

But Mark did come for her when she was at the café. The bell jingled jauntily as he stormed in. Billy was out the back but came striding out as Vanessa's ex made his presence known. 'Walk away, Mark. It's over.' Billy said sternly.

Billy hadn't been able to believe it when Vanessa had told her that she was divorcing Mark. He was ecstatic knowing how much courage it had taken her to say it, let alone have the papers drawn up and ready to sign. They both knew that Mark wouldn't take it well.

'Turn around and leave now, Mark, or I'll put you down again.' Vanessa was impressed by Billy's protectiveness. It made her feel safe despite having Mark there, yelling at her. Luckily, there were no customers to witness his tirade.

'I want to talk to my wife,' he screamed, spit flying from his mouth, glaring from one to the other.

'Buddy, she's not yours anymore and soon she won't be your wife legally either so turn around and get out of here.'

Vanessa stared at Mark, waiting for him to throw a tantrum and try to attack her. Instead, he swore loudly, turned and strode angrily out the door.

'That was a first,' she said softly, 'Mark walking away from a fight. Remember at school he was always getting into fights? I can't believe you were ever friends.'

'More acquaintances, actually. I always liked you better.' She let out a surprised laugh and swatted him on the arm, but secretly she was glad that he had been there; it could and would have gone a different way otherwise. She gently touched her nose, still tender from the break, her rib taped up but healing. There was no point going to a doctor only for them to tape her up anyway and tell her to rest and not overstretch. She liked to work. She loved the independence that it gave her, and she was setting a good example for Wren and Ty. She thought about her boys and their relationship with Billy. They loved him. Adored him, actually. He was the father that both of them had never had. He rarely had to tell them off, choosing to take a gentler approach. Ty did not have the experiences that Wren did, who at first had been shy, but had taken to Billy almost immediately. It had been the beginning of a mutually beneficial relationship. Billy loved them all too, an instant family full of love and hope. And she was ready to open herself up to love and its possibilities. Billy had been patiently waiting for a long time for her to be ready, never once pushing her to hurry up. Their lovemaking had been a huge step forward for her, and it proved just how much she loved him.

Billy came around the corner of the counter, Vanessa meeting him halfway. He took hold of her hand. 'At least it's over. He'll sign the paperwork and you'll be free. Free to marry me.'

Vanessa's mouth popped open and her eyes went wide, and she nervously asked, 'Was that a proposal?' She held her breath.

'Yes, it was,' he said, getting down on one knee and pulling a ring out of his pocket. 'Since the day I ran into you in the street, I have loved you. Actually, I think that I have always loved you. You are the one that I want to spend my life with, the person who knows me best and the woman I love. Marry me, Ness.'

Vanessa was speechless for a moment before looking deep into Billy's earnest eyes. She searched those eyes, looking for any sign of deceit, but all she saw was love. 'Yes!' She squealed, beginning to cry. A normal life with no complications? Sign her up! But Wren and Ty flashed before her eyes. 'My boys. They've had so much upheaval in their short lives – especially Wren, he's seen and done things a little boy should never have to do. This marriage, it has to be forever. I need to know that you'll love them as if they were your own.' This was the most important thing to her. *Stability.*

'Ness, honey, I already do. Wren is my best friend, and Ty is my little dude. I love all three of you – you're the family that I always dreamed of having. I couldn't ask for anything more. I give you my word that I will always be a loving father to them.' It was exactly what she needed to hear. 'Now can I give you your ring?'

She nodded, happier than she'd ever been. Who would have thought she would be accepting a marriage proposal? Obviously Billy had been waiting for the right time.

He slid the small princess-cut diamond in a platinum setting onto her finger.

'It's gorgeous,' she said softly, admiring it before wrapping her arms around him, looking into his eyes. 'I love you, Billy.'

'I love you too, Ness. I've been waiting for this day for so long.'

Vanessa was 100 percent positive that marrying Billy was the right thing to do. Now she just had to convince Mark to sign the divorce papers. She knew that he wouldn't do them on his own; he'd drag his heels until she died of old age. Vanessa wanted to marry Billy and only Mark stood in her way.

Billy left, looking mighty pleased with himself. As soon as he drove away, Vanessa locked up, put up the 'Back in fifteen minutes' sign and quickly walked to the bar where she assumed Mark was, since he had been wearing his standard work clothes. She went up to the counter where she found him cleaning glasses. 'What the fuck do you want?' he hissed, 'and where's your fucking bodyguard?'

'I wanted to talk to you by myself. You need to sign the divorce papers. Now. We need to finish this once and for all. It's been going on for thirteen years and to be honest, we hate each other.' She swallowed, waiting for him to explode. She was acutely aware of the people sitting further down at the end of the bar. Would they step in and help her if things escalated?

'I don't want to sign them.'

'And why the hell not?' She bit back.

'Because you are mine, you have been since you crawled into the back of my van and spread your legs.'

'Fucking hell, Mark. Do you have to always be like this? I'm not yours, actually, I'm engaged. To Billy.' She lifted up her hand and showed him the ring. The finger that he'd never actually put a ring on. Not that it mattered now anyway. She was engaged to the most amazing man.

He looked at the sparkler on her finger. Anger flashed across his face and settled in his eyes. 'Not even divorced yet and already engaged – you're such a slut, Vanessa. I knew I could have you anytime, Maggie or no Maggie. You wanted it, but you'll fuck up his life just as you did mine.'

'Not this again,' she said impatiently. 'Just sign them.'

'Or what?'

'Or I'll show the cops the security footage of you assaulting me at the café.'

'What?' His condescending smile slipped a little. 'There are no cameras.'

'Actually, Toby had them installed after his dad was beaten up and the café trashed.'

She slid the papers across the bar. 'Sign them.' She watched him carefully as he reluctantly signed and initialed every page. 'We'll be officially divorced in six months, maybe less and we'll never have to see each other again.' She slid the signed papers safely back into her bag.

He didn't need to know that there was *no* security footage...

Wren and Ty took the news of her and Billy's engagement exactly how she expected them to: they were both overjoyed that Billy had finally asked her to marry him. Wren shook his hand like the man he was becoming, but Billy pulled him in for a hug anyway, and Ty came racing up to him and threw himself into Billy's arms.

'You know he asked my permission first,' said Wren proudly to his mom.

'He did?'

'Yup. Said that I had been your protector for such a long time and he couldn't think of a better person to ask. I get the feeling that he wouldn't have asked you if I'd said no. He knows that I'm your best friend.'

She felt a swell of love toward her eldest boy. He *was* her protector. He *was* her best friend. Ty came over to her and gave her a hug. 'I'm glad that Billy's gonna be our dad now.' The young boy smiled.

'Me too, sweetheart,' she said, giving him a hug, then tousling his hair.

* * *

The official divorce papers came through six weeks after she'd filed them. Much sooner than she had expected. She looked at the notarized certificate with a sense of pride; she felt like framing it as she kissed it with glee. She was finally, truly free of Mark. He would never want to see the kids, so she wouldn't have to even see him again. She quickly thought of Maggie, safely tucked away at her dad's place. Mark still hadn't found her. She had been there for over two months now and, knowing Mark, he would still think that she would come crawling back to him, unable to make it in the real world.

Vanessa thought of how much her mother would have loved to have seen this day. She missed her so much. Her getting divorced from Mark was reason to celebrate. She couldn't wait to tell Billy and the kids.

She called in to see her dad first. While she sat on the couch, she noticed that he looked... happy and not just to see her, but in general. Vanessa was glad. Sure, they'd had their issues in the past, but she didn't want him to be sad and alone for the rest of his life. 'How are you, Dad? Really?'

'I'm OK, I have my good and bad days. I miss your mom a lot, but it's getting a little easier each day.'

Vanessa had a momentary pang of longing for her mom.

'What brings you over here?' her dad asked, bringing her mind back into the room. 'Not that I'm not happy to see you.'

'Well, I have news, big news. I'm divorced from Mark! You're the person that I wanted to tell first.'

'Oh, honey! That's wonderful news. I'm so happy for you. 'Bout bloody time. Is that man of yours going to make an honest woman of you now?' He got up from the couch and gave her a hug, just the way he did when she was a child, a bear hug.

'As soon as I set a date!' she said, her voice rising higher than usual. She couldn't believe how her life was turning out. She had everything she always wanted.

'So, how are Maggie and Charlotte settling in?'

'About that.'

'Please don't tell me that she went back to Mark.' Fear making her tense up, her shoulders rising, her lips stretching taunt.

'No, no, of course not. But I have moved them into the house. I was doing renovations and we discovered asbestos in the walls of the guesthouse. Can't have them living in that. So they sleep in the two spare rooms.' He looked a little sheepish as he said it.

Vanessa was taken aback and was silent for a long time. 'Dad, are you and Maggie a thing?'

'I can understand why you might think that, but no. I am like a father figure to them both, a good friend. Besides, I like the company. The house was too big and lonely without your mom. I have no interest in romance, Ness, and neither does Maggie.'

'Has Mark found her yet?'

'No. I've been keeping them hidden for a while. They stay inside and I do all the shopping. She's not ready yet.'

'I started all of this, I pushed her to go.'

'No, you didn't. She told me that you encouraged her to leave. Having Billy help her was the best thing you could have ever done. She's finally starting to heal.'

She smiled at her dad. 'Where is Maggie?'

'She's taking a nap with Charlotte. She was up most of the night. Charlotte isn't feeling the best.'

'Sorry to hear that, Dad. Say hi for me when Maggie wakes up.'

She kissed her dad goodbye and drove to the school in a happy daze. She had some very good news for Billy and the boys when she got home.

* * *

Billy asked Vanessa a few times, subtly, when she'd liked to set a date for the wedding, but she always found herself saying, 'Later, down the track.' Somehow, two and a half years went by with Vanessa making no actual plans to tie the knot. Billy was very patient, but it was obvious he couldn't understand why she was stalling and honestly, she didn't have a good excuse to give him. Maybe she was making sure of her feelings, or maybe she was scared. She didn't know herself. Billy had discussed it with Wren in the kitchen one day when they hadn't known that Vanessa could hear them, even over Ty running around the clothesline pretending to be an airplane. He was five now and full of enthusiasm. Wren had suggested to Billy that she was scared and that he should not push her. In her experience, marriage had a way of changing people and not for the better. Wren was fifteen now, a wonderful kid, but Vanessa worried that she had put too much on his shoulders at a young age, that she relied too heavily on him. But he was her everything, her best friend, her protector, as Billy called him. Despite his chaotic early start to life, he was turning out to be a beautiful soul.

She didn't want to lose Billy by not marrying him, but Vanessa thought she was worth waiting for. Once, she would never have thought that. Mark used to tell her that she was nothing, that no one would ever love her. And she had believed him. Until now. But she just couldn't pin down what was holding her back.

She went round to see her dad and Maggie one morning before work. It was clear that having Maggie and Charlotte in the house was making him happy. They had been living in the house with her dad for just over two and a half years now. At first, Vanessa had been worried about the dynamics of their situation, but after so long, she could see how well it worked for all three of them. Her dad had company, Maggie had a close friend and father figure and Charlotte had a grandfather. Vanessa was happy for them all.

'Well, maybe you are scared. You didn't have a great experience with Mark.' Maggie gave her a crooked smile.

'Billy shouldn't be pressuring you, honey,' her dad interjected.

'Oh no, he's not, he just asks the question every now and then. I can't seem to settle on a date, but I love him. It's weird.' Talking about it to people outside their love bubble was proving helpful. They made good points. She *was* hesitant about marriage.

She hugged Maggie goodbye then hugged and kissed her dad goodbye.

'See you, honey,' he said.

She drove to work thinking about marriage, about what Maggie and her dad had said. The rest of the day went by quickly, it was busy so that helped, but she still pondered the question all day. Finally, she made a decision. She pretty much floated with happiness the whole drive home. It was late, as she had to finish off some extra jobs at the café, but Billy was waiting up for her, keeping her dinner warm.

'The kids are in bed already,' Billy said, taking her plate out of the oven.

'Billy?' He turned, oven mitts on both his hands.

'Mmm?'

'I'm ready to set a date.'

There was stunned silence until Billy yelled as loud as he dared, then cupped her face with his warm mitted hands, kissing her all over her face. 'I can't believe this, what changed your mind?'

'I just wondered why I was waiting. I mean I will admit that I'm scared – my last marriage was hardly dreamy – but you are a good man and I love you, and that should be enough.'

* * *

They were married six months later. Wren, sixteen now, served as Billy's best man alongside Ty, who was six years old, much to his absolute joy. He was responsible for the rings and he took his job very seriously, constantly checking his pocket to make sure that they were still there. It was adorable. Both her boys had stepped up, even helping her plan the wedding, right down to the color of her dress: a beautiful lilac.

Her dad had offered to hold their wedding in his backyard, surrounded by her mom's fragrant roses, her memory with Vanessa on her big day. There was a small garden path with a trellis arch at the end and rows of chairs either side. Her dad had walked her down the makeshift aisle to meet her future husband. She winked at her boys, gorgeous in their white button-down shirts and gray pants. Billy, only planning on marrying once, had worn a proper suit. He said he wanted to look his best on their big day. So did she, going with a form-fitting dress with a short train at the back. Her hair was up in a low bun, tendrils floating around her face. Ten minutes after her dad had kissed her on the cheek, she and Billy were man and wife. Their family and friends threw rose petals over them as they made their way down the path to pose for photos in front of the multicolored roses. Vanessa wished with all of her heart that her mom could have been there to share in her joy, but she knew that she would be looking down on her.

Billy held her tenderly in his arms after the ceremony was over and the festivities begun. 'I have never seen you look more beautiful. I love you so much, Ness.'

'Thanks, I love you, husband.'

'I love you too, wife.'

'Mind if I steal her away?' Wren appeared and asked her to

dance. He slipped one hand around her waist, the other one holding her hand.

'What a wonderful day, Mom,' he said.

Vanessa smiled at her son, 'It really has been. I never thought that I could be this happy, that I could provide a better life for you. Wren...' she paused, as if contemplating her next words, 'I love you.'

13

The first day of community college was never going to be easy on Wren, but nor was it going to be a walk in the park for Vanessa either. She would miss Wren so much as he'd spend more time travelling on the bus now. The college could offer much more in the way of classes than Wren's current high school. It would help him get into a good college and Vanessa would do everything in her power to ensure Wren had a good education. Wren was a studious and serious boy, ready to embrace learning and meeting new people. Sometimes she was worried that he was too serious. Had she done that to him? She had so much guilt about what had happened in his early life – she'd do anything for a do-over.

By the time the bus came back from that first day at the college, Vanessa was a ball of nerves. What if it hadn't gone well? But she needn't have worried. When Wren got off the bus, he was mucking around with two boys Vanessa already knew. One was Justin Arden, who had played soccer with Wren for the last couple of years of high school. His mother, Joan, didn't attend the games because she worked all the time – she owned the bar where Mark worked, and her husband worked away, so Vanessa had sometimes taken Justin home to where he lived behind the bar. The other boy was a recent addition to Wren's circle of friends. Wren had introduced him as Wade Fox, a friend that he and Justin had made early on in the year. He had recently moved to town and was a polite kid who also played soccer, something the three of them had bonded over.

Wren and his friends came over to where she was waiting.

'Wade, who's picking you up?'

'Mom. She's not here, probably at home with the baby.' He shrugged. 'I guess I'll walk to my house.'

'Don't be silly. I'll drive you all home.' They piled into the car; Vanessa dropped off Justin, followed later by Wade. Justin lived behind the bar in a nice home, whereas Wade's house was older and was swamped by a large, unkempt garden out the front, weeds showing through the pathway, the front gate rusted open.

The three boys soon became inseparable, and a few weeks into their first semester at college, Vanessa decided a meet and greet with the parents was in order. So, she invited Joan Arden and Philippa, Wade's mom, to coffee at her house. There was a knock at the door and Wren went to answer it. 'Mom, Phillipa's here.' He showed her into the kitchen and introduced her to his mom.

'Sorry about this, I had to bring the baby – I had no sitter.'

'It's OK,' Vanessa said, touching the gurgling child. Joan didn't arrive on time, then didn't arrive at all, so Vanessa spent an awkward twenty minutes trying to make conversation with the woman who spoke in one-word answers. After a while, Vanessa gave up.

'Do you have any questions for me, Phillipa?' The woman looked shocked.

'Um... no.'

Vanessa was a little taken aback that Phillipa had no questions for the woman whose house her son spent so much time at.

'OK then,' Vanessa said. 'Thanks for coming round, it was nice to meet you.'

Phillipa picked up her keys, called for Wade, then left.

* * *

Vanessa pushed open the door to the bar, the cool air wafting round her ankles first, then making its way up and around her body like an insistent lover. She let her vision adjust to the dim interior. If she'd worked here, she'd always be squinting in the dark. She saw Mark wiping down tables, cleaning up spilled beer and restocking the peanuts. She ignored him, but she did notice him glare at her from the corner of her eye. She saw Joan sitting at one of the tables; Vanessa was nervous, but she felt a responsibility to Justin.

'Joan, hi,' she said. She looked up at Vanessa with a totally blank expression. 'I'm Wren's mom.' Vanessa's voice rose slightly at the end of her sentence.

'Wren who?'

How many Wrens do you know?

'Wren Sawyer. Your son Justin is his best friend, hangs out with him at our house all the time.'

'Oh well, thanks for having him.' She turned her eyes back to her paperwork, dismissing her.

'I invited you and Wade's mom Phillipa to have coffee at my house and you didn't show. I wanted us all to get to know each other since our kids are spending so much time together.'

Joan gave Vanessa a withering stare, like she couldn't care less that she missed the coffee date and wanted this conversation to be over so she could go back to her work.

'He's a great kid, you should be proud of him Joan, but you might also want to get a little more involved maybe.' Vanessa tried again.

'Don't tell me how to parent my kid. Ever.' She replied calmly without even looking up.

Vanessa turned, checked to see where Mark was – he was nowhere in sight – and stormed out of the bar.

'I was just so annoyed, no, angry,' she said to Maggie over coffee. She was so happy her and Maggie were close again. It was just like being back in high school, where they would talk for hours, unloading all their worries when they were together. 'The kid is at our house every day, not that I mind, but he spends all of his time with us and she doesn't care what he's up to.'

'Not everyone is cut out to be a parent,' Maggie said, ever the voice of reason. 'Not everyone picks it up easily – some have to work harder at it.'

'Well, she's not working at it at all.'

Rant over, Vanessa made a comment about the cookies she was eating. 'They taste familiar,' she said.

'Actually, they're from one of your mom's recipes that I found.'

The cookie stuck to the inside of Vanessa's mouth for a moment before she swallowed it.

'Your dad said it would be fine if I went through her recipe book. I can only make a few things well – I think he was getting sick of them after all these years, he was just too polite to say so.' She was babbling now, trying to cover up her embarrassment.

'It's fine, Maggie.'

Maggie breathed a sigh of relief. 'I know it's weird sometimes, us living here, but it's working for us all and your dad seems much happier than he was.' Vanessa couldn't argue with her there.

'It's fine, really. You're part of the furniture now,' Vanessa laughed, attempting to make Maggie feel more comfortable. Vanessa stayed a little longer, deciding to enjoy the cookie and memories of sharing them with her mom. She was creating new memories, but they would never erase the old.

14

Wren's seventeenth birthday was rapidly approaching, and Vanessa really wanted to give him a birthday to remember. He had told her that he was happy to have a family party with Justin and Wade over, but she wanted to make it special, so one afternoon when Wren was in the bathroom, she asked Justin what she should do.

'Well, I reckon we throw a real party. He loves parties. No drinking or anything, I swear,' he said, covering his heart for a brief moment. 'But a bunch of his friends, and Olivia for sure. Damn, he loves that girl. He needs to get some,' then Justin remembered who he was talking to and his face went brick red. Vanessa suppressed a laugh.

'How 'bout I organize food and drinks and you handle the music and the guest list?' Vanessa suggested.

'Deal.'

Wren's birthday fell on a Saturday. She had made sure that Ty stayed the night with Maggie and her dad. Billy agreed to be a bouncer in case anyone got rowdy. Wren was oblivious to their plans, and it was all she could do to stop herself from blurting it out. She had also sworn Ty to secrecy, and he was over the moon at being included in the surprise.

Wren was with her when she dropped off Ty, giving everyone a chance to arrive and Billy to do any last-minute adjustments. Wren's thirty friends were waiting. She checked her phone. 'Wren, we gotta go.'

They said goodbye to her dad and Maggie, giving Ty a huge hug on the way out. 'Have fun tonight,' whispered Maggie in Vanessa's ear.

They pulled into the driveway. Wren waited for her as always, but she said, 'You go in ahead, honey. I'll be there in a second.' He headed towards the house and she followed him closely. He walked into the darkened room, and Vanessa reached around him and flipped the lights on.

'Surprise!' shouted everyone.

For a moment there was dead silence and she thought, *Oh shit, I've made a huge mistake,* but then Wren laughed, everyone clapped and the music started, and Justin came over to slap him on the back.

'You did this?' he asked his mom.

'Actually, Justin and I did this. We wanted it to be special.' He was grinning, and she knew she'd done good.

She went into the kitchen where Billy was munching on a mini hot dog. 'You did good, baby.' He kissed her. 'And I'm super proud of our little man for keeping the secret – he was almost bursting.' They both laughed. Ty usually blurted out surprises in excitement.

The doorbell rang, and Vanessa and Billy went to the front door, knowing it was the pizza guy with a stack of different-flavored pizzas. She began randomly handing them out to people followed by paper plates. Vanessa looked around the room at the teenagers. Some laughed, some danced, some ate, but they all looked like they were having a great time. She looked for Wren. He was sitting in a chair with Olivia on his lap. They were kissing and Vanessa looked away to give them relative privacy.

Later that night, Wren, Justin and Wade headed down to Wren's room, Justin doing a terrible job of hiding the bottle of rum under his arm. Vanessa let them go – she trusted her son and besides, she remembered herself at that age. Surprisingly, neither she nor Billy had caught anyone else with booze. She pulled Billy into a sheltered corner of the kitchen and kissed him hard. 'Thanks for helping,' she whispered. 'Why didn't we get together at school?'

'I believe,' he said, raining butterfly kisses down her neck, 'that you weren't into me.'

'My mistake,' she said. 'I wasted all those years.' They didn't speak Mark's name. There was no need for him to be part of their narrative anymore.

'We're together now and that's all that matters. We're married and we're happy.'

Vanessa went down to Wren's room and knocked on the door. 'Time for cake,' she said as she heard rustling and laughter from inside the bedroom. Wren opened the door, and they all filed past her, smelling of rum. She hid her smile.

Olivia was waiting for him at the end of the hallway and he kissed her on the forehead. They were so sweet together. Billy put the cake on the table and rather than make him blow out a candle or sing 'Happy Birthday', they just gave him a round of applause as everyone hugged him.

Later that night when the party was winding down, Phillipa came to pick up Wade. She seemed out of it, and Vanessa asked if she was all right to drive.

'Billy could drop you all off and you could come back for your car in the morning?'

'It's fine, I'm fine,' she said.

As Wade walked past Wren, she heard the words 'prescriptions meds'. Maybe Phillipa was high, all the more reason for her not to drive. But she refused Vanessa's offer. 'I'll be fine,' she said thickly. Justin ended up staying the night because Joan never came to pick him up, even though Vanessa had left a message on her phone reminding her about the party.

Just before he went to bed, Wren came up to her and slid his arms around her. 'You're the best mom ever. I had a great time tonight. Thanks.' He hugged her again, then walked down to his bedroom where Justin was probably already passed out.

The cleanup could wait till the morning. Vanessa had more important things to do. Smiling, she walked down the hallway to her and Billy's bedroom.

PART II

15

Coming to a new school halfway through the year was always going to be painful. Her dad was the principal, which never helped her make friends. She was always the principal's daughter no matter how hard she tried to overcome the stigma. Her dad traveled a lot for work, taking postings all over the country for long and short periods of time, which meant Oliva Holmes had attended more schools in her high-school life than she'd had hot dinners.

As soon as she started at Ashfield High School there had been problems, and Olivia found it worse at this school than any other. New blood to torment was her guess.

First of all, she sounded different after spending the previous year up north. Each place affected the way she spoke, which made her stand out even more. She was just thankful that her dad only took postings *inside* the country. And because of her semi-nomadic lifestyle, she had different interests to the other girls in her class, which made breaking into the existing friend-ship groups very difficult. She was more comfortable in the library and spent a good deal of time there.

She liked a boy, having met him in the library during a free class. His name was Johnathon Peak; he was good-looking and popular, and he was into her. The only thing was that his circle of friends overlapped with the girls that bullied her.

Marcie, Maree, Maureen. The three Ms.

Her enemies. Nice when Johnathon was around, bitches to her when he wasn't. They picked on her day in and day out. Olivia found it hard to keep a smile on her face. She lived for the moments when she was alone with Johnathon, and he made sure there were plenty.

'Gonna run to Daddy now?' Marcie had asked after following her to her sanctuary in the library, calling her names. Olivia tried to stay brave, but the constant bullying was wearing her down, chipping away at her soul. With every cruel word a new crack appeared. She grew weary of the constant barrage of spite directed at her alone. The words, the sneaky shoves from behind. The time she 'accidentally' fell down three concrete stairs, spraining her ankle and hurting her wrist. She took a week off school to recover, and it was the best week that she'd had since coming to Ashfield. She wrote in her diary religiously, detailing the abuse. She couldn't even reread what she'd written, it was too painful, and she couldn't believe that she was putting up with it. She didn't want to go back.

'What is it honey?' asked her dad one night, finally noticing how withdrawn she'd become, and how her only friend seemed to be Johnathon, who admittedly came around a lot. He still hadn't seen the bullying, but she would never confess it to him. He might have been able to stop it, but she wouldn't tell. She would never tell. She kind of wished she could tell her dad so they could move towns, move schools again, so she could get away and start over. At each new school she became someone else, like she was wearing a mask, never truly being herself. Would she ever be?

Her mom would have known what to do. After she died, her auntie had given Olivia her first diary so she could pour her heart into it. Since then she had written page after page, filling book after book. They sat on the bookshelf in the lounge; she knew that her dad would never read them. He'd never invade her privacy like that.

The bullying became worse, if that was possible, the longer she and Johnathon dated. Finally, Olivia worked it out: Marcie had a crush on Johnathon, and Olivia dating him complicated her plans. Johnathon had once asked her why she looked so sad and she had replied, 'I'm happy with you and sad without you.' Her response seemed to satisfy him. Why couldn't he see what was really going on? Was he blind or deliberately ignoring it? Both options weren't good enough.

The physical bulling stepped up after Johnathon took her to a party and Marcie saw them together, saw Johnathon nuzzling Olivia's neck intimately. They weren't sleeping together, despite his less than subtle prodding. Marcie was glaring at them, making her so uncomfortable that she barely touched Johnathon, which pissed him off.

Why did no one like her except Johnathon?

Olivia decided that the best way to get Marcie and the girls off her back was to break up with Johnathon, even though that was the last thing that she wanted to do. She had real feelings for him, but her safety and sanity came first. The day after the party, she caught him at his locker between classes. She needed to rip the Band-Aid off and do it quickly. It was going to kill her as he was her only friend, but it had to be done.

'What's wrong, babe?' he asked, seeing her mouth pursed, her eyes downcast, her arms folded over her chest. 'I... I need to tell you something.'

'Shoot.'

'I just think that we want different things and are heading in different directions.' Every word broke her heart. The look on his face, sadness, then anger.

'Yeah well, I was gonna break up with you anyway – you don't even put out.' He stormed off, punching a locker on his way past, betraying his true feelings. He was upset. And it hurt. She only did this to fix the Marcie problem. She hoped with all her heart that it did.

Marcie stood further along the hallway, watching, her beady little eyes missing nothing. As Johnathon came level with her, she linked her arms with him, throwing a satisfied look over her shoulder at Olivia. Olivia wanted to scream. *You got him by default!*

It turned out that dumping Johnathon made no difference. If anything, it made it worse. School was unbearable now. Johnathon ignored her and started dating Marcie within days of them breaking up. Olivia was devastated. Hadn't he cared for her at all? She moped around the house.

'Love, why don't you call Johnathon to come over. He always cheers you up.'

'Dad, we broke up a week ago – he's dating Marcie now.' She had to bite back the tears.

'Marcie from your grade?' Olivia nodded. 'She's bad news, bit of a bully so I've heard,' he continued. That was her opening, and he looked at her, but when she said nothing he turned away. If only she could tell him.

The bullying followed her everywhere. She shut down her social media accounts, not that she used them much anyway. There was a website put up about her being a slut. Funny thing was, she was still a virgin. She knew that Marcie was behind it: the ultimate mean girl.

* * *

It was a bad day. Marcie had been merciless. 'You know I'm fucking him, right?' Marcie laughed. 'He said it was about time that he got some. He said that I was the best he's ever had.' Marcie was in Oliva's personal space, invading what little room she had left. Olivia ignored her.

'He said that you were a frigid bitch who only let him kiss you. Who does that?' She sneered.

Olivia continued to walk down the concrete path.

'He said you confided in him about your dead mother and he couldn't have cared less. He was texting me at the same time.' A little bit of Oliva's heart broke hearing that. It was the last straw.

She spun on her heel, catching Marcie off guard, and slapped her across the cheek as hard as she could. It felt amazing. Marcie stumbled back into her friend's arms, her hand flying to her face as if she couldn't believe what had just happened, but Olivia had had enough.

'You fucking bitch!' Marcie screamed, lurching forward to grab Olivia by the front of her dress. She punched Olivia in the face, much harder that Olivia's slap. She felt her eye swell up immediately.

'Bitch fight!' someone yelled, as Marcie circled around her.

'Break it up!' yelled a familiar voice as her dad stormed through the crowd to reach the warring teenagers.

'What the hell is going on?' He looked startled to see Olivia as one of the troublemakers. His face registered surprise before his principal mask fell into place. 'Both of you, my office. Now.'

Olivia followed her dad into his office.

'Sit,' he demanded. 'Now, what's going on?'

Neither of them spoke.

'Olivia, what happened?'

'Nothing, Principal Holmes.'

Marcie snickered.

'Marcie,' Principal Holmes said, drilling her with a stare, 'care to illuminate?'

'No, sir,' she said, staring him down.

'OK, lunchtime detention, both of you, two weeks.'

Marcie groaned, throwing Olivia a dirty look.

'Want to make it three?' Principal Holmes countered.

'No, sir,' she mumbled.

Both girls stood up. 'Olivia, stay back please.'

Once his office door was shut, Principal Holmes's body language softened. 'What happened? It's not like you to get into a fight. What is going on with you?'

'Nothing, Dad. It's nothing.'

'Why won't you talk to me?'

'There's nothing to talk about.' *Anymore. She knew what she had to do.*

She left his office and decided to take the rest of the day off school. On the walk home, she wondered how it had come to this. She was beyond help; it was all over. Olivia locked her bedroom door. She removed the first aid kit and took the razor blade from its pouch in the back. Sitting on the bed, she held the razor blade, looking at it. The weight was almost inconsequential. A killing machine. She ran her fingertip across the blade lightly, testing it for sharpness. A bead of blood immediately appeared. *Yes, this would do.*

She moved into the middle on the bed, lying flat. She gripped the blade in her right hand. She looked at the skin on her left wrist: pale, delicate, unmarred. She positioned the blade over her pulse point, her heart rate no longer racing. In fact, she felt calmer than she had in months. She'd read that it didn't even hurt. It was just like going to sleep. Without any more thought, the razor bit into the soft flesh of her left wrist, cutting deep enough that blood spilled from her wrist and ran onto the bed. *How's Dad gonna get that stain out?* The random thoughts of someone trying to kill themselves. She'd better hurry up before she lost consciousness.

She switched the slippery, bloody blade to her left hand, but her fingers didn't seem to want to work, not gripping the blade properly. She couldn't slice her right wrist. *Fuck!* She couldn't even do this right. She lay there and waited to die instead.

Her bedroom door burst open and she had a vague idea of her dad's face looming over hers, screaming her name. He moved into action, grabbing a scarf from her wardrobe and wrapping it tightly around her wrist. He pulled tightly and tied it off. He grabbed her cellphone and called an ambulance, telling them that it was a suicide attempt.

Attempt? She wasn't dead?

She wasn't dead yet. She prayed that the ambulance didn't come in time, but she was still semi-conscious when the ambulance arrived. She barely remembered anything after hearing the sirens.

* * *

Olivia woke up in a hospital bed, her wrist bandaged. Her dad was sitting beside her, head bowed.

'Dad,' she croaked. He got her some ice chips and fed them to her gently.

'Why didn't you just let me die?' she asked quietly, looking down at the white bandage on her wrist.

'I will not lose another person that I love. Especially like that, Olivia. Tell me, what the hell is going on?'

She sighed, a soul-crushing sound of exhaustion. 'I'm being bullied, pretty badly. Marcie and her friends. I don't have any friends, Dad and it's all day, every day.'

Her dad sat there. 'OK, I'm hearing you. I'm going to transfer immediately. There's a community college that I have had an offer from. We'd be living in a small town and going to a bigger town for school. How does a fresh start sound?'

She began to cry silently, and he hugged her to him. 'I'll take that as a yes.'

A few weeks later, they were in their new home in the tiny town, although she was nervous about school, as usual. It never got any easier, but at least this time she was looking forward to it. The bandage had come off and she wore a bracelet to cover up the scar.

16

Walking up the steps of the new school, she almost bolted. Her dad had said that she was ready to start community college, that she couldn't stay home any longer and it would be a great opportunity for a new start. She had disagreed but had eventually decided that he was right. There was only so much daytime TV she could watch. She would catch him staring at her in the morning before he left for work when he thought she wasn't looking. She didn't blame him; she'd put him through hell. She was sorry she'd done that to him, but not sorry that she did what she did. She had been pushed to the edge, over it actually. She had seen no other way out.

Olivia was leaning on the counter at the reception area of the new community college, studying her timetable, when the glass double doors opened and a boy burst through them. He stopped short when he saw her. He smiled and she smiled back. Their connection was instantaneous. He hurried up to her, halting just in front of her. If it had been anyone else, it would have been invading her personal space, but she wanted him to. She wanted him to wrap his tanned arms around her and kiss her. Shocked by her thoughts, she ran a hand down her long hair and blushed slightly.

'Hi,' he said, slightly out of breath. 'I'm Wren. Wren Sawyer.'

'Wren, what an unusual name, I'm Olivia Holmes.' He had an infectious grin, and she found herself smiling like a fool. He was beautiful to look at and she couldn't help but stare. They looked at each other for the longest time, neither one of them feeling uncomfortable.

'You're new here, right? Holmes. Any relation to the new principal?'

'Actually, he's my dad.'

She expected something else but instead he said, 'Cool. You need someone to show you around, Olivia?'

'Well, I'm late for—' she checked her timetable '—English.'

'Sure, I'll show you, and then maybe we could catch up at recess.' He grabbed the piece of paper. 'After math. Just wait for me at your class, and I'll come and get you.' He took her to her classroom, then quickly leaned in and kissed her on the cheek. 'See you after math!' She put her hand to where he'd kissed her. A guy she'd just met, open and friendly, had just kissed her. She was stunned and thought maybe this *was* the place for her. He didn't even know her, she didn't know him, but still...

The usual thing happened – she had to stand up in class and introduce herself. She had never understood this cruel punishment. She always led with the fact that her dad was the principal so people could decide to be friends or not friends depending on her status. She watched the hand on the clock go round in both English and math class, each second brining her one step closer to seeing Wren again. *Wren.* The name rolled from her tongue and it felt good.

The bell rang and she gathered her things quickly.

'What's the rush, honey? I love fresh meat,' said a guy that was sitting behind her in class. He was so close that his breath washed over her. 'Want me to show you around, *Olivia?*'

'No, thanks.' She walked out of the classroom, slinging her bag on her back.

Wren was waiting for her opposite the door, looking for her in the crowd. He smiled when he saw her. She couldn't help but smile back. The boy from class bumped into her from behind. She felt a brush across her lower back but thought it must have been a backpack.

'Hi,' Wren said.

'Hi, yourself.'

'Hey, Justin. Have you met Olivia?' Wren said to the boy behind her.

'Sure, we're old friends.' He smiled at her creepily.

'I'm just going to show Olivia round, being her first day and all.'

Justin touched her shoulder. 'Sure you don't want a real man to show you a good time?'

Wren frowned slightly. 'Don't worry, that's just Justin, you'll get used to him. One of my best friends and a hit with the ladies.'

Not this lady.

'That's right, best friends, so we're going to be spending a lot of time together.' He reached around and pinched her bum, and she was too shocked to do anything about it except turn and glare at him.

'C'mon, don't be so uptight. What's Wren's is ours.' He smiled, but it was the smile of a predator and her alarm bells started ringing.

Wren didn't hear Justin's comment over the crush of kids all talking at once, nor did he see the pinch of her bum. She leaned in close to him and said, 'Can we go now?'

Wren stopped in front a boy, bulky, with a grin on his face. 'Wren!' he said in a deep baritone voice. 'How are you, buddy?'

'Olivia, this is my other best friend, Wade. Wade meet Olivia. She's new here.'

'Wow, you're gorgeous,' he said. 'Just so you know, Wren shares everything.'

'So I've been told,' she said in an annoyed voice.

'You've met Justin already then.' It wasn't a question.

'Right, we're going now, see you later.' Wren pulled her along, away from the boys that made her feel so uncomfortable.

He led her to a bench outside and he sat down. 'What happened to the tour?' she asked.

'Decided I'd much rather get to know you instead. That OK?'

Flattered, she smiled and sat down. 'Sure.'

This place was all about new beginnings. She could be normal here, she was sure of it. She had to admit, she was already hooked on Wren, and he seemed to feel the same way too. He couldn't stop smiling as he looked at her for the longest time. She blushed, the heat rising from her neck to color her face. 'I know we've only just met, but I feel—'

'Me too,' she interjected. She might as well tell him. Coming to this school, and meeting Wren may be the best thing she could have done and suddenly she was thanking her dad for uprooting his life, for her, this time. He would want a blow-by-blow account of her day when she got home, and she already had something positive to report. She'd also met a girl in English class, her name was Lisa, she seemed pretty nice too, but her mind was filled with Wren Sawyer.

'Tell me about yourself,' he said.

'Well, you already know that my dad is the principal. I tell everyone that straight up so there's no confusion, but I'm not a daddy's girl. We move around a lot, wherever the work is for Dad, so I've been to heaps of schools. Some good, some not so good, but I'm liking this one so far.'

Wren smiled in response.

'I'm glad you're here.' He reached out and held her hand. Olivia was aware that they were moving at warp speed, but she didn't care. He was so perfect she wondered if she was hallucinating the guy, but no, his hand, wrapped around hers, was real.

Suddenly someone grabbed her around the waist, breaking her connection with Wren as she gasped.

'Justin, don't be a dick.'

'What? I just want to get to know your new friend here the way you are.'

'Piss off. We were having a moment.'

'Yeah, I could see that – I'm saving you from yourself. You never were good around the ladies,' came the not-so-backhanded insult.

Moment ruined, Justin walked off. 'Is he always so handsy?' Hoping Wren would say no.

'Well, yeah, but he'll settle down once the shine wears off.'

'And when do you expect that to happen?' she said in all seriousness.

He laughed, thinking she was joking. She got a terrible vibe from that guy. 'He just likes the pretty girls, that's all.'

'You think I'm pretty?' she said, emboldened by his words.

'Yeah, I do,' he said, suddenly shy.

Olivia couldn't have had a better first day. She was sure she'd just met the love of her life.

* * *

Olivia dipped her toe in the cool water while lying on a towel close to the bank of the river. They were under the shade of the tall trees whose roots spread out around them, all heading for the water. 'It's beautiful, Wren, thanks for sharing your special spot with me.' He smiled at how happy she was.

'Only Justin and Wade, and now you, know about this place. Oh, and my mom. I've never seen anyone else down here. I guess 'cos it's off the beaten path.'

A shadow fell over her face at the mention of Justin. He was getting worse, grabbing and touching her when Wren wasn't looking or wasn't there. Her disgust must have shown on her face.

'You really don't like him, do you?'

'So, what about your family?' she said, changing the conversation completely.

'There's Mom, my stepdad Billy and my little brother Ty. He's my main dude.' He said with pride. It was obvious that he really loved his brother. It was nice that he could admit that.

'My real dad hasn't been in the picture for a long time.' Now he was the one frowning. 'He's an asshole who used to beat my mom. Haven't seen him in years and don't want to. I used to come here sometimes to get away from him, to escape.

'He used to break into our house and move shit around, and I know he still hurt my mom even after Billy was on the scene. She'd come home from work with black eyes, walking funny. She always said she had just fallen at work. I mean, how many falls can one person have?' He was angry, but a sadness came over his face. 'He's nothing to me.'

Olivia moved so she was curled into his arms. 'I'm sorry, Wren, that must have been really hard on you.'

'What about your mom? You don't talk about her.'

'It's... difficult. Dad takes these jobs to forget. I think he thinks that if he's moving around, then he can't form attachments to people, get to know them and maybe, just maybe, fall in love again.

'I was home one night watching movies with Mom. We were talking, laughing, then all of a sudden, she went quiet. I looked at her; she was staring straight ahead, not blinking. The coroner said she died of an aneurysm. She was there and then she was gone.' She shuddered at the memory, and Wren pulled his arms tighter around her.

'Babe, I'm sorry. I didn't know that happened to you or I wouldn't have asked.'

'No, it's OK. It feels good to talk about it.' Olivia spoke about her mom for a while longer, what she was like, how she loved to do crosswords, what books her mom used to read to her and how much she loved her dad. 'I miss her so much.' She felt the tears well up but pushed them down; it was way too early to be crying in front of her new boyfriend. She was glad that they'd shared parts of themselves with each other: it made them stronger.

Olivia snuggled back into Wren, wanting to feel the closeness of him. She was grateful that he hadn't pressured her for sex the way Johnathon had. Wren was truly a good guy. He started stroking her hair.

They had been together just over six weeks when Wren first said, 'I love you'. They were back down at Wren's favorite spot at the river. Olivia had driven them as Wren didn't have a car yet. She didn't mind though, she liked looking over and seeing Wren in the passenger's seat. It was like he belonged there. They swam with and against the current. Olivia was delighted when she discovered the warm spots that wrapped around her. The river was a bit cool, but it was a perfect relief to the hot day. They came out of the water, Wren like some kind of god, water dripping from his toned body. He shook his head, droplets flying from his hair and skin in all directions. They lay on their towels, holding hands. He rolled over and looked deep into her eyes. 'Olivia, I love you.' He said it so quietly that the breeze almost stole his words.

She gently cupped his face. 'I love you too.' It was a magical moment. She began to laugh.

'What are you laughing about?' he asked, putting his hand on her hip.

'It's just... this feels like it's straight out of a movie. It's so romantic.'

'I guess you're right. It's perfect. We're perfect.'

17

The party was in full swing by the time the three best friends arrived. Wren, Justin and Wade had driven in Justin's V8 car, painted midnight black. Justin was the unofficial leader of the trio, ordering the other two around sometimes, especially when it came to girls. Justin had the first pick of any girl and he usually got them too. There was no real competition: Justin always won.

Justin parked the car on an angle in the dry field so no one would park next to him and scratch his baby. Wren thought if anyone did that, Justin would come close to killing them. Justin was the ultimate spoiled brat; his parents couldn't have cared less about him, so they bought him stuff as a substitute. He spent so much time at Wren's, but Wren's mom didn't know what Justin was really like sometimes. She would have never let him stay otherwise. Most mornings Justin picked Wren up in his throaty car, peeling off from the curb so fast that his breath was always stolen for a second, Wade hulking in the back seat behind Justin. He never asked to sit in the front seat. He knew the pecking order, Justin, Wren, then him.

Wren slid out of the passenger seat, already looking for

Olivia's car. He saw it over in the corner. She was here. His chest tightened; his hands began to sweat a little. He couldn't wait to find her.

Wade yelled out to a bunch of kids from their grade. 'Let's drink some beer and fuck some bitches!' Everyone laughed and he even received a few high fives from the group. Everyone knew Wade was with the two most popular guys at school, who were almost joined at the hip.

Justin seemed a little pissed off all the time ever since Wren had started dating Olivia. They seemed to really have a problem with each other, even though Justin said he thought she was great. He was for sure always touching her. On more than one occasion, he'd seen him 'accidentally' graze her boob. He let it be; Olivia was capable of taking care of herself. She was a strong girl, able to fend off Justin.

'Wren, go get me a beer,' Justin said.

'Screw you. Wade go get us some beers, buddy,' said Wren, delegating the job. Wade walked off to find the alcohol.

'Nice job. Taught you well.' Justin grinned at him. 'Olivia here yet?' he asked.

'Yeah, somewhere. Her car's here, just have to find her.'

Justin, as usual, was the leader; Wade was the muscle, and Wren? Well, Wren was the brains.

'Hey, Wren!' He held up his hand in greeting to a group of girls who laughed when he said hi. They smiled as they walked past and Justin, being Justin, said, 'You know I fucked Tanya?'

'Yeah, you told me.'

Wade came back holding six warm beers, three bottles in each hand. 'Took you long enough,' Justin said. Wade told him to fuck off and received an angry stare in return.

'Drink up boys, I have a feeling that tonight will be a night to remember.' Justin smiled at both of them, winking.

Justin pounded his drink, as did Wade. Wren drank a little more sedately. 'C'mon Wren, keep up. More beer, Wade.'

Justin slammed his back again, Wade copying. This time Wren drank a bit faster and felt a little light-headed. Wade got them each one more beer when Wren would have preferred to stop for the moment. Wren held his in his hand as he went looking for Olivia. Eventually he found her, sitting on a log by herself on the edge of the party, since she only really knew a couple of people here and they were off with their own group of friends. Wren studied her for a moment. Beautiful, desirable, an enigma. She wore a short skirt and a singlet top. She looked better than any girl at the party, any girl he'd ever seen. Casual yet elegant, as if she wasn't even trying to be that gorgeous.

He went and sat beside her. 'Hey, babe,' he said as she turned to face him.

'Hi,' she said over the thumping music that reached her log. She was people watching. 'Ever wonder what's going on in people's minds, especially at a party? *Am I pretty enough? Did I put on deodorant this morning? Why doesn't he like me?*'

Wren laughed. 'You think of the weirdest things. Love it. Love you.' He kissed her and she wrapped her arms around him.

The thing with growing up in a small town was that everyone knew your business. Everyone knew that Colin the postman and Barbara, the married owner of the local grocery store, were having an affair; and they all knew that Mark used to beat his mom and Maggie, yet nobody put a stop to it. It was like living in a fishbowl: everyone could see your business, and everyone remembered everything. Wren wished he could start again, and he had plans to do so when school was over. Everyone knew his embarrassing stories, and nothing was ever lived down. He wished to be free, and he'd finally found a way to do it.

Olivia Holmes.

* * *

Spending time with Wren was better than anything Olivia could ever have imagined. Wren was the love of her life; he was patient, kind. But Justin called her uptight and frigid, just like Marcie had. Never in front of Wren, of course, but enough times to make her think that there was something wrong with her. She didn't want the best thing in her life to end, so she never told Wren about Justin's comments. And then Wade would laugh in that grating voice of his, getting on her nerves. They were as bad as each other. But she would not be the girlfriend who came between best friends. She simply took Justin's behavior as a trade-off for being with Wren. It had been months since they had started dating and she had thought that tonight, she might take him home from the party and give to him something she'd wanted to give him for a while. Wren was the guy with whom she wanted to lose her virginity. She could sneak him in the back door. She had no idea how her dad might react – she'd never tried it before – but she was nearly eighteen.

Wren had invited her to the soccer end-of-season party. She'd heard the parties were held in a field on the outskirts of town. Some people brought their own booze, but there was a keg and most people got rip-roaring drunk. Olivia was not one of them since she had to drive, but she knew Wren would most likely be coming with Justin and Wade and hopefully leaving with her. *Tonight was the night.*

She parked her car in the corner of the field and went to find Wren. She was wearing a short skirt and a singlet top, the heat still warming the air despite the late hour. She had thought about putting her hair up, but Wren liked it down. She was perspiring slightly on her neck under her thick tresses.

She could hear the music from where she was parked and as

she got closer, she could feel the bass in her chest. Laughter carried across the open field, tire marks crisscrossed the dirt lot, straggling weeds fought for survival and the dust floated round her ankles churned-up from the cars.

Olivia wasn't too fussed about these kinds of parties, finding them merely an excuse for people to behave badly. She wasn't a prude and she didn't hate parties or anything, but she rarely drank and especially not while driving, so there wasn't much for her here. Except Wren. She tried to find him, but when she couldn't she went and sat on a log on the outskirts of the party. The music still rang in her ears and if she had to talk to someone, she'd still have to yell. She'd just sit it out until Wren found her, which she was confident he would do soon.

Olivia wasn't sure if her friend Lisa would be there or not. Apparently she'd been grounded for the weekend. Lisa told her that she'd been caught screwing her boyfriend in the garden shed. She had laughed as she said it, and even Olivia could see the funny side, but she knew she'd miss her tonight. Maybe she had managed to talk her parents round, but she hadn't seen her yet. So she sat on the log and waited. And waited. And waited, until finally Wren appeared, sitting down on the log next to her. He was here and all was right with the world again. They had a brief conversation, Olivia barely remembering what they talked about. She was lost in his dark eyes. She pushed back a stray piece of hair and he drew her forward for a kiss.

Suddenly she was pulled backward pressing into something hard, a body. Bands of steel wrapped her waist.

'Justin, put her down, you're scaring her.'

'You're not scared, are you, Olivia?' Justin said loudly in her ear. She nodded her head, too scared to talk. Yes, she was scared.

Justin stood up, depositing Olivia on her feet. She immediately smoothed down her skirt and went to Wren's side, reaching out to hold his hand.

'This party blows,' Justin announced. 'Let's go somewhere and talk.' He exchanged a glance with Wade as he looked from Wren to Olivia and back to Wren. 'C'mon, Wren, we can get to know Olivia properly. Wade even brought her a beer.'

He offered the drink to her, but she refused to take it. 'I'm driving, but thanks anyway.'

'Wow, your girl is uptight, probably frigid too. Tell me, Wren, you been *there* yet?'

'Justin...'

'I know, I know. Olivia can't take a joke. Let's go.'

Despite having a terrible sinking feeling in her stomach, Olivia followed Wren who gripped her hand hard. Maybe he was nervous too, who knew? Or maybe he was just angry at Justin for being such a dick.

They followed Justin further into the field, decorated with tufts of weeds. The music started to fade, the bass no longer thumping in her chest. She was beginning to feel anxious, but she was with Wren; he wouldn't let anything bad happen to her.

'Look at the stars out here, Olivia. Bet you don't get that in the city – too much light pollution,' Wren said. She looked up.

'Yeah, no light pollution here. We got everything we need,' Justin said. Wade sniggered and she wanted to ask them what they found so funny. Wade was a big guy, dwarfing her small frame. She wouldn't want to get on the bad side of him. As she walked, pebbles poked through her ballet flats. She probably should have worn different shoes, but to be fair, she didn't know that she'd be traipsing through a field in the dead of night.

Wren had told her that the three of them were basically

inseparable, something she had found since day one. Olivia had pierced the inner circle, but at times, she wished she hadn't, that she'd stayed outside the bubble. These two made her uncomfortable.

Wren had admitted to her early on that Justin was a bit of a dick, especially to women, especially women he wanted to sleep with. It did not make Olivia feel any better. He had told her that his behavior was because of his home life; His parents, largely absentee, didn't love him. His mom, who owned the bar that Wren's dad worked at, was a workaholic. She didn't seem to care what happened to her son but gave him all the *stuff* he wanted. They bought his silence.

Wade was another story. Wade's dad had run out on them when he was little, the second father figure in his life then knocked up his mom and left. So now she had to be a single mom to a teenager and a baby. Wren told her that she was hooked on pills just to get through the day. She was overwhelmed and didn't have time to parent Wade, so he basically dragged himself up.

They stopped in the middle of the field. Wade still had the drink in his hand and offered it to Olivia again. She still shook her head.

'I'm driving,' she said again. They didn't seem to get the concept.

'Doesn't mean you can't have one,' Justin said. 'Loosen up a little.'

It looked like Wren had had a few already, and his breath smelled of beer. She was used to her dad drinking red wine, smelling like a grown-up; but the boys smelled like boys.

'Leave it, Justin. Olivia doesn't want a drink.'

'Maybe there's something else that she wants,' Justin said, picking up a tendril of her thick hair and running his hand down it. Then he began massaging her scalp. 'Feels good, doesn't it?'

She broke away from him. 'No, it doesn't.'

What was happening here?

She looked at the tipsy Wren, who warned, 'Justin. Leave her alone.'

Olivia was about to walk to the safety and comfort of Wren's arms when she felt someone put an arm around her chest and one behind her knees. She dropped to the ground with a thud.

Justin. She was looking up at him from the flat of her back, the night sky seeming to be pressing down upon her until she realized that it was Justin's boot. It was on her chest, pinning her to the ground like an insect caught by a pin.

He moved his feet to either side of her waist and she seized the opportunity to get up and try to run to safety when he dropped down so he was sitting on her. He wiggled a little, laughing.

'Now we're having fun,' he laughed. Wade laughed along with him.

'Justin! Get the fuck off her!' yelled Wren, moving toward Justin, but Wade's meaty hand of his shoulder halted him. 'Let her go, you fucker.' Wren tried to break free from Wade's grasp, but he hung on, wrapping both arms around the smaller Wren.

Olivia could feel the weight of Justin pushing her further into the ground. She could feel each burr from the weeds underneath her, each pebble as it cut through her thin singlet.

'Stop!' she yelled as he leaned down to kiss her, pinning her arms above her head with one hand.

'No, you fucking cocktease! I won't.' Instead of kissing her, like she thought he would, he reached down with his free hand and ripped her singlet, exposing her chest to the warm night air. Olivia's breaths were coming out in ragged gasps as she tried to fight against Justin. She screamed, a loud sound in the largely quiet night, the sound of the music too far away. 'No one'll hear you bitch. Scream all you want.'

She saw past Justin, Wade holding Wren around the waist as he struggled and tried to get to her.

He's not gonna make it, was her last coherent thought. 'C'mon, Livvy – I like my women feisty.' He ducked his head back down and bit into her breast. She screamed, then his hands were around her neck. The night seemed deeper, darker somehow, like it was rushing down to devour her. She tried to fight, to speak, to beg for her life, but the darkness swallowed her whole.

18

Olivia lay on the ground for God knows how long. The stars above seemed much further away than they had before. Now she felt as inconsequential as a speck of dust. When she tried to stand up, her hands cut by the sharp pebbles, her body felt heavy and in pain. Pain like she'd never felt before. Her heart hurt almost as much as... She couldn't even put words to it. What had happened to her?

She scrambled to her feet after what seemed like an eternity. She walked through the field, burrs crunching underfoot, her shoes forgotten, her singlet ripped, her panties left in the dirt. She felt like she couldn't draw enough breath, her lungs refusing to inflate fully. Olivia couldn't focus on any one thing. She smoothed down her skirt, feeling a lump in her pocket. With fingers that didn't want to work properly, she reached and found her car keys. She looked at them, then looked at her nails, caked with dirt. What had she been doing?

She stumbled through the large open gate filled with tire marks and saw her car, the only one left, sitting there waiting.

Hadn't anyone seen the car and thought, *I wonder if that person needs help?*

She pushed the button unlocking the doors, then slid behind the wheel, hissing in pain as her body came into contact with the chair. Gently, she sat back down and turned on the car, her bare foot pressed against the pedal. She accelerated too fast, corrected the wheel, and nearly hit the gate post. With a short sharp scream, she stopped, let out a shaky breath and tried again. This time she managed to get herself on to the road without any further mishaps.

Olivia didn't remember the drive home. She must have been on autopilot, her body engaging, her mind somewhere else.

The lights in her house were burning brightly. Her dad was still up then. She would sneak through the back and go straight to her room. She parked the car on the street instead of the driveway and walked gingerly through the back door, carefully inserting her key so her dad didn't hear her. She was later than she normally was, but she hoped he was on the couch after one too many glasses of red wine and not watching the time of her arrival.

Easing open her bedroom door, Olivia took in the scene. Her walls were still covered with posters of nineties boy bands of which she was obsessed, unicorn and cloud pillows, a pink-and-white cupcake comforter and lace curtains. It was the room of a girl. Everything screamed innocence. With a cry torn straight from her soul, she pulled the comforter from the bed, throwing it on the floor. Next, she picked up each cushion and threw them wildly, knocking over her pencils, her plant and crashing her laptop to the floor.

She started to sob as she ripped the posters into little chunks that scattered from her hands like confetti.

The door flew open and her dad stood there, staring at her,

then surveying the damage. Her hair was wild, decorated with twigs and her eyes puffy from crying, and tears poured down her cheeks.

'Olivia. What's wrong?' Her dad held out his hand to help his daughter from the bed. She shrank back and stood perfectly still, like the eye of a hurricane passing over her. All the anger went from her, leaving her exhausted.

'Nothing,' she whispered.

He looked at her closely. 'Are you all right?'

She'd never be all right again. She knew this instinctively.

'I'm fine,' her voice hoarse from her cries straining to be heard in the field. Olivia bent down and retrieved her comforter, pulling it up over herself as she curled into a ball underneath it. 'I want to be alone,' came her muffled statement. She heard the door close gently. She couldn't handle another man around her right now. She would have said anything to get rid of him. Men were either liars or they were indifferent: she didn't think there was such a thing as in between. *And there was no such thing as the perfect man,* she thought bitterly.

Hot tears slid down her cheek only to roll off her chin, where they dripped onto the sheet. Her whole body ached now that she had stopped moving. Her mind wouldn't let her think about why that was, the night a blur, and for that she was eternally grateful. Olivia huddled inside her cocoon, finally falling asleep as the sun rose on Sunday morning.

When she woke, she couldn't bring herself to move from her cocoon. Olivia heard her dad walking quietly up to her closed bedroom door, waiting, listening for signs of life then walking away again when he heard nothing. He kept doing it for the next hour before she decided to let him know once and for all that she was OK, even though she wasn't. When she stood, the world swayed, much like it had done... before. Her mind clapped shut, blocking her from whatever memories she couldn't face reliving.

Staring at herself in the mirror in the bathroom, Olivia pulled the twigs out of her hair, not knowing how they got there. She undressed, taking in her ripped singlet. She had a flashback of large hands taking a handful of each side of the singlet and ripping it. She shook her head and moved to the shower. She washed the twigs from her hair, the water dirty from her feet. They were covered in dust and she hadn't showered since... she didn't know when. Surely it was yesterday before she went out? She tried to remember where she'd been. Someone pressuring her to drink a cup of beer. Don't drink and drive: her dad's only rule.

Olivia stood naked in front of the mirror. She noticed bruises on her inner thighs. Her body jolted as her mind kicked out a random memory of the night before. *Fuck! Hold her down, will you? I can't—* She couldn't handle it, her whole body shaking so much that she dropped to the floor, arms wrapped around her knees, rocking back and forth.

She had no idea how long she sat there for, mind blanking time and pain, but eventually she got up and pulled her clothes on, walking back to her bedroom.

Her dad must have heard the shower running because he was hovering in the hallway near the bathroom door waiting for her. 'Olivia, are you all right?' A memory. Hadn't he already asked her that?

'Fine,' she said, not wanting to talk at all.

'Will you be OK to go to school tomorrow? You seem kinda... sick or something.' He was trying, but she couldn't even hold a simple conversation. Her mind drifted away; from what, she was still unsure.

'I just need... I need...' Olivia couldn't finish her sentence. She slipped under the comforter with jerky movements, knowing she should feel something, but she was completely numb. Something had happened.

You wanna go?

Olivia recoiled – from what she didn't know – and buried herself deeper, covering her head. She needed to block out the noise, the terror she was feeling welling up inside of her.

She heard her dad close the door and mercifully, she fell asleep.

* * *

Wren felt rather than heard someone in his room, standing by his bed. He could smell burning toast, the scent of coffee wafting down the hallway. The smell made his stomach turn. Quickly he threw back the comforter and launched himself down the hall to the bathroom. He just made it before landing on his knees and violently throwing up.

'Wren?' The bedroom visitor had followed him down the hall. He heard the small voice say in the doorway. 'Mom said it's breakfast time. She has to go to work.' When no reply was forthcoming, Ty tried again. 'You sick or something, Wren?'

Wren wiped his mouth with the back of his hand. He stood, feeling groggy and unfocused. He rinsed his mouth, still smelling the toast and coffee, still tasting the vomit. 'I'm fine. Coming now, just give me a minute.' He turned to his little brother and pushed him in the butt with his foot. Ty giggled and ran off down the hallway.

Wren looked at his reflection: discolored and swollen eye, cut lip, torn T-shirt. He knew he'd bruised his ribs, they were tender to touch, as was his stomach – probably why he'd thrown up. No, he knew why. *Justin.*

'Wren?' called his mom. 'Billy just left and I have to go soon. Come have your breakfast. I made eggs.' Normally he loved her eggs, but they were always runny and the thought sent him back to his knees where he threw up more beer and bile.

He walked into the kitchen. 'What the hell, Wren?'

He looked down at himself. Damn, he'd forgotten to change and he hadn't cleaned up his face. 'What happened to you?' His mom sprang over to him in two strides and gently grasped his face in her hands. She looked at the shiner, the cut lip. 'You boys need to go easier on each other, you're not kids anymore.'

Wren's stomach was killing him, and the thought of trying to hold food down made him nauseous all over again. He wondered about Olivia. Should he call her? Probably not. He would be one of the last people she'd want to hear from.

'Wren?' His mom snapped her fingers in front of his eyes. 'Sweetheart, are you OK?' His mom knew him pretty damn well. They had been a team since he could remember, a family unit with a connection that couldn't be broken. Even when she married Billy, he'd come in third to her children. 'You look... I don't know, but there's something more wrong than just boys knocking each other around. What is it?' Her eyes stared into his and he was afraid that she'd see his secret. Last night's secret.

'It's nothing, Mom. Breakfast smells good,' he said, trying to stop the interrogation.

'Ty made it,' his mom murmured, seemingly unconvinced that nothing was wrong. 'Maybe I shouldn't go to work today...'

'Mom, I'll be fine, just feeling a bit sore – nothing I can't handle.' *Fuck Justin.*

'Well all right. Make sure you take good care of your brother, OK? And Ty?' She turned to her other son who was sitting at the table eating his breakfast.

'Yes, Mommy?'

'You need to take care of Wren today. Be a good boy and I'll be home in a few hours.' She turned back to Wren. 'You sure you don't want me to stay home?'

'Yeah, I'm sure.' He needed time to think, to figure out what to do next.

He went to the window, ignoring the plate of food, and watched as she drove off in her old car. Billy had often offered to update her car, but she always declined; this car reminded her of how far she'd come. He'd been trying to save for a car of his own by working with Billy.

'Wren?' Ty broke his thoughts and for that he rewarded his brother with a smile.

'Yeah, little dude?'

'Come eat with me?'

Wren sat down at the table and forced himself to finish every last bite of his eggs as his brother looked on, smiling. He loved Ty. He would not let him down.

Olivia. Even her name... He just couldn't.

* * *

Monday morning came around, but Wren couldn't make himself get up. His mom called for him before sending Ty down who Wren promptly sent away. Next, he heard the lumbering tread of his stepdad. Billy came into his room.

'You all right, buddy?' he asked, his brows raised, questioning. 'Your mom sent me to get you.'

Wren rolled over and sat up, barely meeting Billy's eyes.

'I'm fine.'

'You know, if you want to talk about anything, I'm always here for you. No matter what it is. I won't judge.'

Yes, you would. If only you knew.

'Thanks, Billy. Tell Mom I'm getting up now.' He used the bathroom that they all shared. His mom would be heading off to work soon, as would Billy, and Ty would be going to school. As he dressed, he thought about his plan. He would stay home today; he didn't want to go to school. Didn't want to see *them*. How could he?

'Honey!' called his mom. 'Justin's here for you!'

What the actual fuck?

Wren walked down the hallway and into the lounge room where Justin was chatting casually with his mom about her weekend and she was gently chastising him for Wren's injuries. 'What did you boys get up to Saturday night?'

Justin gave her a smile that he used on the girls at school. 'What we always do, Mrs Wright. What we always do.'

They both turned when they heard Wren clear his throat.

'Hey, Wren. Ready to go?'

'What are you doing here, Justin?' The slight hostility in his voice gave his mom pause.

'Came to pick you up, as always. Right?'

Wren looked at his mom, who seemed confused by the tension in the air.

'Right,' she said. 'Well Ty and I have to go. Billy said to say goodbye. Ty, honey, time to go.'

Ty came running into the room, his too-big backpack slapping his back.

'See ya,' he said to Wren with a hug and a kiss, Justin watching on.

'Later, Ty,' Justin said, giving him a high five.

They left and their absence left a void. 'Why are you here?'

'I'm here to pick you up. Let's go, don't wanna be late.' He walked out the door, throwing a look behind him, making sure that Wren was following him. He was.

Wren pulled the locked door behind him, wondering what the hell he was going to do.

Wade was sitting in the back seat, as usual, behind the driver's side.

'Don't forget your seatbelt, Wren,' Wade said, mocking him. It was something his mom said to him often, much to his friends' amusement. Wren pulled the seatbelt over his chest and clicked it in just as Justin took off. Wade unclicked it from his position in the back.

'Don't be an asshole your whole life,' Wren said, his voice filled with annoyance.

Wade laughed. 'Someone's a bit touchy today.'

'Just fucking drive,' Wren said to Justin.

'Wren.' Justin started talking, no doubt aware that Wren wasn't in the mood. 'We all make choices. I make choices and you make choices. And we have to live with those choices. For some, it's easier than others. You'll get there.'

Wren looked out the window as they sped toward the school. Wren had been planning on taking the day off to get his head right, but what if he never saw things the same way again? The car stopped moving and he turned to see Justin already out of the car, Wade slamming his door.

'Get out, Wren. Be normal, for fuck's sake. What the hell is wrong with you?' Justin demanded.

'What's wrong with me? What do you think?' He slammed his door and stormed off, away from Justin and Wade.

He went looking for her straight away. He just had to. There wasn't a particle in his body that didn't need to see her, but she was nowhere to be found. He asked around. That's what concerned boyfriends do. He called her. That's what loving boyfriends do.

After first period, he continued his search for Olivia. Wren heard footsteps behind him. A hand on his shoulder. 'If you tell, you'll be in just as much trouble as we will be,' Justin whispered into his ear. Wren spun around and pushed Justin backward, hands on his chest. Justin stumbled into Wade.

'You're fucking sick. You know that?' People were watching.

'Just being real. You were there too, and you let it happen. Just as guilty as us, man.' Justin and Wade left him alone after that. He sat through the day once he knew that she wasn't there. She wouldn't have wanted to see him anyway. He left school and caught the bus home, something he hadn't done in a while. His mom was home already.

'Hey, baby,' she said, calling out from the kitchen. He walked in. She was facing away from him, taking muffins out of the oven. 'You're home early.'

'Caught the bus.'

She turned around, putting the tray on the side to cool. She came over to him, looked at his black eye and made a small noise in the back of her throat. 'You OK, sweetheart? You've seemed... different these past couple of days or so. Distant, sad maybe. Did you and Olivia have a fight or something?'

Even her name brought up bad memories.

'Nah,' he choked out, 'I'm OK.' He leaned in and wrapped his arms around his much shorter mother. He kissed the top of her head before breaking the hug. He headed for his bedroom, knowing that she would be watching him go, worrying about him. He couldn't deal with that right now. He loved her, she loved him, but he had bigger things to worry about.

That night he couldn't sleep. Worry shot through him every time he closed his eyes. It woke him up, heart pounding like a freight train was running through his body. Finally, around two in the morning, he fell into a shallow sleep dreaming of what happened if she told.

* * *

The next day Wren caught the early bus to school, avoiding Justin and Wade completely. It was recess before he saw them both striding toward him. 'Fuck,' he whispered. He pushed past people, people who said hello to him, people he ignored. He just wanted to get away. Three days and he was feeling... different about, well, everything. Something like this forced a person to re-evaluate things.

He needed to speak to Olivia, but he knew he couldn't. Not now, maybe not ever. He just needed some fucking space. He heard them calling for him, but he ignored them. He needed to decide what to do.

He caught the bus home during the middle of the school day, not even feeling guilty about it. Then he rode his bike down to his special spot at the river.

It was a hot day, the sweat glistening on his brow and upper lip, the birds cawing and wheeling overhead. He glanced up at them, the sun, high in the sky, blinding him. He dropped his bag onto the bank and lay down, using it as a pillow. He stared at the sky through the dappled light that filtered through the tree branches. It was beautiful, but he couldn't enjoy the tranquility today. He realized almost as soon as he lay down that he shouldn't have come here. He'd brought Olivia here not that long ago. They'd swum, traded secrets and kissed until the night cooled.

Wren closed his eyes. He hadn't been sleeping well since the party. He was weary and carrying a burden; a secret like this was exhausting.

He had no idea how long he slept for, but he was jolted awake, aware that something wasn't right. He wasn't alone. He looked around him, the sun beginning its descent over the horizon. He'd be riding home in the dark. Wren hefted his bag onto his back, picked up his bike and wheeled it to the parking lot. Then he saw it. A midnight black car waiting for him, engine off. How long had they been there? Was Justin's engine the thing that woke him?

He walked up to the car and Justin rolled down the driver's window. 'You left school,' he said evenly.

'Why are you here?'

'Your mom – she called me. Apparently, you're out past curfew.' He laughed, Wade laughing along with him.

'Fuck you, Justin.'

'Get in, you big pussy and I'll take you home to Mommy.'

'Fuck no. I'll ride.'

'Just get in the car Wren,' demanded Justin, 'we need to talk,' but Wren had already begun riding away. Pissed off, Justin roared past him, kicking up dust and small stones that plinked off Wren's bike, coating him in dust.

19

It was completely dark now. Vanessa must have peered out the window beside the front door a hundred times. And when she wasn't doing it, Ty was. He was wondering where Wren was too. Billy was doing his best to keep her calm, but she had a feeling that something bad was coming. Billy said she was seeing shadows where there were none. But something had shifted. Something with Wren.

He was shutting her out, they'd always been able to confide in each other but these past few days were hard for her to handle. He was... alone. She figured out on her own that he was either fighting with or not talking to Justin and Wade.

She was just about to look out of the window for the 101st time when she saw a small bright headlight off in the distance. 'He's home!' she yelled to Billy as she saw Wren throw his bike to the ground.

'I told you he'd be fine,' she heard Billy yell from the kitchen. She heard his low rumble again; he must be talking to Ty.

She loved that kid so much, but right now she felt that it was Wren who needed her most.

Vanessa yanked open the door before Wren even had time to get his key out. 'Where have you been?' she demanded, hands on hips, brows lowered. She didn't mean to be angry with him, but he'd scared her. Especially with the way he was acting. Distant, moody.

'Down at the river.'

Vanessa took a deep, centering breath. 'What were you doing at the river? And why did I get a call from school to say you'd missed afternoon classes?'

She heard Billy and Ty talking in the kitchen and caught the sound of a giggle from Ty.

'I was thinking. I left 'cos I needed to think. Can we drop it? I'm home now.' He walked away, not giving her a chance to answer. Calling him back and forcing him to talk to her wasn't going to win her any prizes. She went into the kitchen where her other boys sat eating dinner.

'Wren not hungry?' asked Billy around a mouthful of food.

'Yeah, Wren not hungry?' copied Ty.

She rubbed his head affectionally. 'I guess not. I'll go and see if he wants something later on.' She sat down with the rest of her family, laughed and talked with them, but the frown lines between her eyes didn't fully disappear and Wren was firmly on her mind.

Once the dishes were loaded into the dishwasher, Vanessa decided that enough time had passed for her try to speak to Wren again. Unfortunately, he had other plans; she could hear the music, the bass thumping from the hallway. Clearly he didn't want to be disturbed. She left him to it and went to put Ty to bed. She tucked him in and gave him a good-night kiss. 'You know Mommy loves you, right?'

She tickled him and he giggled. Ty was so easy to understand, not unlike how Wren used to be.

Vanessa crawled into bed beside Billy, their bedroom at the other end of the house to the boys'. Vanessa loved her little three-bedroom house, it had become their home

'I think there's something wrong with him, Billy.'

Billy sighed deeply. 'Love, you need to take it down a notch. Is he acting out? Sure. Is he fighting with his friends? Yup. But that's a normal part of being a teenager, don't you think? You have to give him some growing room to work through these issues on his own. He's not always going to have his parents around.'

'Speak for yourself,' she laughed. Billy smiled and gently started stroking her long hair. He kissed her on the forehead, her cheeks, down her neck and then finally, her lips. It felt so good to be touched by him. She hadn't known that their relationship could be like this, otherwise, she joked to him, she would have married him much sooner.

They made love that night, slow, in-sync lovemaking. Billy awoke in her something that she'd never experienced before. He knew her inside and out, light and dark, and accepted every part of her.

'I love you, Ness. Always have.'

'Love you too. Besides my boys, you're the best thing that's ever happened to me, to us. Before we became a family, I never thought I'd find this. I came with two children and a fucked-up ex-husband. Who'd want to take on that?'

'I did, still do. Besides, neither of the kids has given us any trouble and Mark is in the distant past.'

At the mention of Mark, a shadow dropped over her. She rolled away onto her back.

'I've upset you.' Billy knew her so well.

'No, I just don't like talking about Mark, you know. Talk about him too much and he'll appear, bothering us again. I can't handle going through all that bullshit.'

'Has Maggie heard from him?' he asked, still continuing to dwell on the subject.

It felt like it had been months since she had last seen Maggie, but it had only been a week. 'No, and she doesn't want to. Her and Charlotte are really happy living with Dad and its given Dad's life meaning again. He loves my boys and Charlotte is just another of his grandkids and Maggie a best friend. I'm really happy it worked out for them both.'

'Yeah, your dad deserves some happiness. I'm glad he has them too. Must be nice having a young kid around the house, to play with.' He sighed wistfully.

'Billy! Are you suggesting that we have a child?'

'Maybe,' he said, testing the waters.

'But we've talked about this. We decided on this before we were even married. I was pretty clear that I didn't want any more kids and you said—'

'I know what I said, but things, people, change.'

'So you're not all right with just us now? You want your own flesh and blood? Is that it?'

Vanessa was out of the bed, flipping on the lamp and glaring at him with her hands on her naked hips. 'You always said no to that, Billy. You agreed. I told you that you could find someone who wanted kids, I gave you an out right up to the wedding, but you didn't take it. Now you're lying there saying you want another child?'

'Can I talk now?' he asked mildly.

'I suppose so.'

'Ness, I know I said that thing about the kids, but I guess in the back of my mind, I was kind of hoping I could get you to change your mind. Especially since I'm so good with your kids.'

'*Our* kids,' she interrupted, thunder coloring her face.

'OK, clearly that was the wrong way to phrase that. I didn't marry you with the intention of changing your mind. I just hoped, you know?'

She shook her head, pulled on a nightie, grabbed her pillow and declared, 'I'm sleeping on the couch.' She was so angry. How dare he spring that on her? She felt like she wasn't doing the boys justice as it was. The café was more than a part-time job; she had slowly been increasing her hours there or doing paperwork at home. She didn't like bringing work home but sometimes it was unavoidable. Billy stepped up on those nights, listening to Ty do his reading or cooking dinner. He only knew how to make a handful of meals, but she so appreciated his help. Then there was her baby Wren. Only seventeen, with the weight of the world on his shoulders. She couldn't get out of him what was wrong, and she would have called Justin if he and Wren were still speaking. Maybe that was half the problem; if she knew what it was, she might be able to help. Wren wouldn't want her to call. She instinctively knew that would drive him in the opposite direction.

The following morning, Vanessa was up and had put away any evidence that she had slept on the couch before anyone else was awake. Billy tried to apologize as soon as he saw her, but it wasn't an easy fix of an apology. In Vanessa's eyes he had basically said that her boys weren't enough, and she wouldn't stand for that. He all but groveled, and eventually she accepted his apology, right before he walked out the door. He looked contrite, and Vanessa didn't think he'd be bringing having a baby up any time soon.

20

Olivia had no real understanding of how time passed. It was almost as if she was in a bubble that no one else could penetrate. She knew her dad went to work and when he was home, he would hover around her asking her what was wrong. She would whisper that it was nothing then she would walk back into her room and crawl under her comforter, the only place that didn't feel so aggressive. Olivia had completely stripped her room of everything save the bed. One day she just couldn't stand the thought of looking at all that stuff anymore. It belonged to someone else, someone that she wasn't anymore. She put it all in the hallway and it was gone that very night. Her dad never said a word about it. Maybe he recognized that she just couldn't think, let alone talk right now. She spent most of the days asleep, her nights reserved for staring up at the expanse of ceiling above her.

Olivia knew deep within her that something was terribly wrong. She showered six times a day, trying to remove the stain, scrub the scent from her body. As the minutes bled into hours and the hours into days, Olivia had more flashes of what had happened. It was as if her mind was sending out a trickle of water from the dam, but not trying to cause a flood. It was protecting her, but also wanted her to remember what happened.

The sound of flesh striking flesh, the dirt caked under her fingernails. She remembered that. She remembered losing her shoes somewhere and cutting her feet stumbling back to the car. Where were her shoes and what was she doing out in the middle of that field, alone? She may never get answers; her mind remembered reading an old article once about how the brain will build a barrier around itself and its memories to protect you and may release them in time when you could handle it.

The hand that choked her around her neck surprised her, cutting off any air she tried to breathe in. She panicked, but her arms were pinned down by steel bands. Steel bands that left finger marks. Olivia looked down at both of her arms; the marks almost matched the ones on her thighs perfectly. Another piece of the puzzle. But who would have hurt her?

Her dad hadn't pushed her on going back to school; after what happened last time, he had been very careful not to exert any parental authority over her, besides, how could he know if she didn't fully understand what had happened herself? She went into the bathroom to brush her teeth, studiously ignoring the mirror just in case she caught sight of her reflection. She didn't want to be seen, but when she rinsed her mouth, her eyes connected with the mirror.

She saw Wren, beaten, bloodied, punched, kicked. His eye black and swollen, his lip split and bleeding.

Why? Quickly, she turned away from the mirror and went back to her bedroom. She heard the front door close quietly and assumed that her dad was leaving for work, but she didn't much care, she was beyond caring what he did now.

Then she remembered.

She hadn't checked her phone in days. It sat, uncharged, in

her bag. She pulled it out and plugged it in. A little trickle of life booted it up just enough for her to check her messages. *Wren.* She traced his name with her finger.

Her underwear ripped from her body, shoved deep in her mouth so she couldn't scream again, so as not to be heard by a crowd of her classmates close enough that she could hear the high-pitched laughter of the girls over the music. Would they hear her?

No one will hear you scream. He seemed to get off on it.

Olivia's breath started coming in ragged gasps and she leaned her hands on the end of her bed. She tried to breathe in deeply, but her lungs felt squashed, as they had that night. Shaking, she stood up and felt the immediate head rush. She wondered when she had last eaten or drank anything. It felt like days. *Wren.* His name slammed into her with force. He had been trying to help her. Pieces were slotting into place and with each piece, she became more frightened.

Justin.

She saw him, his image blurry in the low light, but she'd recognize that voice anywhere. *You little fucker! I'm gonna fuck you up, then I'm gonna fuck your girl!*

Wren. The black eye, the cut lip. He'd tried to help. He'd failed.

Olivia shed her clothes in her bedroom, not looking at herself in the full-length mirror, not wanting to be confronted by the haunted look in her eyes that she knew was there, before returning to the bathroom. Pillar and tea-light candles decorated the room, their fragrance perfuming the air. She pulled the matches out of the bottom shelf of the cupboard, lighting one candle at a time, the little flames flickering to life, beginning to melt the wax. She watched the growing swirls, the smell of roses and vanilla rising up to meet her. Soon they would all be ablaze, glowing heartily in the small bathroom. She had spent many hours in here since they arrived, just relaxing in the bath, sometimes reading, sometimes just marveling at how the world had seemed to turn right-side up here: changing towns, schools and meeting Wren.

Wren.

Olivia loved him, didn't she? She wrote it in her diary often enough to believe that it was true. The water gushed from the tap, hot; the large gold-gilded mirror steamed up, finally obscuring the animalistic, feral look in her eyes. When the bath was almost full, she reached her hand into the very back of the cupboard, pulling something out. Something supposed to be hidden, something she had forgotten about but then found in the move.

Her hand tightened around a bottle of sleeping tablets. Olivia reached back in and grabbed a second bottle – the anti-anxiety medication that her previous doctor had given her to cope with the bullying at her old school. She'd never taken any, so thirty little white tablets rolled around when she shook her hand. Her dad probably didn't know where the originally prescribed supply was kept, let alone know that there was more medication at her disposal.

Olivia took the glass beside the tap, filling it to the brim with water. She had to let the tap run for a bit until the water cooled down. She put the glass beside the bottles. Sixty tablets. A couple of handfuls and the pain would end. No dad to save her this time.

She opened the lids and tipped out both bottles onto the sink, mixing them up so she got roughly an even mix. Olivia was making sure she never woke up this time.

She cupped her hand under the lip of the sink and slid at least a quarter of the tablets into her hand. She put them all in her mouth and took a long drink of the water, washing them down. She had no idea how quickly they worked, so she had to swallow and get into the bath fast. She did the same with the rest of the tablets, all sixty of them, then climbed into the bathtub, sliding down into the water so only her head was visible. Her hair was out, floating around her face like a halo, like an angel. She inhaled the scents from the candles, the burning wicks dancing behind frosted glass holders.

Olivia felt like she was suspended in time. That in her bubble, time moved differently, slower somehow. She started to feel… something. Her mind started to drift, and she couldn't seem to control where it went.

She felt the weight of Justin on top of her, she couldn't catch her breath as he pushed her into the dirt. She tried to suck in air and was rewarded with small gasps of oxygen. Wade had a hold of Wren, who broke free from his grasp. Suddenly Justin's weight lifted off her and she sucked in air, gasping, like a fish on land. She was too shocked to move straightaway, but when she did try to sit up, someone's hand wrapped around her neck, pinning her to the ground. She reached up and tried to pry the hand from her body, only to hear him laugh.

He moved around to kneel beside her, putting pressure on her throat; again, she had trouble breathing. Wade moved his face closer to hers, inspecting it, grinning like a maniac. He was enjoying this; his hooded eyes were dark with desire. She heard Justin taunting Wren. *Fuck you, Wren. I'm gonna fuck you up, then I'm gonna fuck your girl!*

Olivia felt each strike of flesh on flesh as Justin punched and kicked Wren to the ground. Her eyes connected with Wren's as he lay in the dirt, panting. Her eyes, wide with horror; his eyes narrowed in defeat. Justin got in one last kick, catching Wren across the cheek. After that, he didn't move. She screamed behind the gag, thinking him dead.

'Where were we, Livvy?' Justin asked, his voice low even though there was no way his voice would have traveled.

She felt like she was slowly choking to death between the gag and Wade's vice-like grip on her throat. Then Wade's hand lifted from her just as Justin spread her legs and thrust inside her. She screamed again, this time in agony. Tears sprung into her eyes, ran down her cheeks, past her ears to patter onto the ground.

This could not be happening. She thrashed from side to side, trying to buck Justin off her, but he had pinned her arms to her sides so hard he left bruises. She realized that he was getting off on her struggling. He liked his women feisty, he'd told her that. So she lay still. He didn't stop, his hips painfully smashing into hers. Her mind was elsewhere. He could take her body, but he couldn't take her mind. She barely even noticed when he finished, when Wade positioned himself between her legs for his turn. She could see his face above hers in the moonlight. Hunger and lust on his face. *They were right, the stars were much brighter out here.*

She looked past Wade to where Wren was still lying motionless. *Her hero. Her fallen hero. She was his angel, his fallen angel.*

Wade pulled out and she felt a warm stickiness on her thigh. He laughed. *They* laughed. Justin squatted down beside Olivia. She was frozen in place, pinned to the dirt by an invisible force.

'Tell anyone, and I'll come back and hurt you again, you don't want that. Nod if you understand.' She nodded. 'Good girl,' he said as he lightly slapped her cheeks.

Olivia didn't realize that she was crying until she could hear the slow, steady drip of her tears hitting the warm water. Now she knew. She put together what her subconscious had been trying to tell her all along.

Wren's two best friends had raped her, left her lying in the dirt, and Wren hadn't saved her.

The tablets were working now that her mind had shown her what she had needed to see, why she felt that she had to do this. She began to hallucinate. That was the only word for it. She saw her mother sitting on the edge of the bathtub, swirling her fingers through the warm water. She stared in wonder. 'Mom,' she breathed. 'What are you doing here?'

'My darling girl, I'm here to welcome you home.'

Olivia smiled as she slipped under the water. Within moments, she was gone, crossed through the barrier of the living and the dead.

* * *

Wren decided that he should finally go and see Olivia. He needed to see her. He needed to make sure that she wasn't going to tell. No police had shown up at Justin, Wade's or his house, so obviously she hadn't reported the... the thing that happened... yet. He was grateful; if she told, he'd go down with Justin and Wade, Justin would make sure of it. He had tried to help Olivia, tried his very best, but Justin had beaten the absolute shit out of him. When he'd finally come to the next morning, they were long gone. He couldn't. He knew what they were going to do to her, and Justin admitted that they had done it. Him and Wade.

Wren caught the bus home from school and then grabbed his bike from the side of the house where it was leaned up against the wall. He could hear his mom inside, bustling round in the kitchen, banging pans together, getting ready to make dinner. He hadn't told her where he was going or even that he was leaving. He knew he should have, especially after the other day when he'd been by the river; she was so worried about him, always scrutinizing him when she thought he was unaware. He knew that she wanted so badly to ask his friends what was wrong, but he knew that she would never betray his trust like that.

He pedaled through the streets at a fair clip, going from one side of town almost to the other – not that there was a whole lotta town, but there was definitely a divide between the quality of housing.

Olivia lived in a lovely house. He'd been there a few times, having met her dad both in school and out of school. He seems like a nice, fair man, Principal Holmes. Certainly better than their last principal, a man with something to prove. The front path was lined with fragrant roses in a few different colors. Once, he'd picked a rose for her and put it in her hair, smelling the heady scent while kissing her. They had kissed a lot, but they had never slept together the whole time they'd been dating. She'd once confided in him that she was still a virgin. He said he'd wait. Olivia said she wanted to wait until she knew it was right, despite having said 'I love you' and spending all her time with him. She spent her weekends with him and after school, doing their home-work together. She would talk about their plans for the future, for when they went to college together and moved into a small house nearby. She had their future all mapped out, right down to when she expected to get married and have kids. When she had mentioned marriage and babies, he'd been a bit surprised, taken aback. He had grown up knowing all about marriage and babies straight out of high school and it hadn't ended well for his mom.

The warm wind whipped around his face, making his shirt billow behind him. He rounded the corner to Olivia's street, trying to rehearse what the hell to say to her when he noticed something going on at the end of the street. He stood up and pedaled harder, screaming his bike to a stop and jumping off, throwing it to the ground.

There was a throng of people standing out in front of Olivia's house. He pushed through them, desperate to see what was going on. A scream split through the buzz of people talking, everyone stilled. Coming outside the front door was a gurney, rolled by two official looking men in uniforms. He had a terrible sinking feeling in his stomach. The yell had been from a man.

He saw Principal Holmes walking beside the gurney, holding Olivia's hand as she was rolled along the path.

What the fuck had happened?

'Principal Holmes!' he yelled, catching the eye of the wild-looking principal as they loaded Olivia into the van. 'Principal Holmes!'

'I heard she hung herself.'

'No, she slashed her wrists.'

Wren turned and glared at the two gossiping women beside him before running toward Principal Holmes. The older man grabbed him in his arms, leaning heavily on Wren as he sobbed.

'She's dead, Wren. She's really dead this time.' Wren was stunned into silence. He wasn't sure what to say, let alone do.

'What happened?' he finally stammered. 'What did she do?' Principal Holmes had stepped back from Wren's embrace but held onto his forearm, seeming to need the physical contact.

'She... she... took tablets, lots of them... she drowned in the bathtub,' he whispered, trying not to let the neighbors hear him.

'Jesus, Principal Holmes. I'm so sorry.' Wren knew why she'd done it, and now he knew how she'd done it. It didn't make it any easier. He had played a huge role in this terrible incident. He should have called her, should have made her listen to him.

He heard people talking loudly behind them, speculating what had happened. The tragic death of a seventeen-year-old girl would be gossip for years to come. Olivia would be immortalized in death by her final act in life.

'What do we do now?' Wren asked.

'I need to go with Olivia and you need to go home.' Wren nodded, that was the smart thing to do. He pushed through the crowd, some of whom were taking photos and videos, and grabbed his bike from the footpath, slowly riding home.

His mom's car was in the driveway, but Billy's was missing. He jumped off his still-moving bike, threw it to the ground once again and yelled as loudly as he could. He was kicking his bike when his mom flew out the door. She ran down the path and grabbed his hands.

'Wren!' she said, 'What's wrong? Are you OK?'

'She fucking killed herself!' he yelled.

'What? Who? *Olivia?*' she asked, shocked. When Wren didn't answer, she asked again. 'Olivia? You mean Olivia's—'

'Dead.' He flung his arms around her and dropped his head onto her shoulder for a brief moment before pushing her away. 'She took a bottle of tablets and drowned herself.' His voice was devoid of emotion and tears now. His mom looked at him strangely for a second before trying to hug him again, but Wren was having none of it. He saw the hurt flash across her features before sadness settled in.

'Sorry, Mom, I just need... I don't know what I need.'

'Come inside, sweetheart, I'll get you a drink and we'll talk.' She gently wrapped an arm around his shoulder and this time he let her. She led him inside and sat him on the couch, then went to put the kettle on in the kitchen. She came back with a warm mug and sat down next to her son.

'Was she depressed, Wren? Was she going through something?'

'I don't know, I don't know!' he said, knowing exactly what had happened.

She hushed him as Ty was asleep. They'd think of a way to

tell him tomorrow. He was very close with Olivia; she treated him like a little brother.

'Her dad...' He couldn't finish.

'Oh God, Principal Holmes. Is he, I mean...? I should call or go round there or something tomorrow. I doubt he's had time to make friends yet. That poor man.'

'He was going with... with... Olivia.'

'Oh, honey, I'm so sorry.'

Wren looked at her, the weight of guilt on his shoulders. He should have done something.

Wren heard Billy's pickup pull up at the curb, its rumble as familiar as the flicking metallic noise the chain on his bike made. His mom patted his knee, then went to meet Billy at the door. He heard a hushed conversation and Billy swearing a bit louder than a whisper. He heard Billy's heavy footsteps heading toward the lounge room. He came over and took the seat next to Wren, his mom standing in the doorway, looking on.

'I'm so sorry, son.' Billy took his hand in his. He had never been afraid to show affection to any of his family members; he loved them all. He pulled Wren to him in a crushing hug.

'It's my fault,' Wren managed to get out.

'No. It's not. Olivia made this choice on her own. Loved ones often feel like this, but it actually has nothing to do with you.'

Not true.

'I think I need to be alone. Thanks for the talk, Billy.' Wren felt a little dizzy he stood up, handing his mug to Billy. He over-balanced a little when his mom caught him in a hug as he passed her. 'Love you, Wren,' she said simply, her face conveying all that her words didn't. In that moment, he wanted to confess what had happened, but then the moment passed. This was something he would take to his grave. He went into his room, passing Ty's room, the door half ajar, the lamp on. He loved Olivia, but his mom would have to break the news to Ty, he just couldn't.

He grabbed his laptop and sat down on the bed. He typed: *What does it feel like to drown?*

He had a need to know. There were conflicting symptoms, but all agreed that sometimes you hallucinated. He wondered if Olivia did, and if so, what did she hallucinate? She would have breathed water into her lungs, then sunk to the bottom of the bathtub. He thought about the pain that her father was in right now. He had lost his entire family. One to a freak accident and the other to an unexplained suicide. Wren closed his laptop and put it back on the desk. He felt like going to the river, but it was well after dark and there's no way his mom was letting him out of her sight tonight. *Tomorrow.*

21

Wren slept but didn't sleep; he was in an emotionless void. He dreamed of Olivia; lucid dreams, he guessed you'd call them. In one she was hanging herself using rope she'd found in the garage from a camping trip, in another she slit her wrists. Then there was the one that was the truth. The one where she swallowed a bottle of tablets and drowned.

He woke just before dawn; he opened his curtains and watched as the sky blossomed on the first day without Olivia. Justin flitted through his mind. Would he know by now? How would he feel about this? He had caused this – well, all three of them had. He was just as culpable as the other two, so Justin had reminded him many times. He was right, though. He'd let her be raped. He should have fought harder for her. She might still be alive. He felt like a real shit when it crossed his mind that now she definitely wouldn't tell. Couldn't.

Dressing quickly, he left the house, grabbing his bike from out front where he'd dropped it last night. It was cool, the sun yet to warm the air. He rode to his special spot at the river, the one he'd shared with Olivia. He could swear he could hear her laugh. He sat down cross-legged on the ground and watched the river, the water lapping at the bank. It was normally peaceful here, but it couldn't calm his turbulent mind. Eventually he decided he'd better go home. His knees popped painfully as he stood. He found riding a bit difficult until his legs warmed up a bit.

When he rode down his street, he could see his mom out the front of the house in her pajamas, her dressing gown tied against the cool morning air. He wondered how long she'd been waiting there. Probably since she'd discovered that he'd left the house without leaving a note, something he rarely did. He never liked to worry his mom, she always looked out for him and he wouldn't hurt her for the world. He felt a pang of guilt, loaded on top of the mountain he was already feeling.

'Where have you been, honey? We were worried.' He knew that she was concerned that he'd done something stupid. He'd heard of suicide clusters; sometimes it only took one to become more. He could see the question in her eyes.

'Don't worry, Mom, I wasn't doing anything stupid and I won't.' It was as close to a promise as he could get. She looked a little more relaxed, but the pinched expression was still on her face. She opened the door, waiting for him to follow her inside.

'He's back!' she called out. Billy must have been worried too. Now he felt even worse, if that was possible.

Wren was about to head down to his bedroom when his mom stopped him. 'We need to tell Ty,' she whispered. 'You know how close he is... was... to Olivia.'

Ty was sitting on the couch. The TV was on, but he was gazing blankly at the wall above it. The sound was off.

'Ty, honey? We need to talk to you.' His mom sat down on the couch beside him, Wren on the other side and Billy leaning up against the door frame.

'You don't have to tell me, I already know,' he said so quietly that Wren had to lean sideways to hear him.

'What did you say, Ty?' he asked.

'Olivia.' He whispered her name and Wren felt a chill travel the length of his body. 'She's dead.' He said it so matter-of-factly.

Wren looked at his mom. They knew better than to question where he'd overheard the news. Sometimes Ty just knew things. Sometimes ahead of time, sometimes you didn't have to tell him, he just knew stuff. It could be coincidence; make enough guesses and you're bound to be right every now and then, but it was spooky nonetheless.

'I'm so sorry, buddy. Yeah, she passed away last night. I know you loved her. We all did,' Wren said.

Suddenly Ty launched himself at Wren, who caught him easily in his arms.

Ty was crying as he said, 'I don't want you to die too, Wren.' Wren caught the worried look on his mom's face.

Wren felt the cold prick of sweat on the back of his neck. What the hell was his brother saying? That he was worried he'd do something stupid or that he was actually going to die?

'Ty, why'd you say that?'

'I don't know,' he said, looking contrite at his outburst. Maybe Wren had heard him wrong, but he knew he hadn't, and it scared him.

'I'm going back to bed,' Wren announced quietly as he stood up. His mom grabbed for his hand as he walked past, but he moved from her reach. She looked wounded, but Wren didn't have the energy to care. He walked past Billy, who said nothing. Normally he would have put him in his place gently about brushing off his mother. He did everything gently, but not today; he didn't say a word.

He fell asleep almost immediately and, of course, he dreamed of her. *Olivia.* He was watching her as she slipped under the water, her last breath bubbling to the surface. He woke up in a cold sweat. Had she thought of him? Of how he hadn't helped her? Or was her last thought a loving one?

The shadows were starting to touch his bedroom. He'd obviously been asleep all day and everyone had left him be. He redressed, pulling off his sweat-soaked clothes and changing into a fresh, clean set. He went out the back door, grabbed his bike and rode over to Olivia's house. Was it still Olivia's house, or was it Principal Holmes's now?

It was gloomy, but Principal Holmes had the lounge light on and Wren could see the man hunched over on a couch. In one hand he held a framed photo; in his other, a glass of wine. Wren put his bike down. The least he could do was offer a shoulder to lean on. He owed her that. Wren rang the doorbell and waited. The door opened and before him stood not the strong, commanding Principal Holmes, but a man broken with grief. His shoulders hitched for a moment before he got himself together. 'Wren,' he said flatly.

'Principal Holmes.'

'What are you doing out so late?' Principal Holmes asked.

'Not sure. I just ended up here. Can I come in?'

Olivia's dad seemed to think about it for a moment. 'Yes.' He opened the door wider and stood to the side.

He walked into the lounge. A bottle of red wine and the half-filled glass sat on the table, the framed photo of Olivia close by. Wren was staring at it when Principal Holmes walked back into the room.

'Beautiful, isn't she?'

'Yes, sir, she is.'

'I keep wandering into her bedroom to check, to make sure

that this hasn't been some huge mix-up; that she'll be sitting on her bed, legs tucked up under her, watching a movie on her laptop. You know how she loved a good movie. Horror was her favorite.' Wren knew this but nodded, the man needed to talk, and he would listen. He owed him that.

'I'm so sorry, Principal Holmes.'

'We're bonded in a way we never were before. We're bonded in grief. In our shared love of Olivia. And I know she loved you.'

Wren looked down, then put a finger in his mouth, chewing on a nail. He looked up slowly, sure that Principal Holmes would see the guilt on his face, the blood on his hands, but he was staring at the photo.

'I don't understand why,' he said, his eyes wet. The man struggled not to cry. 'We moved here for a fresh start for her. She was happy here. Yes, she had been different for the past week or so. She was upset, but she wouldn't tell me why. Do you know anything about it?' he asked.

'No, I don't,' Wren said, swallowing the lie.

'Well, did you have a fight? She didn't talk about you like she normally would. Did you break up?'

'Not really,' he lied. 'She said she needed a break, not a breakup, just a break. I got the impression she was working through some stuff.'

'She could have told me anything,' Principal Holmes said sadly, and Wren knew it was time to go.

'I'd better go. I didn't tell my mom where I was going – she'll be worried.'

'Thanks for coming round. Olivia would have appreciated you checking in on me.' His voice was thick with pain and Wren said goodbye hurriedly, picked up his bike and left.

* * *

Wren's mom offered to drive him to school the next day, but he refused, saying that he'd rather catch the bus. He knew that she felt him pulling away and it would upset her, but he couldn't help it. He didn't want to be touched or pushed gently to confide in her like he always had. This was a situation that he'd never been in before. As he hopped on the bus, all conversations ceased and he guessed that Olivia had been the topic of conversation. He didn't care. He took a seat and they resumed talking around him. He heard his name a few times, but he tuned it out. It was all background noise, white noise: they didn't matter. He needed to talk to someone that actually mattered. He needed to find Justin.

It wasn't hard to find him. He and Wade were in the courtyard, talking to a small group of friends.

'Wren! Been looking for you,' said Justin.

'Well here I am, motherfucker.'

Justin's eyes narrowed. ''Scuse us.' He grabbed Wren by the forearm and dragged him away from the group, who watched on with interest. Wade followed them.

'What the fuck is your problem?' demanded Justin.

'What's my fucking problem? What do you think? Olivia killed herself.'

'I heard. Good for us – now she can never tell what we did. We're home free. Stupid bitch.'

'You mean *you're* safe. You and Wade, I didn't do shit.'

'Sorry, buddy, but you were there too and didn't stop it. You're just as responsible as us.' Justin sneered. 'I'll just tell people that you let us have sex with her.'

'At least call it what it was, Justin. *Rape*. You and Wade raped her and then she killed herself.'

'Calm the fuck down, Wren. You want people to know what we're really fighting about? Remember, we're in this together.' Justin's eyes blazed with anger, Wren's with righteousness.

'I'm not with you at all. Just forget you know me.' Wren glared at Justin, then at the silent Wade.

22

The insistent knocking woke Vanessa from her pleasant dream. It was still dark outside and Billy slept beside her, taking up most of the bed and snoring softly as he exhaled. She thought about waking him up in case it was Mark at the door, but he'd been working so hard lately and was so tired, she decided to leave him be. The knocking began again.

'Coming,' she muttered to herself. She wondered if Wren had forgotten his keys again and needed to be let in. Surely he would have knocked on her bedroom window rather than the front door, though? So maybe it wasn't Wren. She quickened her step as she hurried down the hallway, hoping that Ty wasn't woken up. It was always hard to get him back to sleep, especially if Wren wasn't home; sometimes he was the only one who could get him to drop off.

She looked out the window beside the door and her breath was stolen away. Two uniformed police officers stood at her front door. She put her hand to her heart and immediately thought of her dad. She was his next of kin. He could by lying on a hospital bed injured. She quickly unlocked the door.

'Mrs Vanessa Sawyer?'

'Yes, but I remarried. It's Wright now.'

'May we come in, Mrs Wright?'

'Sure, of course.' She unlocked then opened the screen door, inviting them both inside before closing the door again. She began to feel funny, like your stomach does as you're going up the steep climb of a rollercoaster and you know that at any moment you're going to tip over the edge and free fall. 'What's happened?'

'Let's sit down. I'm Officer Jason Miles and this is my colleague Sergeant Jasmine Wicker.'

Vanessa was frozen with fear, wishing that she could stop time and prevent the words that she knew with absolute clarity that they were about to say.

Yet, he spoke anyway. 'Please sit.'

Her legs felt like wooden logs, refusing to bend in the middle. Finally, she dropped onto the couch and waited for someone to speak. Vanessa picked up the hem of her nightie and began twisting it and untwisting it in her fingers. She looked at the clock. It was two in the morning. Nothing good happened after midnight.

'Mrs Wright, there was a car accident tonight at approximately midnight out on the old highway. The accident involved your son, Wren Sawyer.'

She waited at the top of the rollercoaster.

'The ambulance crews did everything they could, but I'm afraid he didn't make it. He died at the scene.'

Free fall.

Time refused to move for her. She could see their lips moving but could hear nothing. Then slowly words instilled themselves into her brain.

Accident. Catastrophic injuries.

She screamed. Not the scream of someone enjoying the ride

on the roller coaster, that of someone who'd come off the tracks completely. A raw and primal scream burst forth from her lips again, as the female cop, her name already forgotten, moved to sit with her, to do her job and comfort her. Vanessa heard heavy footsteps running down the hallway and Billy burst into the room, hair sticking up wildly. He took in the scene and immediately ran to his wife, wrapping her shaking body in his arms.

'What's happened?' he asked bluntly.

'Are you Mr Wright, Wren Sawyer's stepfather?'

'Yes, what's happened?'

'He's dead?' said Vanessa, shaking like a leaf. 'He can't be dead. Are you sure?'

'Yes, I'm afraid. There was a car accident.' the female officer repeated for Billy's benefit. 'He wasn't wearing a seatbelt.'

'It's not Wren then. He always wore he seatbelt. He was good like that.' Vanessa tried to convince them that they'd got it wrong. 'Oh God, Justin? Wade? Are they dead too?' she asked, guessing that Wren was with them and that they had been in Justin's car.

'No, they're both alive, in hospital with severe injuries but expected to make full recoveries.'

So only her Wren had died.

'We will need someone to come and identify his body.' Delicately said but still a knife through the heart.

At this, Vanessa started wailing, the sound of a heart breaking. She kept repeating, 'No, no, no, no,' over and over again.

'I can do the identification,' Billy offered.

'He's my son, I'll identify him,' she said weakly. She barely registered the hurt look cross Billy's face. Wren was his son too. She'd said as much.

'I'll ring Maggie and ask her to come over and take care of Ty.'

Within a few minutes, Billy re-entered the lounge, now dressed in pants and shirt. All eyes swung to him. 'Maggie will be here in ten minutes to watch Ty – Ty is our other son.' *Remaining son.*

Not even five minutes later, Maggie burst through the door, using her own key to get into the house. She'd been crying, her eyes already red and puffy. Billy hugged her; Vanessa just watched. She didn't have the tears right now; they had dried on her face, not even wiped away, like glistening trails. Maggie came over to where she was sitting and bent down in front of her. 'Ness, I'm so sorry.' Vanessa looked straight through her, ignoring her like she wasn't even there.

Billy had a quiet conversation with Maggie, probably about Ty and what to tell him if they weren't back when he woke up. Just how long does it take to identify someone?

'Ness, are you sure you want to go? Do—'

'Yes,' she snapped.

'Well you'd better get dressed then. Do you need help?' Billy asked.

He was treating her like a child, an invalid or something, his voice a higher pitch than normal, his face lined with concern. She pulled on the first things she could find: black pants crumpled on the floor and a thin red cable-knit jumper draped over the chair.

'Are you ready to go, Mr and Mrs Wright?' the young officer asked.

She was never going to be ready for this. She was doing this because she owed it to Wren.

Rather than letting either of them drive, the officers gave them a lift to the hospital, morgue. No one said anything. Maybe they were trained not to say anything, maybe they didn't know what to say. She looked out the window past the dark night, then she saw her reflection and started gently banging her head on the glass. Suddenly she banged harder and Billy reached across, grabbing her by the shoulders and all but pinning her down.

'Don't you touch me,' she hissed. She had wounded him. Well, so what? She had been dealt a fatal blow tonight too.

The officers took them through a back entrance, down a short hallway and into the morgue itself.

'Are you sure you want to go in?' Billy asked, giving her one last opportunity to have him do it, but Vanessa had to see Wren, had to know it was him and that all hope had been lost.

'I'm sure.'

'Are you ready, Vanessa?' Asked the female officer.

'Yes.'

She waved her hand and a gurney was rolled over. The sheet was pulled up over the body and Vanessa needed to both see and not see what was under the sheet. The attendant didn't just remove the sheet, yanking it down with a flourish as she'd seen them do in the movies. He took his time, peered under the sheet first, then lifted it up high and back, smoothing it just under Wren's neck. Vanessa saw why. The right side of his face was still her beautiful Wren, but the other side was covered with carefully placed bandages.

'Wren!' she screamed, her heart beating wildly in her chest, a bird desperate to be set free. She stared at his face, surrounded by hard stainless steel when he should have been at home, surrounded by family and friends. Vanessa collapsed. No one managed to catch her before she went down, her world destroyed.

* * *

Vanessa woke up, aware that there was something firm yet soft underneath her. She struggled to sit up. She saw Billy sitting in a chair beside her in what looked like a hospital room.

'Shh, Ness,' Billy said, gently helping her swing her legs over the side of the bed.

'What happened?' she asked, her mind giving her a few more blissfully unaware moments.

'You fainted while you were... identifying Wren's body.' He cleared his throat and Vanessa could hear the emotion thickening his voice.

'It wasn't a nightmare?' she asked, unfeeling wood replacing her emotions.

He shook his head. 'I'm so sorry, honey. He's gone.'

She put her head in her hands, fingers finding purchase on the strands.

'Are you all right?' Billy asked.

'No, I'm not fucking all right. My son just died.' She went to stand up, but she lost her balance, falling back against the bed. Billy put out a hand to steady her. 'Don't touch me,' she snapped.

The officers were waiting outside the room for her – she couldn't have been out for long – and offered to give them a ride home.

It was quiet the whole way back. Vanessa stared, unseeing, out the window while Billy kept his eyes firmly on Vanessa, the officers once again not saying anything.

When they got to the front door, Billy realized that he had left his keys inside and knocked on the door. Maggie opened it. 'Ty's awake,' she said immediately. 'He wanted to know where you all were and why I was here. I told him you'd speak to him about it.' She hung her head and swiped at her eyes. 'I just... Ness... both of you. I'm just so damn sorry. Wren was an amazing young man. Someone who you could always count on—'

Vanessa pushed between Billy and Maggie and walked slowly down the hallway to their bedroom. Ty would have to wait. She couldn't handle talking about Wren's death just yet. Soon enough it would be out there, and people would know. They'd ask questions like the busybodies that they were, giving her empty platitudes that didn't help. No, she would leave telling Ty to Billy. He was good at that kind of stuff.

'How bad was it?' she heard Maggie ask Billy in hushed voices.

'Fucking awful. He had bandages over one entire side of his face.'

Vanessa listened from the doorway. She had no idea what the officers had said to Billy while she'd been out of it.

'Did they tell you, like, *how* he died? You said it was a car accident that killed him. Did you get any more information? Specifics?'

Was Maggie being a gossip or just a person who loved Wren deeply and needed to understand and make sense of this tragedy as much as Vanessa did?

'There...' She heard Billy take in a deep breath. 'There was a lot of damage done. For some reason Wren wasn't wearing his seatbelt when the accident happened, and his air bag failed to go off. It... it made for injuries that he couldn't have. It'll have to be a closed-coffin service.'

Vanessa stuffed her fist into her mouth to keep from crying out. What injuries? Did Billy know? Her beloved baby. Taken from her.

She couldn't even think about his... funeral. She would have to put him in the cold, hard ground, alone. Abandoned. And where had she been while he'd lain there dying? Safely tucked up in bed. She hadn't even waited up for him. She assumed that he'd been with Justin and Wade, safe.

Maggie spoke, her voice carrying down the short hallway.

'But *why?* Why did they crash? What happened, Billy?' Her

voice broke as she asked the question, and she imagined that Billy had laid a comforting hand on her arm.

'The police said that Justin swerved to miss a deer, but they ran off the road and into a tree.' Billy paused, then kept talking. Vanessa clung to the doorframe for support, knowing that she couldn't hold herself up without help. She could have called for help, but she needed to hear the rest of the story. Billy might water it down for her, to protect her, but he was being straight with Maggie. 'When they hit the tree, Wren wasn't wearing his seatbelt. He went through the front window.'

'Oh God,' Maggie gasped.

'He had a broken eye socket, a fractured skull, broken neck, and deep lacerations on his arms and torso. He... he lost an arm too.' Billy rattled off the litany of injuries her baby had suffered.

Maggie began to cry, mirroring exactly what Vanessa was doing. She turned away from the conversation and her crying best friend, wanting nothing more than to die right along with her son. Before she closed the door, she heard Billy say, 'They don't know if he died right away. He could have lived, seconds maybe, but those few seconds...' His words choked off.

Those few seconds must have felt like years to him. The agony he must have been in.

Vanessa laid down, hollow-eyed from grief. She couldn't cry anymore; her tears were trapped behind a wall made of glass. Billy opened the door quietly and sat on the edge of the bed.

'Ness? We need to tell Ty what's going on. Please, he needs his mom there too.' Billy didn't often beg but he was now.

It was the last thing she wanted to do. Talk about Wren's death. It was so fucking raw and she was exhausted. It was the longest night of her life and it stretched before her like an eternal highway of hell. Billy put his arm behind her back and lifted her up.

'I can't,' she whispered.

'You still have another son to take care of,' he said quietly. Vanessa thought it insensitive and she glared at him. If he noticed, he didn't react.

'I can't, you'll have to... tell him. I just can't, Billy.'

He looked down at his lap for a moment. 'He's going to be devastated. He idolizes Wren.'

Vanessa didn't reply, she couldn't form any more words. It was like she had used up her daily allotment of speech, and that was it. No more.

Billy stood, tugging her with him into a standing position. He wrapped his arms around her, trying to give her a centering hug like he'd done a hundred times before, Her arms hung limp at her sides. He let go, then opened the door, ushering her out.

Maggie and Ty were waiting for them at the kitchen table. Maggie stood up when she saw her, throwing her arms around her best friend. Maggie was whispering words that didn't make sense into her ear, patting her back like she was a child.

'Mom?' A small voice cut through the tension and Vanessa's heart. She would never again hear Wren call her *Mom*. She swallowed her tears, not wanting to fall to pieces in front of Ty. She looked over at Ty, but instead of looking at him, her gaze settled on a point above him. She could see Billy and Maggie staring at her from the corner of her eye.

Billy pulled out a chair across from Ty, which scraped across the floor. Vanessa winced at the sound; it grated on her already frayed nerves. She felt like a stone; she couldn't move, yet she wished more than anything to run. From this conversation, from this situation, from this life.

'Ness? Want to sit down?' Maggie whispered.

Vanessa looked at Ty.

He looked so small, sitting at the table that he'd sat at thousands of times before, opposite from Wren. Billy was sitting in Wren's chair and she wanted to scream at him to move, but she didn't have the energy to.

'Buddy,' Billy began, Maggie hiccupping slightly. Vanessa glared at her; she caught the glare and covered her mouth. 'We need to talk to you.'

Vanessa looked at her youngest son – her *only* son – and wondered if she could even be in the same room as him when he heard what Billy was about to say.

Billy grabbed his hand gently and bowed his head. Vanessa stared at them, almost removed from the situation yet dreading the words that came next. She didn't know how to act, what to do with her hands, so they fluttered up to her neck, danced around her collarbone before dropping to her sides again.

'You may have seen that Wren isn't with us this morning,' Billy began. He looked over at Maggie, then up at his wife. Vanessa met his eyes, but what Billy saw in them made him turn away quickly.

'Where is he? Where's Wren?' Ty's little voice went up an octave as he asked the question, he looked around frantically as if maybe Wren was just misplaced. 'Is he OK?' He gripped onto Billy's hand tighter. Vanessa watched as Ty's small fingers flexed around Billy's large ones, turning white, the tears already building in his little eyes as if he knew what was coming. Maybe he did. Vanessa thought back to the whispered words to Wren when he found out that Olivia was dead. Sometimes Vanessa thought Ty really could see the future.

'He's not coming back, is he?' He began to cry, tiny little sobs that escaped lips that tried to hold them back. 'He's dead, isn't he?' This time, he sobbed louder, and Billy moved around the table, picked him up and put him on his lap, wrapping his huge arms around him.

'Yeah, buddy. I'm so sorry.' Tears rolled down Billy's face as he stared up at his expressionless wife, frowning. Maggie reached over and gripped Ty's hand, Billy put his hand over the top of hers, the three of them crying.

She couldn't handle it, Ty's face, their faces; she was numb. A veil had been thrown over her emotions, but she knew it wouldn't last, although maybe it was a better state to be in rather than abject pain and heartbreak. She walked from the room, no one stopping her, and went to the safety of her bedroom.

She could hear Ty. She covered her ears, but it didn't block out his gut-wrenching sobs. Vanessa heard the knock on the front door. So it had begun.

She heard her dad's voice. Quiet, yet still overpowering, filling the small space of her kitchen and leaking its way down the hallway to reach her ears. He knocked on her door.

'Ness? It's Dad, honey. I'm coming in.' Not a question, a statement. Would people always make decisions for her from now on?

'Hi Dad,' she said quietly in the still room.

'Ness.' He sat on the edge of her bed and picked up her hand, patting it gently. 'I'm so sorry. You... I... I have no words, honey. Your mom would have known what to say. All I can do is tell you that I love you.' Vanessa watched as he shed his tears. Vanessa felt herself welling up. Her dad hadn't cried since her mom had died, and it hurt her. He stood up. 'I'll leave you be, I just wanted to come by and, I don't know, see you.' He gave her a kiss on the forehead and closed the door gently on his way out.

She heard him murmuring, no doubt to Billy. She'd overheard that Maggie was going to stay for a little while and help take care of Ty since Vanessa was in no fit state to do so. She hadn't even been able to hug him when he'd found out that his big brother, whom he adored, had died. What kind of mother did that?

'Ness?' Maggie poked her head through the door. She rolled over to face toward the window, away from Maggie. She felt her hovering by the door, wanting to speak but not knowing how to. 'Billy...' She cleared her throat. 'Billy wants to call Mark. You know, before Wren... before he's on the news.'

Vanessa didn't roll over, but she did nod in agreement. Mark. Wren's dad in name only. A drunk, wife-abusing bastard who hadn't ever been interested in his sons. Would he even care that Wren was dead? Let them call, she didn't care. She stared at the wall, but all she saw was Wren's face.

23

Vanessa dressed with care. She rolled on her pantyhose, smoothing them up her long legs. She pulled on her black dress and zipped it up slowly. She watched herself in the full-length mirror mounted on the wall opposite their bed. Beyond the safety of her bedroom walls, she could hear Billy talking with Ty. Maggie and Billy were probably getting Ty fed, dressed and ready. Moving into the bathroom, Vanessa began applying layers of war paint. She put on her foundation, smoothing out her blotchy complexion, hiding her grief. She finished off by adding a thick layer of waterproof mascara. She had no idea why she was putting on makeup when she rarely wore it, but she guessed she felt she owed it to Wren to look her best. It made no sense, but it was what she needed right now, what she clung to. Tears filled her eyes as she looked at herself in the mirror. She ran her fingers underneath the bottom of her eyelids, removing the droplets of tears that decorated her lower lashes, hanging like tiny crystals. Her eyes were vacant: she knew that nothing would ever be the same again.

Vanessa pulled her hair back into a tidy bun, securing it with pins. Vanessa changed her everyday small gold earrings to her more formal silver studs. She studied herself. She was dressed for the part of the grieving mother, but she was so much more than just a mother. She was a best friend, a confidant, something... more. She would never be ready for this day, but the knock at the door told her it was time to go anyway.

She was scared. Scared of a future without Wren in it. Scared of how she could live without him. Scared of how she could have failed him like that. She hadn't given him what he needed these past few weeks before he'd died. She had known something was wrong with him, and she had failed to get it out of him.

Billy opened the door. 'It's time to go now, honey. The car has arrived to take us to the church.' He spoke slowly, as if she didn't understand what he was saying and in that moment, she wanted to slap him. She had all this anger and nowhere for it to go. Wren's death was an accident, a terrible tragedy. Who could she blame for that?

Standing in front of the coffin, sliding her hand along the warm polished wood, she imagined she was touching Wren's face. Billy had promised her that Wren would get only the best. She hadn't really been listening, she rarely did these days; one foot in a fading reality, one foot in a world of longing. She turned and saw Ty sitting in between Maggie and her dad. He looked as lost as she felt. Their eyes met briefly, and she gave him a sort of sad half-smile, then she had to look away. She couldn't stand the look of pain in his face, the face that looked so much like Wren's did when he was that age.

It was like everything had come into sharp focus, in high definition with the volume turned right up. She could hear people from the back row whispering, the minister turning pages, preparing for his sermon. She even imagined that she could hear the falling of Ty's tears. She couldn't move; she was rooted to the spot, touching Wren's coffin until Billy came and grabbed her hand, one arm around her waist, and sat her down next to him.

She could hear people crying and sniffing throughout the service. Billy put his hand on her stockinged knee. She looked at it like it was a giant bug that had crawled up her leg and settled there. She brushed his hand away. She didn't want to be touched. It hurt too much to have someone else do something that her son would never do again – comfort her. She knew in her pain-numbed mind that she should touch Ty, say something soothing to him, but she just couldn't. Her world kept jumping from crystal-clear focus, to blurry again. A funfair mirror, distorting the truth. She was no good to him like this; better that Billy and Maggie took care of him.

She heard snippets of the minister reading passages from the Bible. She wondered why when no one in their family were churchgoers, or indeed even believed in God. She hadn't organized the service – Maggie and Billy had done that, done everything. She was in no condition to do anything but stare at Wren's photo and cry, disconnected from reality.

* * *

She lost time. Vanessa had been sitting in the front pew staring at a photo of her Wren. He was smiling and happy, two things he hadn't been when he died. It had seemed like the whole town had tried to pack into the church. She had actually seen people lining up. Lining up to get into a funeral. How disgusting. Who did that? She wanted to slap each one of them, not thinking that they were there for Wren; no, just to be ghouls, she suspected.

Then she was at the gravesite with no clear memory of how she got there. She remembered Billy's arm around her shoulders and the desire to shake the heavy cloak that was his presence off her.

There was a man handing out colored roses to everyone that came near the coffin. People were taking them with thanks and a small smile. Didn't they know that Wren's favorite flower was the sunflower, just like hers? He'd loved them ever since he was a boy and had grown his first one in a pot. She remembered fondly a young Wren with his oversized watering can, sprinkling the budding flowers with water. She also remembered his tears when one day Mark had ripped the heads off them all and kicked the pots over, dirt and sunflower stems spilling out onto the ground. She wondered if Mark had dared to show his face here today.

She had wanted to see Wren one last time before the funeral, even though it was a closed-coffin service, but Billy had put his foot down, saying it wasn't good for him to be remembered that way. She needed to remember him as he was in that photo: smiling and happy.

Billy handed her a rose that should have been a sunflower. She looked at it, unsure what she should be doing with it. As they lowered Wren into the ground, she began to sob, feeling arms slide around her again. Billy. As he descended, music played. 'Stairway to Heaven'. It played softly in the background, the sound of collective crying almost drowning it out. As she listened to the haunting music, she watched as people walked forward and threw their roses into the hole where her baby now lay.

She wanted to throw herself in after him. Her husband, as if reading her thoughts, grasped her arm firmly. 'Ness,' he whispered close to her ear. 'Put your rose in, honey – people are staring.'

Let them fucking stare.

She brought the fragrance-less rose up to her lips and kissed it gently, as if she were kissing Wren's cheek for the last time. She couldn't look at the gaping hole, so she threw her not-sunflower in blindly where it would forever lay on top of Wren, the two of them decomposing together.

Two familiar faces were missing from the crowd of mourners. Justin and Wade. Both still in hospital. She'd hadn't been fit to go and see either one of them yet; she wasn't ready to see the survivors of the crash that had taken her boy from her. Why hadn't Justin just hit the fucking deer? Why did he have to swerve? Why didn't Wren have a seatbelt on and why didn't the airbag go off? Why was he depressed? Did they even notice? What had happened with Olivia? So many questions, but still no answers.

Vanessa noticed that neither of their moms showed up either to represent the boys. Joan, she hadn't expected to see, but Phillipa? Yeah. Had the roles been reversed, Vanessa would have been there to support them.

She turned to walk away, her back to Wren, when she saw him. He was standing there, hands by his sides, a haunted look in his eyes. Their eyes connected. She shrugged Billy's hand off her shoulder and walked quickly over to the man.

'Mrs Wright, Vanessa,' he said, before slipping his arms around her. She finally gave herself permission to cry. This man, arms wrapped around her, understood her completely. She was touched that Principal Holmes had come at all, given how hard this must be for him. She had been told that Olivia would be buried in two days' time. There had to be an inquest as she had died at home and due to the circumstances surrounding her death. Vanessa had decided to attend the funeral, no matter how difficult it would be for her. They hadn't been in town long. He had no wife and now no daughter and no answers. She hugged him tighter.

She had no idea how long they stood there, wrapped in their bubble of disconnection, but eventually she became aware of eyes on them. She stepped back and turned her head slightly. Only her family remained, Billy watching them intently. With a hoarse voice she said, 'Thank you for coming, Principal Holmes. I know how hard this is for you to be here.'

'Please call me Ryan.'

They were bonded by their grief now, and Vanessa knew that they would help each other through their shared tragedies.

She walked away from Ryan and back toward Billy. 'Time to go back home to the wake, love. Just hang in there a little longer. Maggie is already at the house taking care of people, but we really should go.'

Can't be late for her own son's wake.

She didn't speak until they were close to home. 'Can't we just keep driving?'

He looked at her with pity in his eyes. *Pity.* 'No, love, we have to go inside.'

They pulled up at the curb because her dad and Maggie had parked in the driveway. Just another reason to be angry. She felt like she was going to explode if one more thing happened to her. She got out of the car and was about to head into the house when someone stepped out in front of her. She gasped.

'What are you doing here, Mark?' demanded Billy.

'I'm not here to cause trouble. My son died too,' he said quietly. 'I want to mourn with my family.'

'Oh, now he's your son and they're your family? Well, they're not your family anymore, Mark,' said Billy furiously. 'Go home and sleep it off.'

Mark looked at Vanessa. 'I haven't touched a drop since I

found out about Wren. I'm done with that stuff.' He stepped forward to touch her, but Billy put out a hand, preventing him.

'I just want to give the mother of my children a hug on the day that we bury our eldest son. You wouldn't stop a father from doing that, would you?' Vanessa hadn't even bothered looking for Mark at the funeral.

'It's OK, Billy,' she said quietly. She opened up her arms and her ex-husband walked into her embrace, touching her for the first time in years. She folded her arms around him.

'I'm so sorry,' he wept, 'for everything. I was a terrible person, an awful father and an even worse husband. I made your life hell. Can you forgive me?'

She thought about all the things that he had put her and the boys through. 'No, I can't forgive you, but I will let you grieve with us.'

Billy looked at her with confusion and disbelief, but Vanessa felt it was the right thing to do. No one should be alone today. The three of them walked up the path to the house and watched the looks of surprise on people's faces when they saw Mark with Vanessa. Those of them who knew about Mark and his violent nature toward her and the boys, her dad and Maggie especially, wore identical looks: something akin to horror.

She left Billy and Mark in an uneasy stand-off and walked down to Wren's room. She closed the door behind her with a quiet click. She didn't want to see or hear any more people. Why were they all talking in hushed tones when all she wanted was them to scream as she wanted to? She didn't want silence and hushed tones anymore. She needed something else. She wanted Wren and his noise. The best she could do was plug in his phone into the docking station and press play. She had no idea what the song was called, but it was one of Wren's favorites. She turned it up. Loud. She knew from experience that those in the lounge room and kitchen would have felt the bass thumping through the walls. She just wanted a moment of normalcy among the madness. She lay down on Wren's unmade bed, vowing never to make it again. His pillow still smelled like him and she touched it, feeling just a little closer to him. Everything in his room was waiting for him as if this was all a huge mistake and any moment now, he would come strolling back through the front door like nothing had happened. But she knew that would never happen.

Someone knocked on the door. 'Go away!' she yelled, not even bothering to turn the music down. The door opened. Billy.

'Ness, people are starting to leave now – you have to come and thank them for coming. Could you please turn off the music and come out and say goodbye? Even if you don't feel up to it, it's the right thing to do.'

'The right thing to do? You do know that I buried my son today? The right thing be damned. Tell them to go fuck themselves for all I care.' She closed her eyes. waiting for him to leave, but she felt him standing there. 'What?' she snapped, opening her eyes.

'Do the right thing and go and say goodbye to the mourners that came to pay their respects to *our* son.' He didn't yell exactly, but it was clear there was no way he was leaving this room until she came with him and did as she was told. Shooting him a filthy look, she turned off the music, her ears stinging in the sudden silence.

Billy forcefully had her by the wrist and basically dragged her to the spot he wanted her to stand. She shook limp hands and listened to their drivel.

'He's in a better place.'

No, he's not.

'He wouldn't have felt a thing.'

How the fuck would you know?

'God has called him home.'

Fuck you and your uncaring God!

Billy was shaking hands firmly with the men, kissing the women on their cheeks. Even Ty was doing a better job at saying goodbye to the mourners than she was. *Mourners*, that was a funny word. It didn't even begin to describe the grief she was feeling. Eventually they were all gone, and it was just the family left. Maggie offered to make tea, probably just to keep her hands busy. Vanessa leaned against the wall and Billy, her dad and Ty sat down at the table. Mark had left early on, obviously feeling out of place. Vanessa had barely eaten or drank in days, but when Maggie suggested food, she almost threw up. She shook her head no.

'You have to eat, Ness.' She put her hand on Vanessa's shoulder. She shrugged it off. She didn't need her sympathy. She needed them all to piss off and leave her alone to go back to Wren's room and fall asleep on his bed.

Her dad was making room in the fridge for some of the cooked meals that people had brought with them. Why do people bring food? Was it because they thought the bereaved had forgotten how to cook? Or do they think that their grief is so palpable that they just can't stand to cook, clean, or do anything but be numb? Well, she was numb, all right, but clarity would come soon. Super laser-focused clarity. She would want – no, demand – answers, but for now all she could think about were those wrong flowers rotting atop her son's coffin. She gave a little sob and everyone turned to look at her. She wanted to tell them she was fine so they'd stop looking at her, but it was a lie and they knew it. She was not fine.

Her dad went home around eight, Maggie was staying to help with Ty and took the spare room, and Billy put Vanessa to bed, removing her dress and wiping the makeup from her face. She lay awake beside him as he drifted off, snoring lightly beside her. She was exhausted but couldn't sleep. She knew what she had to do.

She had to find out everything there was to know about Wren's final two weeks.

24

Vanessa hadn't slept properly that night or any night since losing Wren. Things had continued to move along around her. The funeral, the wake; Ty went back to school and Billy went back to work just days later. Life went on for other people, but it had stopped for her. All she really cared about was discovering the secret that Wren was hiding. The secret to why he had been so down in his final weeks. In the dark recesses of her mind, she realized that she should be more concerned with how little Ty was coping with losing his brother. She did care, she just couldn't express it properly. Her grief was stronger than her concern and she knew that between Billy and Maggie, who had come to stay, leaving Charlotte with Vanessa's dad, would take care of Ty.

After Billy had gone to work, Vanessa got up and headed down to the kitchen to see Ty before he went to school. Maggie was making breakfast. She was making pancakes, which were Wren's favorite breakfast food, not Ty's. Vanessa froze.

Maggie saw the look of shock on Vanessa's face and realized what she had done. 'Oh God, Ness! I'm so sorry, I just wanted to do something nice for Ty.' She covered her mouth with her hand, trying not to cry. Vanessa did the same. Ty looked from one to the other, obviously confused with what was going on.

'Mommy?'

She looked with great difficulty at the boy who looked so much like the boy she'd lost. She turned to face him. She was silent for a long moment before finally saying, 'Yes, Ty?'

'I miss Wren.' His little face was flushed with emotion.

Vanessa's heart stilled. She felt like all the breath had left her body and she could barely stay upright.

'Why don't we go and get ready for school, Ty?' suggested Maggie, but Vanessa spoke.

'I miss him too, Ty. I really do.'

Ty got up from the table and came to his mother.

'He's OK, Mom, I know he is.' Vanessa didn't even try to stop her tears. They fell from beneath her closed lids even as she drew Ty into her arms. She saw Maggie turn around, giving them privacy, her own eyes welling up.

'C'mon, Ty. Go get dressed, sweetheart.' Ty went down the hallway to his bedroom and Vanessa picked up her bag.

'Are you going somewhere?' Maggie asked in surprise. Vanessa hadn't left the house since the funeral.

'Yeah. I need to do... something.' She didn't elaborate, even though she knew Maggie wanted to ask.

This time she didn't wear black, nor did she put on makeup. She arrived at the graveside service of Olivia Holmes, one of only ten people who were there. She went straight up to Ryan, who was talking to the minister. He saw her coming and excused himself. She held out her arms and he all but fell into them, gripping her tightly, his head bent, mouth so close to her neck that she felt his warm breath on her skin. She rubbed his back.

'How are you holding up?' she asked. She knew that it was an empty question, but she also knew it had to be asked, just in case he wanted to answer it.

He looked at her, his face pale under his tan, his good looks hidden behind a mask of pain. The minister started the service and Vanessa found herself holding Ryan's hand with no recollection of how it got there. Still, she didn't let go, knowing the excruciating agony this day brought with it. The service was short; Olivia Holmes, aged seventeen, was buried without any fanfare. She had roses too, and Vanessa had to ask if she liked them.

'Yes, she did. She got her love of gardening and roses from her mother, who died many years ago – Olivia never got over her passing.' He smiled sadly. 'I guess I didn't either and now I've lost them both.' His voice rose higher as he tried to hide the tears in his voice and in his eyes.

'How 'bout I drive you back to your house? You can pick up your car tomorrow.' She didn't think it was a good idea for him to be driving himself around. She knew that after Wren's funeral she could barely walk in a straight line, let alone drive. She didn't want Ryan to hurt himself. He nodded.

No one followed them back to his house. 'Are you not having anyone come over?'

'Who would attend but you? I really appreciate you coming today. It has made an unbearable day slightly more bearable. Olivia would have liked that you came too. She always said you were a lovely person and a great mom.'

Vanessa smiled sadly as Ryan opened the front door.

'I know it's kinda early,' he said, looking at the clock that showed eleven thirty, 'but I need a glass of red. Would you like one?'

She really should go home, but she knew she couldn't leave

him alone; he'd just buried his only child for fuck's sake. 'Sure, just a small one, though.'

She watched as he poured a generous glass for them both. Lucky for her that Maggie was looking after Ty. She would pick him up from school and she could stay here with Ryan for a bit longer. The wine hit her fast as she still wasn't eating.

She stood up, wobbling slightly, and went around the lounge room, looking at the framed photos. There was one of Olivia and her mom. 'She was gorgeous, your wife. Olivia looks just like her.'

'Yes, she was beautiful and yes, Olivia does – did – take after her mother. You're beautiful too.' he said boldly. She pretended not to hear the compliment. Grieving people often said things that they didn't mean and it meant nothing; the ramblings of a drunk man, high on grief. Vanessa picked up a photo of Wren and Olivia. His arms slung around her, laughing into the camera. She didn't expect to see it, so she was caught off guard, sucking in a breath before beginning to cry.

Ryan was at her side in an instant. 'I'm so sorry, Vanessa. I should have put that one away just in case you came over.'

'I just wasn't expecting to see it is all. He looks so happy.' She was aware that Ryan was standing very close to her. She thought of Billy. Her wonderful, savior, kind-hearted, not-a-mean-bone-in-his-body Billy, and she moved away. Grief made people do silly things, but she would not do that.

'I should go. My son Ty will be home soon. I'm trying... it's not going so well yet. He looks so much like Wren.'

'Can you come back tomorrow?' Ryan almost begged.

Vanessa wondered if it was the best idea, but the man had no one else. He hadn't any friends to lean on, and they were thrown together by circumstance. She owed it to Wren to help Olivia's father.

'Sure, I'll come back.'

He hugged her goodbye. 'See you tomorrow.'

As she got into the car, she realized that except for seeing Wren's photo and that little hiccup, that she hadn't cried for three hours. It was a huge step forward for her.

But it didn't last long. She pulled her car into the driveway and walked up to the front door.

'Mom!' yelled Ty. She felt deflated as soon as she walked into the house. She used one arm to hug him, then gently pushed him away. She saw Maggie's disapproving look and just knew that she was going to tell Billy all about it. She figured Billy must have asked Maggie to keep an eye on her and report back. She seemed to watch her a lot, especially when she thought Vanessa wasn't looking. In one way it was sweet, in another it pissed her off. She was a grown woman and she'd do what she pleased when she pleased. She was grateful as hell to Maggie, but she was still grieving for Wren and wanted to find out why Wren had been so depressed, even before Olivia had committed suicide. She would have to ask Ryan if he knew anything, but now was not the time.

* * *

The next day Vanessa left the house while Maggie was dropping Ty off at school. It was a sneaky way to do it, but she didn't want to answer the inevitable questions until she was home and it was too late to stop her. She wanted to talk to Ryan about something delicate. Did he know what had happened, if anything, between Olivia and Wren? Olivia hadn't been around to their house for over a week or so before she'd died. Wren had stopped talking about her, so she figured that maybe they had had a fight. He hadn't confided in her, which had been very unusual considering how close they were, but maybe Olivia had confided in her dad. Maybe Ryan could help shed some light on part of the puzzle.

She still needed to talk to Justin and Wade, but she knew they were both still in hospital and they weren't going anywhere in a hurry.

She knocked on the door and he answered quickly, like he'd been waiting for her arrival. He looked as rough around the edges as she felt. He wore casual pants and a T-shirt with buttons halfway down the front in a deep mulberry color. Vanessa was pale from lack of sunlight and had bruise-like smudges under her eyes from lack of sleep. She wore jeans with her black knee-high boots and a casual black T-shirt, given that it was over eighty-five degrees outside. Her long hair was out and wild, flying around her face in the breeze. He quickly stepped back so she could come in as she grabbed at her hair and smoothed it down. There were a few strands across her face and before she could fix them, he had reached out and tucked them behind her ear.

Dangerous territory.

He then pulled her into a hug. 'Ryan—'

Her phone vibrated in her pocket. She pulled it out and was surprised to see a text from Mark. She must have made a noise in the back of her throat because Ryan said, 'Problem?'

'Just a text from my ex-husband.'

Just wanted to make sure you're OK. Call if you want to talk.

It still shocked her that they had spent time in the same room after the service without incident. Who would have thought that they could have done that, what with their history? She didn't answer the text. He would have seen that she'd read it, but that wasn't her concern. Right now, she needed to ask Ryan for information. He went to the kitchen to make them both a cup of coffee. She hovered awkwardly in the living room until he returned five minutes later. He set both coffees down on the table.

She saw him put a healthy dose of bourbon into his cup. She wasn't going to say anything; whatever helped ease the hole in his heart where his child should be. She got the impression that this was not the first nip he'd had this morning. Again, no judgment.

'Come, sit,' he said, heading to the low, comfortable-looking couch. Again, he sat closer than normal; she figured he was craving human companionship since he'd lost his daughter. She understood that.

Vanessa took a sip of the scalding liquid, which burned like molten lava the whole way down. She began to cough, her throat on fire. Ryan went and grabbed her a glass of water, which put out the fire inside her. He patted her on the back while she coughed.

'Shit, that was hot!' She swore before even thinking about it. Ryan smiled softly at her, it felt like he had attached himself a little to her and that was fine, she'd probably imprinted a bit on him too. She understood – his daughter and her son were lovers after all; they shared their hurt in not knowing what the hell had happened. She knew Wren died in a car accident – her mind mentally stumbled over the word *died* – but what about beforehand?

'Ryan, did the kids have a fight at all? I mean, before Olivia... passed away?'

'She never actually came out and said if they did or not. I've been trying to recall and analyze every conversation with her, and I would have remembered that one. I do remember Wren saying she asked for a break. But if I'm honest, Olivia pretty much raised herself at this point. She was nearly eighteen – I didn't know much about her life anymore. Didn't you find that with Wren?'

'Wren and I – we shared an incredibly close bond. Something was bothering him before his death, before Olivia's death, but he wouldn't talk about it with me.'

Dammit, still no answers.

'I can't believe all this,' Ryan said quietly. 'How are they both gone within weeks of each other?' His voice was thick with emotion and she felt for him, she really did. She wanted to help him. He had no one. He was truly alone in the world.

She liked Ryan, and not just because they had bonded over their children, but because he was a good person.

She sighed, swallowing one final mouthful and standing up. 'I have to get home, I just wanted... to... check on you, I guess.'

He looked at her with longing in his eyes, but she glanced away.

'One thing,' Ryan said, rising to stand with her. 'Olivia kept diaries – she has since she lost her mom. I've been wondering if there's anything in there that would shed light on why she did what she did.'

Suddenly, Vanessa could think of nothing else. She had to read those diaries.

'If you're finding it too hard, I'd be happy to read them for you, see if I can't find a clue in there. Maybe she wrote about her plans or reasons, or something, anything.'

'You'd do that for me?'

She nodded. He stared at her a moment longer, then fetched a bag and pulled a pile of books from the lounge-room book-shelves. They had proper spines and were made to look like real books. He handed over the bag and she took it with a small smile. 'I'll read through them and let you know if I find anything.' She held the bag against her chest reverently, aware that these were the last words of his daughter. 'I may find what happened with her and Wren. It's been... consuming me, I guess you could say.'

'Thanks, Vanessa.'

'No problem. I'll call you in a couple of days to check on you, OK?' She was desperate to get home and start reading, now that she had a tangible place to start. Ryan had been the only other person besides her dad she'd really spoken about Wren's death with. She was probably the only one he'd spoken too. He must have felt so isolated, and she needed to remember that.

'Bye, Ryan.' She waited to see what he was going to do, but he left his hands down by his sides, the smell of coffee and bourbon the only thing between them now.

* * *

When Vanessa arrived home, Maggie's car wasn't there; she must have either got caught up at the school or gone to do some grocery shopping. Either way, Vanessa was glad to be alone. She sat down on her bed and sorted through the diaries, finding the first one, then putting the rest back in the bag.

She read the looping, girly handwriting for over an hour. Reading about the bullying that Olivia was subjected to was brutal; it brought back memories of her own experiences. Vanessa had to stop a few times to wipe her eyes and take a deep breath. Olivia was a beautiful writer, capturing her torture with a mixture of objectiveness and sadness. She might have gone on to be a professional writer one day, so detailed and evocative were her entries.

She felt tears welling up again when she read about the fight Olivia had had with Marcie. Olivia thought that the torture would stop once she and Johnathon broke up, but it was just another thing to bully her about.

Vanessa couldn't read any more today, so great was the girl's heartbreak. She came out into the kitchen only to find Maggie standing by the sink.

'We need to talk,' Maggie said, pulling out a chair and

motioning for Vanessa to do the same. She did so reluctantly. 'Last night Ty asked me if Wren was in heaven or hell.'

Vanessa said nothing, not knowing what to say.

'Don't you have anything to say to that?'

'What did you tell him?' she asked, looking in Maggie's direction.

'Of course I told him that Wren was in heaven looking down on him, but you need to talk to him. He is suffering and you doing this whole absentee thing is not good for him. I'm taking care of him, but I'm not Mom. With questions like that, the answers should come from you,' she rammed home, but in a soft voice, meaning to cajole her into being a present mom.

'Maggie,' Vanessa sighed. 'I'm mourning the loss of my eldest boy; I literally can't think of anything else. I have no room for anything else. There is nothing but Wren. I love Ty, I do, but I can't be there for him right now.' It was more than she'd said on the subject since Wren had died. She needed Maggie to know that she just couldn't deal with anything else at the moment. She had questions that needed answers, and then, and only then, could she be a mother and wife again. She knew that Billy, Maggie and her dad talked about her, no doubt trying to decide how to bring her back from this limbo world that she was stuck in.

Vanessa stood, signaling the end of their conversation. She walked down to the bedroom, pulled her boots off and promptly fell into a tense sleep. She woke with a start when Billy put a hand on her shoulder. More like nearly leapt through the roof.

'What the fuck, Billy?' she said, before she had a chance to engage her brain. She wanted to take it back but, it was out there now.

'I was just coming to tell you that Maggie has made dinner. How are you feeling today?'

She just stared at him.

'I guess I shouldn't ask that question anymore, huh?' He asked, slight bitterness to his voice. She knew she was hurting him by being this way – she wasn't completely blind – but she also knew that she couldn't do anything about it right now. It was still all about Wren.

'Come and eat something. You'll feel better.' He pulled back the comforter and put her slippers on her socked feet. She sat down on the chair that Billy pulled out for her. She knew that she looked a mess. Hair untidy and unwashed, her shirt now crinkled from sleeping in it. Ty beamed at her as she sat down. 'Hi, Mommy,' he said brightly, and she felt a pang of loneliness. Wren should be sitting at the table next to Ty, ruffling his hair or tickling him under the arms. She sighed deeply before making her mouth smile at him. 'Hey, Ty.' That was all she could give, but it seemed to be enough for him, but not Billy and Maggie.

She tried to eat, but it made her stomach churn so much that she was afraid that she was going to be sick. She went into the kitchen to make herself a weak tea, which she was able to stomach in small doses. She could tell when she came back to the table that they'd been talking about her. They looked kind of guilty, except Ty, who looked like he was about to cry.

'I miss Wren!' he said before pushing his chair back and running down the hallway. The other two looked at her, but she sat there, staring at the wall until Billy eventually stood, angrily pushing his chair across the floor and heading off down the hallway to comfort Ty. It seemed his initial excitement at seeing his mom had worn off and his grief had come pulsing through.

* * *

Distant though they were, Billy tried to hold her hand in bed that night. She pulled away and he sighed in the darkness. 'Are you ever going to come back to us, Ness?' She didn't answer, just rolled over and looked into the darkness. She couldn't answer that. She didn't want to tell him that she may never come back, and she certainly wouldn't be coming back the same. She was forever changed, and not for the better. This grief was like a stain on her soul, blackening part of it, killing it off, poisoning it from the inside out.

In the safety of her own room, she thought about transference and her relationship with Ryan. As long as she kept it above board with him, telling him when he came close to the line, she didn't see any reason to stop their friendship. Billy had asked about her spending so much time over there and was hurt when she said that he understood her. He kept his mouth shut, but she knew exactly what he wanted to say but had yet to say it.

The next day, Vanessa snuck out of the house with two diaries and a bottle of water and drove around aimlessly, looking for a place to sit and read. She didn't want to go to the library; she couldn't handle people today, and besides, every time people saw her, she received condolences and she just couldn't handle it. Another drawback to living in a small town. You'd think she'd appreciate the support, but unless they had information about Wren and his state of mind before the accident, they just didn't exist to her. Eventually, she knew where she wanted to go. She sat down on the hard-packed dirt of the riverbank: Wren's favorite spot. His sanctuary. She wondered if he had brought Olivia down here. She knew the boys had been.

The boys. The survivors.

She wasn't ready to see them just yet either, but they weren't going anywhere. She knew where they both lived. For a moment, she watched the fast-flowing river as it sped past her, momentarily blinded by the sun dancing across its surface. She watched as fish jumped out of the water, arching gracefully before diving under again. The primal smell of the mud filled her nostrils, and she could see why Wren loved it down here so much. Secluded and quiet. She was completely, blissfully alone. Finally.

She took out a diary and opened it to where she had left a bookmark. Olivia was in the process of moving schools after her dad had taken the position at Wren's community college. While she felt guilt that her dad had to change jobs and towns again, it was the first time that she had been happy to move towns, schools. A fresh start. She loved the quaint little town with its small population, where neighbors knew each other and the corner store still sold boiled lollipops for twenty cents each. She wrote about her trepidation of starting another school, but she seemed optimistic. She hoped with all her heart that she made a friend this time round. And she did, before she'd even left the front office. She wrote about a boy that she met on the first day. A boy who she felt an instant connection with. A boy whose name was Wren.

Vanessa cried out when she saw his name even though she knew it was coming, it still hit her in the stomach, hard, when she read it. She traced his name with her fingertip, a couple of her tears dropping onto the page before she moved the book and wiped her eyes. It was still so raw. It became clear after reading a bit further than Olivia was smitten with her son. So far, Vanessa couldn't think of a single reason why Olivia would commit suicide.

Ryan called her, the ringing cutting through the peacefulness of the river, and she had an insane urge to apologize. 'Hey,

Vanessa, how are you?' He sounded down, the pain in his voice coming through loud and clear.

'The same. You?'

'Same. Just wondering if you've had a chance to start the diaries?'

He'd only given them to her yesterday. 'Yes, I've started – I'm up to where she has just started at the community college and met Wren.' She was quiet, and couldn't speak for a moment.

'That must be hard for you to read. You're so much braver than I am,' he said quietly.

'I read about the bullying, which was hard to read. Did you know about that?'

'No. Not until... the end. I'm just happy that they had each other, much like we do. No, not like that. I value you as a friend, and I appreciate your support and guidance.' It was just what she needed to hear from him.

'Thanks, Ryan, you too.'

She just wanted to help him. A girl who had written about what sounded like just about every facet of her life would certainly write about her impending suicide.

The cicadas chirped their songs so loudly in the background that she could barely hear Ryan's goodbye. The sun was blazing down on her head, her hair hot to the touch. She thought about a quick dip in the river, but she didn't think she could handle the memories of swimming with Wren. She packed up her bag, the diaries and her bottle of now empty water and headed back to the air-conditioned comfort of the car.

The ever-present Maggie was waiting for her when she got home. 'Hey, where have you been?'

'Nowhere.'

'Ness, you have to talk sooner or later. Wren's death has been hard on us all, but we've been coping, leaning on each other. You're not living this way.'

'Then maybe I should just die.' She walked off down to her bedroom. She heard Maggie murmuring something in a low voice before she closed the door. Was it to her? She didn't know nor did she care.

Later, when Billy arrived home, he came straight down to their bedroom, smelling of fresh lawn clippings and summer. 'Dinner is ready and you're coming down to eat with us like a normal family. Your son needs to see you, hear from you and you will give him that.' Billy rarely laid down the law with her, so she dragged herself off the bed and followed him down to the kitchen, taking her place at the table. Maggie had a mug of weak tea and some dry toast put in front of her chair instead of the roast that the rest were all having.

'There are some leftovers in the oven if you want it.'

Normally there were no leftovers: Wren would eat everything in the house.

'Hey, Mom,' said a very subdued Ty. She wanted to ask what was wrong, but honestly, she couldn't deal with the answer if it was to do with Wren.

'Hey, Ty.' She may not have been talking much, but she reached her hand across the table to hold his. He smiled slightly and put his hand in hers, and she gave it a brief squeeze before letting go.

It was two days later when Maggie approached her again. 'It's time to come back to your family. I've said it before, and I'll say it again. They need you. I can help out all you want, but they want and need you.'

'I need to find out what happened to Olivia – she didn't commit suicide for no reason. I need to help Ryan and Wren...' She couldn't finish her sentence.

'Why does a stranger come before family?' Maggie asked, running her hands through her hair in frustration, a trait that Vanessa and Wren also shared.

'Because Wren loved her. It's as simple as that. I'm doing the best that I can. Now if there's nothing else, I have to go out.' Vanessa didn't make any mention of the fact that Ty was home because he wasn't feeling very well. She didn't look back at Maggie as she picked up her bag and left.

She went outside only to find Mark leaning on her car. She had a flashback that left her breathless.

* * *

Wren was always a good boy: a good son and a great friend. Her best friend, in fact. They had been through so much together in their lives. Not for one second had she ever wished she hadn't fallen pregnant with him. Not even in her darkest days. He was the one thing that kept her going, got her out of bed in the morning, and he nourished her soul with his love. He was her soulmate and she knew that he loved her just as much.

He tried his best to protect her from Mark's temper, sometimes trying to deflect blame and even a few times, stepping in to try to help him mom while his dad was attacking her. He knew right from wrong; he was a *good kid*. Vanessa would have liked to shield him from the harsh realities of life but, living with Mark, she couldn't do that. He saw the worst in humanity, but it never warped him; if anything, it made him a better person.

There had been one particular night when Wren had tried his best to rescue her. Mark had come home from work in a foul mood. She didn't know what had caused it and she didn't much care, she just tried to keep out of his way and keep Wren in his bedroom. She was cooking his dinner – meat and three vegetables – which obviously wasn't cooking fast enough for his liking.

'For fuck's sake, woman, hurry up. I'm starving and you're fucking around.'

She bit back the retort on her tongue. She was trying to keep the peace, and keep the peace she would, no matter how much he baited her. 'Not that your cooking is all that anyway. Pretty shit, actually.'

She ignored him.

'I said, it's pretty shit. Isn't it, Vanessa?' His voice was low, dangerous. She didn't dare turn around.

'Yes. Of course.'

'Say it.'

'My cooking is shit.' She felt so low in that moment and wanted nothing more than to disappear right then and there. She heard the chair scrape behind her as he pushed it noisily away from the table. She could feel him behind her and she froze, not daring to move at all.

She heard Wren walk into the room and wanted to scream at him to get away. She turned around, moving away from Mark. She turned back just as Mark reached over and grabbed the handle of boiling pan of broccoli, cauliflower and carrots. He cocked his arm back and threw the contents of the pot. As the boiling water hit her chest, the pain took her breath away. She screamed in agony, dropping to the ground.

'Mommy! Mommy!' She lay curled up on the floor, moaning loudly. She looked up into Mark's angry face.

'Fucking hate meat and three veg.' Then he walked out the door not looking back.

She cried harder.

'Should I call Nannie? Mommy, what do I do?' screamed Wren, his voice hysterical.

She couldn't tell him what to do. Her vision started to fade then everything, including the pain, mercifully disappeared. When she woke, she was in hospital, her chest covered in bandages. Her mom, Wren on one side of her, was asleep in a chair next to her bed. They both were asleep but her mom heard Vanessa let out a low moan. Her mom's eyes popped open. 'Wren, Wren, look who's awake. He opened his sleepy little eyes, finally focusing on his mom. 'You're OK,' he whispered.

'Yeah, I'm OK.' Her chest felt like it was on fire, so she pressed the button for the nurse. She came bustling in. 'Pain is it?' Vanessa nodded. 'Glad to see you're awake, scared your little boy half to death, burning yourself like that.'

Wren had obviously covered for Mark, doing what Vanessa had done numerous times. He was just following her lead. She hated what she was doing, teaching him to protect a bully, an abuser of women. Wren held her gaze and shook his head gently. Now was not the time to confess. He knew it and she knew it. Wren touched the back of her hand.

'I'm sorry, Mom, I—'

'Don't, Wren. Just don't, baby.'

* * *

Vanessa put her hand on her heart, which was thumping painfully in her chest. 'What are you doing here?'

'Just coming to check on you.'

'I'm no longer your concern, Mark. I'm not married to you anymore and I'm not your property.' She was still affected by all those years. 'The only thing we share in common is Ty and you've never shown any interest in him.'

'Actually, we have Wren and our shared grief in common. And I do want a relationship with Ty, that's why I'm here.'

'Oh is it?' she said sarcastically.

'Yeah. Losing Wren... it's been hard. I know it has been on you too. I regret so many things in my life, but what I regret the most is not fighting for my kids. I don't want to make that mistake again.'

'And does that include Charlotte?' Vanessa asked. 'Maggie's inside if you want to talk to her about it.'

'Both my kids, Ness.'

'Don't call me that,' she snapped.

'Sorry. Could I come in and see Ty?'

'It's a school day, but he is actually off school because he doesn't feel well.'

Vanessa thought about what he'd said. He did seem changed. He wanted to see his kids and he was sober, wearing clean, possibly new, clothes. She then noticed that he'd combed his hair, and she realized that he was trying to make a good impression. Like a job interview where the job was being able to spend time with your kids.

'OK, but only for ten minutes – like I said, he's sick and you need to go slow. He's a special little boy and he's still not coping that well.' She was only guessing, and that was terrible.

She unlocked the door. 'That was quick,' yelled Maggie.

'Actually, I didn't get out of the driveway. We have a visitor and he has something to say.'

Maggie came out of the kitchen, wiping her hands on a tea towel. Then she saw Mark standing just behind Vanessa.

'What the hell are you doing here?' Maggie demanded. Her furious gaze fell on Vanessa. 'Explain yourself,' she said, like Vanessa was a naughty school girl.

'I think I'll let him do that,' she said in the face of Maggie's anger. 'Mark.'

Mark rubbed a hand over his lightly stubbled face. 'Maggie, I know I've done wrong by you and done a lot of damage to you, both of you actually. I'm here to say I'm sorry, so very sorry that I hurt you both and our children. I want to make things right with the kids, both of them. If something should happen, I want them to know that I tried. That I wanted to be a proper dad. I've changed.'

That part seemed true. He had never expressed any desire in seeing his children before. Maggie looked at Vanessa skeptically. 'What do you say to this?'

'I guess if he's adamant about trying to have a relationship with Ty, then I should at least give it a go. He is his father, after all.'

Maggie's brows lowered as she swung her gaze back to Mark. 'You do this, you commit to these kids. You have to see it through. No disappearing on Ty and Charlotte. Especially Ty.' She looked at Vanessa. 'He's been through so much and needs stability.'

'Ty!' Maggie called out. They heard his footsteps coming down the hallway and Vanessa felt a sense of dread.

'Yeah?' he said as he came into the room.

'Ty, do you remember your dad? Mark.'

'Billy is my dad,' he said matter-of-factly.

'Well, yes, Billy is your stepdad. Mark is your biological dad, your first dad, I guess. He was married to your mom when they had you.'

Vanessa thought about the night Ty was conceived. She pushed the thought away. She'd never be able to let Mark have a relationship with Ty otherwise.

Ty tried again. 'But I only want one dad. Billy. Mom, are you making me go away?'

Vanessa was stricken with his question and went round to put her hands on his shoulders. 'I would never make you go away. I love you,' she choked out the words, then let him go.

She looked at Maggie, pleading for help.

'Maggie will be here for ten minutes while Mark visits with you. Then he can come back another day.'

Maggie came closer to her. 'You don't want to run this by Billy first?' she whispered.

'My child, my choice. All right, I'm off.'

Maggie looked surprised. 'Where are you going?' she asked.

'I... uh... have things to do.' She could see the disapproval on Maggie's face, but she didn't care. The comradery they just shared was gone. Vanessa didn't have the energy to care. She loved Maggie, but like Billy, she was pushing her.

Again, Vanessa drove around, not really knowing where to go, before finding herself turning onto the old highway toward the crash site where Wren had lost his life. Reading the diaries out there would make it seem like the lovers were together again. She hadn't been to the site yet – Billy hadn't thought she was strong enough – but she was over other people making decisions for her.

She pulled up and walked across the road toward the tree with the flapping blue and white tape on it, Vanessa thought it strange that there were no skid marks as you would expect. Justin had told police that he swerved to avoid a deer and that it all happened so fast he didn't even know what happened.

So why no skid marks, Justin?

Just one of the questions she'd be asking him when she eventually confronted him, then Wade. Vanessa followed the flattened-down weeds toward the tree, tracing the path that the car had taken. She hesitated, then stopped. Was Billy right? Was she ready for this? To see the actual spot where Wren had drawn his last breath? Could she do this?

Yes.

She started walking again, slower but still inching closer. Soon she was just in front of the tree, standing on broken safety glass, thick and glinting in the morning sun. There were deep gouges in the tree where the car had impacted with the thick trunk. Vanessa reached out a trembling hand and traced the marks with her fingertip.

She swept the glass out of the way with her hand, then sat down with her back against the tree trunk. She pulled out a diary and inhaled deeply. She looked up into the perfect blue sky, and the perfect fluffy clouds drifting on a lazy breeze.

Her life was far from perfect. She now sat in the very place her son died.

Tears welled up in her eyes again, but she did not let them come. Instead, she began to read.

Olivia had wanted to stay a virgin until she was sure that Wren felt for her what she felt for him. She was adamant that she be sure. He never pressured her, like her previous boyfriend, and Vanessa felt a sense of pride, knowing that she raised her boy to be respectful of women despite what he'd grown up with. It was a worry that the violence he'd seen early on in his life would leave a lasting impact on the man he'd become, but it wasn't the case. Wren was wonderful. As Vanessa read more pages, she became convinced, as did Olivia, that Wren *was* the one.

She couldn't understand. If he was the one and they were so in love, why the fuck did she kill herself? She was tempted to skip ahead, but she had promised Ryan. She also promised him that she'd call when she had something to tell him.

The sun hung low in the sky and she had to shade her eyes on the way home. Billy was going to be so mad and not just about her missing dinner. She drove home and saw Billy's pickup parked out the front and had a sinking feeling in the pit of her stomach.

'A word,' he said sternly as soon as she walked in the door. He had been waiting to pounce on her.

She followed him down the hallway to their bedroom.

He sighed. 'Look, I don't appreciate being kept out of the loop on such an important decision. Ty told me *his dad* came to visit him today. He gave him a carved wooden car that he's carrying around with him everywhere. Maggie said that Mark came over wanting to make amends for everything that he's done. And you're just, what, going to let him see Ty after everything?' She could see that Billy was working himself into a state, his fists clenching and unclenching.

'Well, why shouldn't he be given a second chance?'

'How many fucking chances does that bastard deserve? Do you remember what he did to you? To Wren? You were broken when I ran into you,' he hissed. 'Now you're letting him back in? This won't end well.'

'Maybe, maybe not, but I need your support on this.'

'Sure, I'll help you with Mark, but if he puts a foot wrong, I will kill him. He shouldn't be allowed near Ty,' he said, his parting shot as he went to leave the room, then he stopped, his back to her. 'Maggie says you go out nearly every day. Where do you go, Ness?'

'I just drive around. Usually, I end up at Wren's spot at the river.'

'Maggie told me about some diary of Olivia's that you've been reading.'

Damn her!

'Yeah, Ryan asked me to. He can't read it himself – it's too painful. He wants to know if she explains why she killed herself.' She didn't mention that there was more than one.

'Ness, that's a very intense and personal thing to be doing. You're still so fragile. Are you sure?'

'And this is why I never told you about it,' Vanessa said, angrily sweeping her hair to one side to massage her stiff neck.

She was stressed and it was manifesting in knotted muscles. 'It's important to Ryan.'

'And just how much time are you spending with Ryan?' His eyes were narrowed in suspicion.

'Are you kidding me? I go over there sometimes, but we usually talk on the phone and it's limited to him calling me to see if I've found anything, which isn't often. In fact, once.'

'Is this really the best use of your time?' he asked. 'Wouldn't you be better focusing on your grief, moving through it and coming back to us, whole?'

'Billy, I'll never be whole again, I thought you understood that. The woman you married is gone. This is who's in her place now. I have to get to the bottom of this. As I explained to Maggie – who I'm sure passed it on to you – I can find out what was wrong with Wren by finding out what was wrong with Olivia. Why don't you get that?' She was crying now, tears of frustrated littered her face.

'OK, OK, I don't want to fight with you anymore. I just want to make sure you know what you're doing, what you're giving up.' With that, he walked away from her. Part of her wanted to run after him, but the stronger part said, *Let him go.*

Her phone rang. She picked it up without looking at the name on the screen.

'Hey, it's me.'

'Hey, Ryan.' She could hear the floorboards shift outside the door and she knew someone was listening. Well, they wouldn't hear anything.

'Just calling for an update,' he said hopefully.

'So far I have nothing that would indicate she's anything other than happy. I think it would help bring you closure if you read what she's written. They really were in love.'

'I was kind of hoping for an explanation, a confession, something.'

'Look, I haven't finished. She writes just about everything that goes on in her life. Listen, I have to go.' The footsteps moved away. She slowly hung up the phone and placed it back into her bag.

25

Vanessa was back at the river again. This time, she parked underneath the dappled light coming through the trees. She lay on top of the bonnet, feeling the sun – still warm in the shade – dancing on her bare arms, the almost hot bonnet underneath her. She pulled out Olivia's third diary. There were two diaries left, so she hoped that Olivia would get to the point soon. She read about general school things for about an hour until she found something interesting buried within.

I don't like Wren's friends.

That's all she wrote. One line about such a complex and obviously troubling issue. Why didn't she like them? What had they done to warrant a mention in her diary? She didn't say anything more, which in itself was odd since she was so detailed with everything else. It just didn't fit. She didn't like his friends. That meant Justin and Wade. The two boys she couldn't face yet. The survivors of the crash that took her boy. Crushed skull. Closed coffin.

She kept reading. Twelve pages later, she was rewarded by another tiny piece of the puzzle.

I should talk to Wren about them, but I just can't find the words.

What words? Why was she being so cagey? Why not just come out and say it? Vanessa kept reading, enthralled now. She read for another hour, looked at the time and thought she'd better get back. There were two cups sitting on the sink, so Vanessa surmised that her dad had made a surprise visit today, but she hadn't been home. They'd been avoiding each other, neither one of them knowing what the fuck to say.

For the first time since the service at their house, Vanessa felt up to going into Wren's room again. She hesitated, her hand on the doorknob. She both did and didn't want to go inside. But eventually love and curiosity won out and she turned the knob.

It was just as he'd left it. A boy's room, bed unmade, clean clothes on the floor not yet put away and soccer boots thrown in the corner. She ran her hand over his laptop. She closed the lid to protect it from dust. There were stickers all over the lid; he'd customized his school laptop to better reflect who he was. Vanessa sat down on his bed and picked up his pillow. It had lost his scent and she lost her shit. Bursting into tears, she howled at the unfairness of it all. Why him? Why was *he* taken? Eventually her howls turned to light sobbing, and she lay curled up on his bed, clutching his pillow. She fell asleep and woke up in a panic to a silent house. Maggie and Ty should have been home an hour ago. So, where were they?

Vanessa had a frightening thought: a tree, gouge marks. She panicked, the heaviness in her stomach turning to a hot ball of fear. She tried ringing Maggie's phone, but it went to voicemail. The fear within her started to take over, radiating out from her heart. She rang Mark's phone. He answered on the fourth ring.

'What's up, Ness... Vanessa?' he corrected.

'Is Ty with you?'

'Sure, him and Maggie and Charlotte are all at my place. Why?'

She sagged against the doorway and couldn't answer for a moment, the words lodged in her throat. She cleared her throat, but still no words.

'Vanessa? Did you forget they were coming to my place today? You did say it was OK.' He spoke softly, so unlike the old Mark that she had known. He sounded almost tender.

'I don't even know what day it is, Mark.' She hung up without saying another word and Maggie was home within the next twenty minutes, full of apologies.

She had called Billy when she began to panic, and he was the one that suggested she call Maggie's phone. Once Maggie was home, Vanessa called Billy back to let him know Ty was home safe and sound.

'See, babe, nothing to worry about. He's fine, though, I admit I am glad you were worried.'

'What's that supposed to mean?' she snapped, not under-standing why he would say something so hurtful to her.

'Nothing,' he backpedaled.

'No, tell me.'

'It's just that you haven't shown much interest in Ty since Wren died. It's nice to see you still care.'

'Fuck you, Billy,' she said quietly and hung up.

How dare he say that to her? She loved Ty, even if she had a little trouble showing it right now. *A little trouble?*

Billy didn't know how she felt, not really. Ryan did. She was debating whether it was a good idea to call him when the phone rang in her hand. *Billy.* She declined the call. She was too angry to talk to him right now. He had basically accused her of not loving Ty. After Wren, how could she not be the way she was? It didn't mean Ty wasn't on her mind, in her heart.

Somehow it felt right reading Olivia's diary in Wren's room, surrounded by his things. Olivia's entries had captured Wren's room right down to the last little detail. She had truly captured the essence of who he was. She had loved Wren. What had gone so horribly wrong?

Vanessa heard the front door open. Billy was home. She closed Wren's door on the way out and walked down to see him. She wanted and expected an apology. She was seething, still so angry. She had the diary clutched in her hand.

'What's that?' he asked. No apology. He didn't even seem contrite for what he had said.

'Olivia's diary.' She wondered why she didn't say Olivia's *diaries*.

'You shouldn't be reading that; it's only going to cause you more pain. I already told you that.'

Vanessa didn't like his tone; it reminded her of things better left unsaid. 'I told Ryan I'd read it and I intend to keep that promise. He needs to know why she killed herself. Can't you understand that?'

Suddenly Billy snatched the diary from her hand, seized a cover in each hand and ripped it in two. She screamed. He ripped it again, then threw the pieces to the ground. Vanessa dropped to her knees, gathering the fragments into a messy pile. She cried as she tried to pick them all up, scooping them possessively toward her. Maggie came running into the room, saw what had happened and walked out again, choosing to leave husband and wife to work it out.

'Why did you do that?' Vanessa screamed at him. Her tears burning track marks into her cheeks.

'For your own good.'

She stood and launched herself at him. She slapped him

across the cheek as hard as she could pages fluttering to the ground. He stood there and took it. 'And I'd do it again. You're only going to find heartache there.'

Vanessa left the pieces lying on the floor and grabbed her bag and keys. She looked back, something telling her to turn around. She saw Ty hiding in the doorway of the lounge room. He must have heard her scream. She wanted to go and comfort him, but she couldn't go back into the house, she couldn't even think, she just knew if she didn't leave, she was going to say or do something that she couldn't take back. Better for her to go.

Vanessa drove around for a while, trying to work up the courage to go to Ryan's place and own up to what Billy had done. Every time she thought about it, she burst into tears. He had no right to do that, no right at all. Who was he to tell her what was best for her?

Eventually, she pulled up out the front and rang the doorbell. Ryan answered after a long time. Maybe he was in Olivia's room, touching her things like she'd been doing in Wren's room.

'Vanessa. Nice to see you. Come in.' He stepped back to let her pass but noticed the look on her face. 'Are you all right? Did something happen?' God knows if anything worse than the death of your child could happen – could anything even come close to that?

She nodded, wanting to fling her arms around him, but knowing that it wasn't a good idea. 'I came here to confess and to say how sorry I am.' Her eyes were downcast, tears slipping from beneath her lids. She couldn't even meet his gaze.

'Jesus, Vanessa, what the hell happened?' He touched her arm and she looked up at him through a haze of tears, her face drained of all color. She felt faint, dizzy, like she was either going to puke or pass out.

'Billy saw me with one of Olivia's diaries and he snatched it from my hands and ripped it to shreds. I'm so sorry.' She completely lost it, bawling, covering her face, muffled cries coming out from under her hands.

Ryan gently took her hands and held them in his. 'It's all right.'

'No, it's not. I'm furious that he'd do that. There could have been a clue in there! He doesn't know that there's one left, I'll hide it so he can't find them. I promise.' She was supposed to be bringing him answers, not bad news about something that could have been avoided. Billy thought he was protecting her, but did that give him the right to destroy someone else's property?

He hugged her to him, but there was distance to it; just a friendly hug to let her know that everything was fine between them.

'You know, this place is like a sanctuary to me,' she said, pulling back. 'Here I don't feel judged about how long it's taking me to work through my grief.'

'I'm glad you feel that way. I seriously don't know what I'd do without the support you give me.'

* * *

She was still fuming with rage when she went home hours later. Someone had left the front light on for her – probably Maggie. They were getting used to her coming and going at all hours of the night. Vanessa no longer slept much and when she did, it was fitful and full of nightmares. She imagined the crash as if she'd been there. Then there was the one where she was stuck in the funeral, like a time loop, reliving that day over and over again and again until she woke, covered in sweat and crying. It was burned into her memory forever; she couldn't escape it, even in her sleep.

While Billy slept, she pulled out the next diary and began flipping through it. It was only half full. She wondered if it stopped when Olivia died and if this diary would finally give them both the answers they sought. Billy snorted in his sleep, scaring her so much that she shoved the diary under the bed. Once Billy had settled again, she pulled the diary back out and read it using the light on her phone. She finished the diary within half an hour. It didn't hold the secrets they were hoping for, but it did have a note in it for her dad. Vanessa had felt like she was invading Olivia's last words to her dad, but she just had to read them. She felt like she knew the girl now, and what if she said something about Wren?

Dad,

I know you won't understand why I'm doing what I'm doing but know that I had a very good reason. It's not like before. I won't be waking up and you won't be rescuing me this time. I will be gone. I'm sorry that I'll be leaving you on your own. I know that you'll struggle to cope at first, but you'll find a way. You're strong, much stronger than I am. I am taking the coward's way out, the shortcut right to the ending. It just hurts too much to go on living.

I love you, always and forever,
Your Olivia

Vanessa sat there, stunned and unable to move for a few minutes, tears of frustration streaming down her face. Ryan was going to be absolutely inconsolable. Her note explained absolutely nothing. It was more infuriating than having no note at all. Still, she had to show it to him.

* * *

Yet again, she rang Ryan's doorbell and yet again she had bad news. He looked prepared for it this time.

'Did your husband destroy the other diary?'

'No, it's something else. Olivia, she left you a note. It's like she knew you'd read the diaries at some point, so I'm sure she's omitted some things.'

She handed him the diary with the letter page open. He read it slowly, then again.

'That's it? That's all she left me? It doesn't even explain anything. How could she? She took her secrets to the grave with her and now I'll never know.' He began to cry silently, shoulders hunched up, body tense. She wrapped him in her arms for a moment until he started to calm down.

'I'm sorry.'

'Don't ever apologize for being human.'

'You always seem so strong,' Ryan said.

'Trust me, I'm not. The littlest thing can see me unravel. I break down too, you're just not there to see it. I carry my grief alone.'

'That must get very lonely. You can always talk to me.'

'If I'm going to talk to anyone, it should really be my husband.' She thought of Billy and his usually caring ways. Ever since Wren had died, she felt like he had changed. Become a harder man. Then again, she had changed too, become distant and angry. 'But he wants me to hurry through the grieving phase and come back to being his wife. The trouble is, I'm not ready to let go just yet. I have things to do. I haven't spoken to Justin or

Wade yet – I need their stories and to ask them questions. They lived and Wren didn't – that's all I really know at this stage, but I intend to find out everything.'

'Well, if you need backup...'

'I know where to find it.'

She left soon after. Tomorrow, she would pay Justin and Wade a visit.

26

The day didn't exactly go as planned. Vanessa had wanted to go and visit Justin and Wade, talk to them at length, find out what they knew. She knew exactly what to do. Then Billy had thrown her a curveball.

Maggie had got Ty ready and driven him to school, and Billy had showered and dressed, but he still didn't leave the house. It got to ten o'clock and he was still there.

'Billy, do you have a late start today?' Vanessa asked, noting that he wasn't wearing his work clothes.

'I'm not going in today. I thought we could spend the day together, some quality time. Maggie is going home for the day to spend time with Charlotte and catch up with your dad. He comes to see you, you know, but you're never here anymore – hence taking the day off.'

'I wish you'd asked me first; I had planned on doing something.'

'With Ryan?' he asked, eyes narrowed. Billy rarely got jealous, but this was a whole new Billy.

'No, I was going to see the boys, Justin and Wade. I am going to ask them a few questions. They were still in hospital for Wren's funeral and I was in no state anyway, so I'm going to pay them a little visit.' She waited for him to explode.

'What do you need to see them for? Why do you want to open old wounds?'

'Because they're not healed!' she yelled. 'And I want to know what happened in Wren's last moments. What's so wrong with that?'

'His lasts moments as he lay on the grass dying?'

She was stunned. 'I've never known you to be so insensitive ever since I met you. What is it with you?' She felt the tears prick behind her eyes.

'I told you, I want my wife back.' He glared at her and she glared back at him.

'Well, this is the wrong way to go about it, let me tell you that. I haven't even forgiven you for ripping up Olivia's diary.'

'It was the right thing to do,' he said, jaw set, eyes blazing.

'It wasn't your property *or* your call to make.'

'Ness,' he said, trying hard to keep his anger in check, 'we've been through this. It wasn't healthy for you and this Ryan guy shouldn't have asked you to do it.'

'Actually, I volunteered since he couldn't do it himself. Got anything to say about that?'

'I want you to drop it. Don't go and see Justin or Wade.'

'I can't promise you that,' she said defiantly.

'I forbid you to talk to them.'

'Wow,' Vanessa said. 'You know who you sound like? *Mark.*' She walked out of the room.

Billy followed her. 'I'm nothing like him and on that subject, is it really a good idea for him to see Ty alone next week?'

'Yeah, it is, he's changed Billy. Are we really going to do this right now?' Vanessa asked.

'I just don't think it's a good idea, that's all.'

'Well, Billy, that's not your decision, is it?' Argument won, she stared at him.

'You've changed, Ness. So much.'

'I told you,' she said, frustrated and angry still. 'I'm a different person. You don't understand, do you?'

'I do.'

'How can you? You've never lost a child.' She knew it was a shitty thing to say, but she couldn't help herself. Billy had always thought and treated Wren as his own, he'd always promised her he would. She knew it was fucked up to say that.

He looked crestfallen. 'I've always considered Wren my own. I miss him every day, Ness. You know that.'

She glanced at him, her face a mask of rage, mouth snarling, eyes wide with annoyance. 'I'm sorry, Billy, I'm just not myself, I know that. I need you to be patient with me and let me do what I have to do. Can you do that for me?'

'I can't condone you bothering those boys. They will already feel so guilty and bringing it up isn't going to help anyone.'

'Fuck!' she yelled. 'You *still* don't get it. I'm talking to them whether you or they like it.'

Angry as she was, she knew she wasn't in the right frame of mind to confront Justin and Wade. She needed to be non-threatening, not the ball of white-hot rage that Billy had turned her into. She would go tomorrow, no excuses.

Later that night, they lay beside each other, but they were worlds apart. She could tell what Billy was thinking – he wanted to protect everyone from further heartache – but she couldn't move on until she had spoken to Wren's friends to see what they knew.

She went to sleep and had the dream again. She was back at Wren's funeral in her uncomfortable black dress, pantyhose and black heels. She never wore heels, but she needed to look her best, as perfect as she could, because that would be people's lasting impression of her, of Wren. This time, however, the nightmare changed. She was in the car, sitting in the passenger seat. She could feel Justin swerve to miss the deer, feel them speeding toward the tree that she knew they were going to hit. She pumped her foot on the imaginary brakes, trying to slow down the runaway car, but nothing worked. They hit it head-on.

Vanessa must have been moaning in her sleep because the next thing she knew, Billy was shaking her awake.

'You OK? You were having a pretty bad nightmare there.'

'I was in the car, I watched Wren die,' she sobbed, rubbing her eyes angrily.

Billy pulled her under his arms, snuggled her in and said, 'No more bad dreams tonight, Ness.'

Despite being so angry with him, she let him hold her. She was too afraid to be by herself, to be stuck in the nightmare again.

* * *

Vanessa woke up the next morning a little later than usual. The sun was streaming in through her window. 'Shit.' She dressed hurriedly, pulling on jeans and a jumper.

'Morning, sleepyhead,' Maggie said when Vanessa walked in the kitchen. 'Want a cup of coffee?'

'No thanks – gotta run, late already.' She spoke fast so Maggie wouldn't be able to get a word in edgewise. 'See you,' Vanessa said, taking a banana from the fruit bowl. She flew past a speechless Maggie.

'Are you going to see Justin and Wade?' she yelled after Vanessa.

Vanessa stopped in her tracks. 'How do you know that?' she asked, hands on her hips.

Maggie looked sheepish. 'Well, Billy is worried that this will set you back, that's all.'

'And how do you know that?'

'He voiced his concerns to me about how you were coping, the diary, Ryan, you know, everything that's been going on.'

Vanessa was fucking furious. How could they be talking about her like this? By the look on her face, Maggie knew it was wrong too.

'I'd appreciate it if you no longer spoke about me behind my back,' Vanessa said coldly. 'If you have something to say, say it to my face.'

Maggie looked surprised by the frosty tone. 'We didn't mean anything by it. He asked my opinion, that's all.'

Vanessa softened; she unclenched her fists. 'I don't mean to be snappy at you, at anyone else, but I just feel that those who I love are working against me, stopping me from what I've got to do. Do you understand?'

'I understand. Next time we have concerns, we'll come to you. I thought I'd take the kids to see Mark after school. Would that be OK? Your dad will be there too, if you want to come round.'

'I'll think about it – I have things to do today.'

Vanessa drove around the corner and parked. She needed to make a call and hadn't wanted Maggie overhearing. She scrolled through her phone until she found Justin's mother's number. She dialed, but it just rang and rang and there was no voicemail. Vanessa decided to go to the bar and talk to Joan in person.

The first person she came across was Mark who was working. He saw her, surprise on his face. He dropped his cloth and walked over to her.

'Is Ty OK?' he asked immediately.

'He's fine. I'm here to see Joan. Is she here? Do you know where she is?'

Mark laughed. 'Joan's not in the habit of telling her employees where she's going or what she's doing. Maybe at the hospital?'

'So Justin's still in hospital then?' she asked casually.

'Are you going there? To the hospital?'

'Why, you gonna try to stop me?'

'Whoa, I was just going to ask if you wanted company – I can get someone to cover my shift.'

Vanessa really needed to calm down, but the thought of someone potentially stopping her from seeing Justin pissed her off.

'Thanks, but I need to do this on my own.'

'Let me know if you need help.' He smiled at her, then went back to what he was doing. So that was one person who wasn't going to hassle her. Good.

It was hot outside, the sun fully beating down and tainting the air with its dryness. She drove over to the hospital in the next town. She liked the anonymity there. There she wasn't the mother of Wren Sawyer who died in a horrible accident, smashed beyond repair. Here, she was just another faceless, nameless person going about her business. She drove past Wren's old high school, going out of her way to see it. Ty would go there one day – how was she going to handle that? How was he? She found it hard to catch her breath as she slowly drove past, looking at all the teenagers swarming out the doors for lunch. Healthy-looking. *Alive.*

She found a parking space at the hospital ten minutes later. Cracking her knuckles and smoothing back her hair, she walked inside where the air-conditioner kept the hospital slightly too cold.

'Hi,' she said to the woman behind the reception counter. 'I'm looking for a patient named Justin Arden. Which room is he in?'

'Are you a family member?' she asked.

'Yes, I'm his Aunt, I've just arrived in town.'

A few clacks of the keyboard later and she had a room number. 'Ward C, Room 101.'

She took a deep breath and walked into the room. Joan was nowhere to be seen, but Justin was lying on the hospital bed. His eyes were closed, but they opened slowly when she said his name.

'Justin?'

He blinked. 'Mrs Wright?'

'Yeah, hi. How are you?'

'Sore.' He tried to smile, but it seemed to hurt him. There were half-healed scabs on his face.

'I've come to ask about the accident.'

'Accident?'

'Wren. You were driving. Justin, do you remember?' He seemed pretty drugged up, but maybe he'd be more forthcoming.

'Wren,' he said sadly.

She swallowed the lump that suddenly appeared in her throat. 'It was an accident,' he said slowly. 'Swerved to avoid a deer, hit a tree.'

'That's what happened?'

'Yeah,' he said thickly.

'Justin, there were no skid marks – why didn't you brake?'

'Happened too fast. No time to think.' He was falling asleep while talking to her. She wasn't going to get much more out of him, and she still had questions.

'Why wasn't Wren wearing a seatbelt?'

'Not sure,' he said slowly.

'What are you doing in here?' came the strident voice of Joan

Arden. 'You can't be in here. Leave now or I will call security.' It was an over-the-top reaction, and Vanessa had to wonder why.

'I was just coming to see how Justin was doing, but he is a little out of it.'

'I don't want you talking to him.'

'Why not?' Vanessa replied, folding her arms across her chest.

'Because Justin has been through something traumatic and I don't want him to be reminded of that. He has a lot to recover from – he may never walk the same again. He has a concussion, a crushed leg from being pinned under the steering column, and memory-loss issues. He's in no shape for visitors.'

'Joan, I understand he's in pain, but my son is dead, and I need answers. Justin may have them.'

'Fuck off, Vanessa.'

Vanessa was taken aback by her words, her tone, her demeanor, but left anyway. She was going to have to try a different tack with Justin. She'd think on it some more.

She drove back to their small town and headed over to Wade's house. The front yard was unkempt – weeds up to the knees, toys half hidden among the out-of-control foliage. She knocked on the door and heard the baby crying; someone was definitely home. A harried-looking Phillipa opened the door. 'What do you want?' she demanded.

She decided to be direct. 'I want to speak to Wade. I want to ask him a few questions about the accident.'

'I'm sorry for your loss, Vanessa, I really am, but Wade had nothing to do with it.'

'He was in the car with Justin, who was driving, and Wren, who died. Why can't he speak to me?'

Phillipa sighed. 'He has concussion, a broken arm and a fractured wrist. He smashed his head against the side widow and hasn't really been himself since.'

Why were these two women using injuries to stop their sons from talking to Vanessa?

'He feels guilty – it could be about Wren.'

You think?

'Can I talk to him, please?' Vanessa almost begged.

'It's not a good time.'

'OK, can I come back when he is feeling better?'

'No. I don't think that's a good idea. He... he doesn't need to remember.'

'Things don't add up, Philippa. If it was Wade, wouldn't you want to know?'

'Go away, Vanessa,' she said as she went to shut the door in her face.

Vanessa was shocked. Mild-mannered Phillipa had just told her to go away! Vanessa stuck her foot in between the door and the jamb. 'Did Joan call you? What did she say?'

Philippa looked down. 'No,' she said, clearly lying.

'If they did nothing wrong, then why can't I talk to them? What are they hiding?' She was so frustrated with Joan and Phillipa. What was their problem? 'Next time I come back, I'm not taking no for an answer.'

Vanessa walked away and drove off without looking back. She was angry and emotional, and the only person who would understand was Ryan. She drove over to his house and rang the doorbell. He answered the door with a glass of red in his hand. She took it from him and drank three healthy gulps.

'Been one of those days, huh?'

'You have no idea.'

'Tell me about it. That's why you're here, right? To vent?'

'Something like that. I just don't understand. Why can't I talk to them? It's making me angry and desperate. I went to the hospital to see Justin, but I didn't get much out of him, then Joan kicked me out. Same at Phillipa and Wade's house. I just want to talk to them, see if Wren confided in them.'

'Maybe they just feel guilty for surviving, Ness.'

'Maybe, but it won't stop me.' She took another sip of the wine, just a little one this time. 'They must know something,' she said to herself.

'Do you need to sit down? You look a little pale.'

'Maybe just for a minute then I have to go home. Billy will know what I've done by now. Fucking small towns.' She gave a bark of laughter.

27

'Thanks for listening to me babble, Ryan. I appreciate that I can come here and feel safe. It's like a haven.' Vanessa smiled at him. 'I'd better go before my husband sends out a search party.' She felt calmer now than when she had arrived. She was sure the red wine and the venting had helped.

Billy was in the lounge when she got home. 'You missed dinner. Again.'

'I know.'

'You missed Ty's bedtime too.'

'I know. I'm sorry. I got caught up and lost track of time.'

'I rang Mark to see if he'd seen you. Turns out he had. Did you go to the hospital?'

'Yes,' she said firmly.

'I thought we'd decided you weren't going to do that.'

'No, we didn't decide that, *you* decided that. I never agreed. I need answers. Billy, there was something wrong with what happened to Wren and they know something, I know they do. I have to find out what it was.'

'So you're going to stalk them till they talk?'

'What a great idea, Billy. Thanks,' she said sarcastically.

'Can we not fight for just one damn day?' demanded Billy.

'Sure, then stop provoking me.'

'I'll say it again – moving on is best for you.'

'That's provoking me.'

'When my mom died, I moved through the stages pretty fast. That's all I'm saying.'

Vanessa looked at him with complete shock on her face. 'Your mom was an old woman who'd lived a long and happy life, *Billy*. My mom was younger, but I dealt with that. My son was a seventeen-year-old boy who was stolen from me and those boys know something. We're having the same argument again and again. I love you, Billy, but this is getting to be too much.'

'What's that supposed to mean?' He clenched his fists at his sides.

'I don't know. Maybe we need some space from each other. Just until the dust settles, until I'm better at grieving. We clearly have differing opinions on what that looks like.'

'You're kicking me out? Jesus fucking Christ, Ness.'

'No, you can sleep on the couch.'

'Fine, I'll sleep on the couch as long as you deem fit.' He went and grabbed his pillow and a blanket from the linen press. He pushed past her shoulder as he came down the hallway, and she felt like utter shit, but it was the only way she could do what she needed to do and not lose her marriage in the process.

She moved down the hallway to Ty's room, pushing open the door and heading inside. He lay, one leg out of the covers, an arm flung across his forehead. She smiled gently, then kissed his cheek good night.

When she came out, Billy was watching her.

She spent the rest of the night lying awake in her bed, alone.

So many times she wanted to go to Billy, but she didn't. She had to stand her ground.

By the time the sun came up, she was exhausted, weary and feeling sorry for herself. She shuffled into the shower and put her face under the spray, waking herself up. Billy was already gone – probably deliberately so he didn't have to see his wife.

* * *

Another week passed without her getting any closer to an answer. She hadn't tried again to see the boys; she needed to formulate a plan first. Vanessa figured she'd have more of a chance of talking to Justin when he was recovering at home. Joan wouldn't be with him; she wasn't that kind of mother. Justin would be on his own soon enough. Just to be sure, she rang the hospital and was told that Justin had been discharged. He was at home, alone – ripe for the picking.

She dressed quickly and slipped out the front door while Maggie was showering. She couldn't just stroll up to the house to see Justin, and she couldn't just wander into the bar to see if Joan was there. They lived in a house out the back of the bar at the end of the block. She called Mark. 'Hey Vanessa, what's up?' She could hear him shelling then eating peanuts.

'Is Joan there?'

'Yeah, she is in the corner doing payroll, why?'

'This is going to sound crazy, but I'm going to break into Justin's house and confront him, but I need your help.' She held her breath. Would he help her? 'Mark? Will you help me?'

'Will this help give you closure?'

'Yes.'

'Fine, I'll help.'

And it was that easy. 'OK, just text me if Joan gets up and

leaves. Then I'll quickly leave their house, she'll never catch me there.'

'Yeah, sure.'

She drove to the bar, parking down the block just in case Joan recognized her car. She walked up the driveway at speed but not quick enough to attract attention. Her heart was pounding in her chest as she tried the front door. It was unlocked. Luck was on her side. She could hear the TV and followed the sound to the lounge. Justin looked up in surprise, then fright when he realized she was there. 'Mrs Wright,' he said. 'What are you doing here? I'm not supposed to talk to you.'

'Why not?' she demanded.

'Dunno, Mom said.'

'That looks painful,' she said pointing to a metal contraption along Justin's leg.

'It is. Can barely move. I was crushed by the steering column. Concussion, lost some memories.'

Vanessa's heart sank. 'Justin, what happened?' She made it clear that she wasn't leaving until she had her answers.

'I don't really remember, it's a bit fuzzy.' *Convenient.* 'We were driving round, like we normally do. We drove past the river. Wren was talking about what was going to happen when we graduated school. We were having fun. Then a deer flew out in front of us. I swerved. I hit the tree, Wren didn't have his seatbelt on.'

'Justin, why not? And why didn't the airbag go off?' That was one question she definitely needed an answer to. He may have lived had it deployed as it was supposed to. She could feel herself getting angry, getting worked up. 'Justin, why didn't you brake? Why didn't you brake? You crossed the other side of the road into a tree and you didn't brake.'

'I think you should go now, Mrs Wright. I don't feel well.'

'What was Wren depressed about? Even before Olivia killed herself. He was different. Why?'

He looked away. 'I don't know. He was different, sure, but he wouldn't talk about it to us.' His eyes shifted away. 'It's what happened, ask Wade. Please leave, Mrs Wright.'

Her phone buzzed in her pocket and she knew it was time to go. She left, running down the driveway to her car. She still didn't have all she needed, but she was close.

She headed to Wade's house, determined not to take no for an answer this time. She knew Justin was lying about something, she just didn't know what or why.

Mark called her on her way to Wade's place.

'Did you get what you needed?' he asked.

'No. He's lying to me. I need to find out why.'

'Anything I can do to help?' It was nice that someone was being helpful for a change.

'Not yet, but I'll let you know.' It was surreal to think that one day she may rely on Mark, need him.

She drove to the Fox household and knocked loudly on the door. Phillipa opened it, her face falling as she saw who was on her doorstep. 'Vanessa, what are you doing here?'

'I need to talk to Wade.' She pushed past Phillipa and barged inside.

'You can't just come in here!' she replied, outraged.

'What are you protecting him from?' Vanessa demanded, striding down the hallway.

She threw open the door and startled Wade. 'Mrs Wright,' he said, looking around guiltily. 'What do you want?'

'I want to know why Wren was depressed in the weeks before he died. He was unwell before Oliva killed herself and it only got worse afterwards.'

'Maybe ask Justin.'

'I did, he said to talk to you.'

'He did?' Wade asked, surprised. He threw back the cover awkwardly with one hand, his other wrist in a cast. He looked like he was going to piss his pants. 'I don't know anything,' he mumbled.

'Wade, why didn't Justin try to stop the car from hitting the tree after allegedly swerving to miss a deer?'

'He swerved to miss it; he didn't have time to brake. It all happened so fast.'

He had been coached. It was identical to what Justin had said. 'Vanessa!' screamed Phillipa. 'Get out of my house now or I will call the cops.'

Vanessa backed away. 'I know you're lying, Wade, I just don't know why,' she said quietly. 'But I'll find out.' She walked down the hallway and out to her car.

Disappointed, she drove to Ryan's house. She needed a glass of wine and didn't want to be judged at home by Maggie for her drinking. She should be worrying about it too, but it was just a coping mechanism – God knows she needed one. She was barely hanging on as it was. She had slightly more information than before, but it wasn't enough. Ryan let her in and poured her a glass immediately. She took a grateful sip.

'They both said the same thing, almost word for word. I still don't know why he wasn't wearing a seatbelt, why his airbag didn't go off and why he was depressed.'

'I'm sorry you didn't get what you wanted, Ness.'

'Oh, I'll find the answers somehow, I know I will.'

'You are so brave.'

'Ryan, you're strong – you lost a child too.'

'You know, I kinda blame Wren for Olivia's death.' Vanessa's heart just about stopped.

'What did you just say?' She wheeled around, thunder in her

face, eyes snapping like a live current ran through them. 'What the *fuck* did you just say?'

'I didn't mean it like that, Ness,' he backpedaled.

'Then what did you mean? Explain yourself.' She slammed the wine glass onto the bench, the stem breaking, wine dripping down the counter and onto the floor, looking a lot like blood.

His face was flushed, whether from the wine or embarrassment, she didn't know. 'Just if she'd never met Wren, all this might not have happened. Something clearly went on between them, something bad, we just haven't talked about it yet.'

'I can't believe you're blaming Wren. How could you?' She was so angry that she could barely spit her words out.

'Well, she might still be here otherwise. Maybe they broke up and that's why she did what she did.'

'Well, thank you very much for sharing how you really feel, you fuck wit.' She grabbed her bag and went to storm out, but he grabbed her arm. 'Get your hand off me,' she screamed, 'or I'll call the police!'

He let go and she shot forward, out of the house and into her car where she sat, stunned. Then she burst into tears. This whole time they had been trying to figure out what was wrong with their kids and he had been thinking that about her Wren. Comforting her but thinking that he was to blame. His place had been her only sanctuary, now that was fucked. She would never speak to him again for what he said. *Never.* He was dead to her. Finally, she felt strong enough to drive home.

After having no luck with Justin and Wade and then the bullshit with Ryan, she was spent. Now she had to go home and pretend that her world wasn't shattered all over again.

Billy jumped on her as soon as she came through the door. 'I got a call from Joan today. Apparently, you broke into her house and verbally interrogated her son.'

'For starters, I didn't break in – the front door was unlocked, I let myself in. Secondly, he lied to me. And Wade was lying to me too. But why? What are they hiding?'

'Ness, it's time to stop now. I'm getting calls from angry parents and you're turning yourself inside and out with knots and worry.'

Fuck, she was having a bad day. She couldn't win, no matter what she did.

She knew that she shouldn't be taking her anger out on Billy, but he was just the last in a long line of people who were pissing her off today. 'Don't tell me what to do,' Vanessa hissed, then stormed off to their bedroom, slamming the door.

She sat on the edge of the bed, her hands fisted into the sheet, twisting them this way and that. Tears threatened to come, but she would not give any of them the satisfaction. There was a soft knock at the door.

'Go away!'

Billy could take his apologies and shove them.

'Mommy?' questioned the voice.

'Oh, Ty.' She pushed her tired body off the bed, feeling like she was heavy with weights. It seemed to take her an age to cross the floor, but eventually she managed to open the door, her small son waiting patiently for her.

'Hey, buddy, how was school?'

'Not so good.' Eyes downcast, she knew she had to be careful here. Ty was still grieving too, and he was a little boy. He was not the enemy.

'Why's that?' she asked.

'We had to draw a family tree and I didn't know if I should have put Wren in it.' Tears spilled down his face and Vanessa tried and failed to hold back a sob.

She grabbed him and pulled him close to her. 'Oh baby. I'm so sorry. Wren always goes in the family tree, love. Wren may be gone but we'll never forget him, OK?'

Ty nodded against her breast.

'All right, go find Maggie and she'll give you dinner.'

'Aren't you coming?'

'I'm not hungry.' Ty's shoulders drooped as he walked down the hallway and Vanessa wanted to yell at him to come back, that she loved and needed him, but she couldn't say either of those things. She just let him walk down the hallway, dejected, feeling unloved and probably unwanted by his mother.

Her phone vibrated in her pocket.

Ryan.

I am so sorry for what I said to you. I didn't mean it. I don't blame Wren. He made Olivia's life better. Please forgive me.

She read the message a second time before she deleted the text. Angrily, she deleted the entire thread. She didn't want to see his name anywhere, she was still so damn furious. How dare he say what he did! Wren, with his beautiful nature, his caring heart, his ability to make people feel at ease. So many things that she loved about her boy. A wonderful and loving son, a best friend, a big brother who was never too busy for his baby brother. How dare he!

* * *

Vanessa opened the door as if something was going to jump out at her. Memories. Memories sprang at her, assaulting her from every direction. Wren's room was full of them; they made her want to both laugh and cry, curl up in a ball and rail at the world. She sat gingerly on the bed, looking at the posters tacked to the wall, the shoes piled untidily in the corner, the dirty washing on the floor. Vanessa had allowed no one entry into his room. It was hers. It wasn't just an unwritten rule; she had told them all that Wren's room was off limits.

Maggie had wanted to come in before she left to go back to her house, but Vanessa just couldn't let her. She was appreciative of everything that she'd done for her family, but she just couldn't. She did manage to thank her and when Maggie had thrown her arms around her, she returned the hug.

She touched Wren's laptop. She didn't even know the password to get into it. His phone was lying beside the laptop. She knew the pin to that one: Ty's birthday. She smiled. A nice touch.

His phone had been returned along with his wallet. Could she do it? Could she actually go through Wren's private messages and emails? She'd had no problem going through Olivia's most private thoughts. *But that was different.*

The phone opened and a lovely photo of Wren and Olivia popped up. She felt a wave of sadness pass through her. The app for messages was on the front page. With a shaking finger, she touched Olivia's name. There was nothing past that Saturday, just under two weeks before her death. He hadn't spoken to her at all. Maybe they did break up after all. It was a mystery to her. She clicked on Justin's name. The last message from Justin read:

I'm coming to get you.

It was dated the day that Wren died. There was nothing before that until around the same time as Olivia's last message. Either they weren't talking for a bit or they were doing it in person – after all, Wren was with them the day he died – and if they weren't talking, what was Wren doing with them in that car? Justin said they were just driving around, but why were they out in the middle of nowhere? Out past Wren's favorite spot at the river? Still so many unanswered questions, questions that she'd probably never find answers to.

Vanessa didn't realize that she was crying until she felt the wetness on her cheeks. Gently she wiped them away, then wiped her wet hand on her jeans. She left Wren's bedroom, clutching the phone and closing the door with her other hand.

These days it felt like home wasn't home anymore, and the less time spent here the better. She gave her dad a quick call just to say hi. It was a short and awkward conversation. She didn't talk much and he didn't ask any questions. Again, she wished her mom was there and she'd bet a hundred bucks he was thinking the same thing.

Maggie was still picking Ty up every afternoon but now she was taking him home to her place and keeping him there until Billy picked him up after work. They were both still picking up her slack. She felt more than useless. Was Billy right? Did she need to drop all of this? Leave the past in the past?

She drove down the road and pulled over a short distance from the corner store and headed towards it. She was going to get a newspaper and some candy when she looked up and saw a familiar figure.

Ryan. He saw her too. He reached up a hand and waved, but she turned and walked away.

'Vanessa!' she heard him call after her. She started running.

'Vanessa, wait!' She could hear him getting closer; he was running too. She made it inside her car, slamming down the locks and starting the engine. Next, he was banging on the window. 'Please, Ness, please let me in, let me explain.'

'Fuck off, Ryan!' she yelled, then gunned the engine and took off, not caring if she ran over his foot. There was a bit of a crowd, people who had seen him running after her. She didn't care. She had to get away or she would have slapped him stupid.

Her phone beeped as she drove, and she glanced at it. Ryan again. She ignored it without reading the message, she'd do that when she stopped driving. She was sure he'd be pleading for her to listen to him, to give him another chance. She wasn't going to do that; she was *never* going to do that. Not after what he said.

Her phone beeped again and she was about to throw it across the car when she saw that it wasn't Ryan. It was from Wren's school. They had an app that sent messages directly to parents' phones about upcoming tests and assignments and class trips. This one was reminding the parents that the English oral presentation was due today. She tried hard not to cry. No one had told the school to take her off the mailing list. It was a horrible, gut-wrenching stab to the heart.

She ended up driving back home; there was no one there anyway. Ryan kept texting her, variations of the same message and so many that she wanted to throw her phone in the wardrobe. She had lost just about every friend she had – which was a small circle to begin with – and she didn't see her regulars from work because she hadn't gone back yet. She missed her independence, not to mention making money. She just couldn't go back; Billy thought it would be good for her, that it was time, but who was he to tell her what to do? Suddenly she was irrationally angry at Billy again. But what else was new?

Her world had started dying the day Wren took his last breath, the color and happiness leaching from everything around her. She knew she was bitter, but she couldn't help it. Justin would walk with a limp forever? Well, Wren was *dead*. So who got the better deal here? She didn't want these boys dead; she wanted her son *alive*.

Later that night, after a tense dinner which Vanessa barely touched, she went into the lounge and gave Ty a kiss goodbye.

She returned to the kitchen. 'Where are you going?' asked Billy in surprise. 'It's past seven.'

'Thanks, I can tell the time.' Sarcasm was not a good look on her, but it seemed like one thing she couldn't avoid these days.

His face hardened. 'Do what you want.' He stood up and began to scrape the leftovers into the bin, all but throwing the plates into the sink. His body softened. 'Ness?' he said quietly as she picked up her bag. She stopped. 'Do you want company?' His offer of support.

She could see he was trying, today at least, but she wanted – no, needed – her space. 'Billy... I don't want to hurt you, but you've got to let me go. I need to be alone. One day I'll take you with me again, but today's not that day.'

His face sagged with her rejection. She desperately wanted to tell him that she still wanted to be married to him, but the words got stuck somewhere between her mind and her lips. Instead of saying all the things she wanted to say, she just left.

She revved the car out as she was reversing and ran over the curb on her way out. This time she knew where she was headed.

She rang the doorbell and the front light flicked on.

'Vanessa?'

'Hey, Mark, can I come in?'

'Sure.' She followed him inside his new place. It was clean and tidy – two things he'd never been when they were married. Actually, it looked nice.

'I like your place.'

'Thanks.' He looked at her, really looked at her. 'You OK? You look like shit.'

She burst out laughing before covering her mouth like she'd committed a sin. 'You're the first one to tell me that.'

He smiled. 'Want a drink? Of tea, of course.' She knew he didn't drink anymore. It also showed in his body, which was beginning to lose its beer gut. He put the kettle on. 'So, what's up?'

'I don't have anywhere else to go.' She burst into tears. His arms were around her in seconds, her head on his shoulder, closer than they had been when they were together.

'It's all right. Let it all out.' He patted her on the back while she cried. Finally, she pulled back and he handed her a tissue.

'Sorry. I just... I thought I'd found a safe place with Olivia's dad Ryan, but it turns out that he blames Wren for his daughter's suicide.' She sighed. 'Can you believe that? Now he's harassing me to forgive him. Well, fuck him.'

Mark let her talk. He went into the kitchen and brought back a cup of tea, which he sat on the dining-room table. There was a drawing that Charlotte had done, just a scribble of color, but it made Vanessa smile. 'Nice drawing.'

'Actually, that's me,' he said proudly. 'Ty's is already on the fridge. He drew him and Wren. Nearly lost my shit at that, it was brutal.' He paused. 'Ness?'

'Mmm?'

'You were right to leave me. I haven't admitted it to myself before but you were. I hated you for a long time, but you were just doing what was best for our boys and I should have understood that. I don't know how you're even friends with me.'

'Well, we're not at the friends stage just yet, but we are parents to a beautiful little boy. Speaking of, I'd better get home. Thanks for the tea, and the talk.'

When she got home the door to the spare room was already closed, so she crept down to Ty's room with the intention of kissing his little face. He was still awake, staring at the ceiling.

'Honey, what are you doing awake?'

'I just wanted to make sure that you were coming back to me.'

It broke her heart. She took hold of his hand. 'Baby, I will always come back to you.' He smiled and she kissed his cheek, then left the room.

She whispered, 'I love you.'

'I love you' covered a multitude of sins. I love you because you're mine. I love you because you're beautiful. I love you because you're my son. The list was endless. I love you, I'm sorry we fought. *I love you* – something she'd never say to Wren again.

When she was heading to her bedroom, it occurred to Vanessa that if Wren didn't know Olivia was suicidal, then her close friend might. She had come round to Vanessa's house with Olivia one day. Lisa something. *Lisa Peterson.* A new plan falling into place, she drifted off to sleep.

28

Vanessa had sworn that she would never go to Wren's school. This was the place where Wren had hung out with his girlfriend, his best friends, took classes and played soccer. There were just too many memories.

She pulled into the parking lot and headed to the main building. She went up to the receptionist's desk and waited.

'What can I do for you?' asked the ancient lady behind the counter.

'Hi, I'm wondering if you wouldn't mind paging a student for me. Her name is Lisa Peterson.'

'And you are?'

'My name is Vanessa Wright, and I need to speak with her. It's very important.'

'Are you a family member?'

'No, but, as I said, it's important.'

'I can't just pull a student out of class because you want to chat.'

Vanessa's eyes welled with tears. 'My son recently died in a car accident. Two weeks beforehand, his girlfriend committed suicide. I think the two are related, and I think that Lisa might be able to shed some light on why two seventeen-year-old kids are dead. That good enough for you?'

She was breathing heavily by the time she'd finished, gripping the edge of the counter tightly.

The lady pressed a button and called for Lisa Peterson to come to reception.

'Thank you,' Vanessa whispered as she went to sit down on one of the couches pushed up against the wall.

She saw Lisa coming down the stairs. 'Mrs Wright?'

'Hi, Lisa, how are you?'

'Fine,' she said, looking confused.

'Can you sit for a moment? This won't take long.'

She sat next to Vanessa, smoothing down her dress.

Vanessa hadn't really thought much about what she was going to say, so she just winged it. 'I know you haven't seen me in a while or know me that well but I'm hoping you can help me and Olivia's dad. Did Olivia ever tell you that she had thoughts about harming herself?'

'No. Never. I would have told somebody.'

'Of course you would have. So do you know why she was acting strangely in the weeks leading up to her death? Not going to school, not wanting to see friends?'

'I don't know about any of that, all I know is that she stopped returning my calls and texts after the party.'

Vanessa tried to think of which party she meant. There were so many, so she asked.

'The end-of-year soccer bash?'

I didn't go, I was grounded. I heard she spent the whole night with the three boys, but that's not unusual. I'm not much help, am I? Mrs Wright? Are you OK?' Vanessa could feel the blood draining from her face.

'Uh... I'm fine, thanks for your help. I have to go now.' Vanessa staggered out the front doors and over to her car. Once inside the car, she needed to take a few deep breaths to calm herself down. She held down the horn for a few seconds while she screamed.

She knew what happened.

Olivia went to a party, disappeared with the three boys, didn't speak to anyone again, then two weeks later, she committed suicide. It was so obvious now. Why hadn't she seen it before?

Justin and Wade had raped her. It was the only scenario that made any sense.

It all came rushing back to her. Seeing Wren that Sunday morning with a black eye, a split lip and holding his ribs as he walked funny. He said he'd been mucking about with the boys, that it was just normal boy stuff. But Wren had actively avoided Justin afterwards and to her knowledge, he never spoke to Olivia about the party, about what happened. It all made sense now. Wren had taken a beating trying to protect his girlfriend from being attacked by his two best friends. Justin would have initiated it; Wade would have just followed. Vanessa wept, remembering her own experiences with Mark. The pain, the fear, the isolation. Olivia wondering what she'd done to deserve that. She would have been so scared. Vanessa sat in the car, crying for Olivia. For the young girl who'd had her innocence and her dignity taken from her.

She finally wiped her eyes. *Wren, you poor darling. It must have been hard carrying this weight alone, and then when Olivia died, it was so much worse for you. Why couldn't you have told me?*

She wished Olivia had told someone, got the help she needed. Why hadn't Wren told anyone? Was he protecting his friends, or had they threatened both him and Olivia? It would make sense as to why neither of them spoke up.

She had finally put the pieces of the puzzle together, but she didn't feel any better. In fact, knowing the truth made her feel worse.

Wren and Olivia had been so in love, their whole lives ahead of them, but that had been stolen from them in an instant, the moment when Justin and Wade had raped Olivia. But how would Vanessa prove it? All she had right now was her theory, which *she* knew to be the truth. Short of getting one or both of the boys to confess, she didn't know how to get others to believe her. Their secret had died with Olivia and Wren. *How convenient.* Suddenly her eyes widened. Was it possible? Surely not. Yet still, convenient. Wren died in a car driven by Justin. He had swerved to miss a deer, yet there had been no skid marks and they had ended up slamming into a tree and there just happened to be a faulty airbag on Wren's side. The question was, how far would Justin go to protect himself and Wade?

Vanessa was looking for her boots in her wardrobe. They were her favorite pair and, for some reason, she was taken over by the desire to wear them. Did it really matter what she wore anymore? She didn't give a shit most of the time and right now, she looked like crap. She was half in, half out of the wardrobe when someone spoke to her. She gave a little squeal of fright before backing out of the wardrobe. She was so jumpy, unable to concentrate since she'd worked it out, but she'd yet to tell anyone what had really happened to Olivia and Wren. She needed concrete proof, otherwise no one would believe her.

'Can we talk, Vanessa?' asked Billy. He was running late for work and she guessed it was because he wanted to talk whereas she just wanted to find her damn boots.

She knew she was in trouble because he never called her by her full name. 'Sure.'

'I can't deal with this anymore,' he said, glancing at her then looking away.

'Are you leaving me?' she asked in a flat tone.

'That's so blunt; it's much more complicated than that and you know it.'

'Is it the truth though?' She felt her heart beat fast, the rushing of blood in her ears almost drowning out her words.

'I'm not sure. All I know is that you're hardly ever here and when you are here, you're not. Ty misses you, I miss you and we both need you.'

'Well, that clears it right up for me, doesn't it?' She put her hands on her hips, staring intently at him. 'Enlighten me, Billy. Please.'

'All right then. You want the truth, I'll tell you the truth. It's like we, Ty and I, don't matter to you anymore. Like Wren has the biggest piece of your heart and always will. You're walled off and I'm worried it'll be forever. He's gone, Ness, and though we all mourn his passing, we're not. We're still here. Ty and I are still here. Waiting. For you. I just don't know how much longer I can wait.'

'Are you leaving me?' she asked again, painfully aware that this was truly an option, but not willing to back down.

'I'll give you one more week. One more week of my heart and soul, then I have to do what's best for me. I'll back away and you won't see me anymore.' He seemed to not know what to do with his hands; he clenched his fists, then crossed his arms, then put them down by his side. Once he'd finished giving her his ultimatum, he left the bedroom.

Vanessa sat back on the floor and picked up the one boot that she could find. She should have been thinking about what Billy had just unloaded on her, but she was thinking of Wren, of how devastated he must have been. Frustrated, she blew out a breath that sounded more like the raspberries that she used to blow on Wren's tummy, listening to him giggling with delight. Instantly, she was transported back. Rolls of baby fat; skin as soft as velvet; wide, inquisitive eyes. Wren had been her salvation. Every day she was thankful that she had him. She suppressed a sob; she didn't want Billy to hear her crying. It would show too much weakness. She thought about what he'd said, but the desire to finish what she started trumped everything else. Vanessa crawled back into the wardrobe, still looking for her other boot. She touched something hard and felt round the edges. It felt like a book. She grabbed it and pulled it out.

It was one of Olivia's diaries. It must have tumbled into the back when she'd thrown them into the wardrobe so Billy didn't destroy any more. Great, she'd have to return it to Ryan. She wondered if she could just post it. It seemed like both the coward's way out and a great idea. She looked at it a bit more closely. The other ones had broken spines; you could tell they'd been used. This one, however, was pristine. Like it had never been written in. She opened the book to the first page. There were two words written down.

Wren knows.

Wren knows what? A sinking feeling settled over her. Her body turned into a mass of pins and needles that punctured her skin. What did Wren know? That Olivia was going to commit suicide? Maybe she confided in him and that's why he was so depressed, because he knew what was coming and there was nothing that he could do about it. She put the diary with its offending words down and dove back into the wardrobe, looking for Wren's phone, which she'd discarded in there after reading his messages.

She found the phone and held it in her hand for a long time before putting the phone and the diary into her bag. She made her way down the hallway and out to her car. Billy had already left after he'd spoken to her – well, *at* her.

She had a week's grace. A week to solve this mess, to wrap it up and get a confession from Justin and Wade so she could take it to the police. If she hadn't finished it by then, she had two choices: keep at it and lose Billy, or keep Billy and lose Wren. She wasn't prepared for either of those options.

She resisted the urge to take out the phone and start playing with it. She was headed for the river, then changed her mind and began to head to where Wren had died. Vanessa pulled over to the side of the road, carefully crossing before sitting where she had last time. Someone had been here since; a teddy and a bouquet of flowers sat leaning against the side of the tree. She walked around to the back and found more. Had these been there last time? How had she not noticed them before? There were more teddy bears and cards. She read them all, thanking each and every kind soul for caring so much. Finally she came back around and sat back down.

She took out the last diary and opened the page again.

Wren knows.

She knew she should tell Ryan that she suspected that Wren may have known Olivia was going to kill herself but that would just confirm his theory that he was ultimately responsible when she didn't know for sure. Justin and Wade were the ones who needed punishing, not Wren. Crucify them, not her baby.

She believed with her whole heart that Wren had wanted to confide in her but didn't know where to start. Maybe he would have told her eventually, but then Olivia had gone and done what she had done. He would have been feeling so much guilt. Olivia had committed suicide because she had been raped. It was as simple as that. Wren didn't rape her, his friends did. Wren was an innocent bystander who'd tried his best to stop what had happened to Olivia but had been beaten down. Perhaps he'd lost consciousness as well. She'd never know but it made perfect sense.

Her son was a hero, she knew that. He'd always been her hero. He'd taken a beating trying to save Olivia. A real hero. Did she blame him? *Wren knows.* It wasn't an accusation, just information. Vanessa ran her hand down her long ponytail, feeling the tangled strands in between her fingers. She couldn't remember the last time she brushed it, just chucking it up in a bun every morning. What did it matter anymore anyway? She massaged her temples, resting her elbows on her crossed legs. She had the beginnings of a whopping headache and she had no painkillers on her. The hot sun wasn't helping. She'd have to go home soon.

She pulled Wren's phone out of her bag and then remembered the message she'd received from the school. Wren had an English oral presentation due today. He would have practiced it on the voice recording app. He always did that, just to time his speech and to see how he sounded. She was trying her best to remember what this speech would have been on.

She searched for the app and finally found it on the last screen – always the way. It felt good, holding his phone in her hand; something so important to him, something that was always on him. She looked at the recordings log. There was his speech, recorded a few days before he died. He may have been depressed, but he still did his homework. But then there were two more recordings after that one.

One from the night of the party.

One from the night of Wren's death.

Vanessa's hand flew to her mouth, playing with her lips. What the fuck was happening here? She didn't know what to do. Why were these recordings on his phone from those particular dates? What did Wren record? She was too scared to listen; she didn't want to know, but she *had* to know. She put her headphones in and plugged them into the phone. With a shaking finger, she pressed the first recording: the speech. The sound of Wren's deep, melodious voice filled her ears. She could almost feel him with her, sitting beside her, holding her hand. She listened to the words, beautifully written. Wren had always had such a way with words, whether it was making an argument for staying up late or comforting her after another one of Mark's beatings. The speech finished; Wren's words now gone. She was going to listen to it again, but decided to see what the other recordings were.

Hesitantly, Vanessa touched the next recording from the night of the party.

At first there was nothing, then Vanessa heard a loud scratching noise, like when you have a phone in your pocket when you accidentally butt-dial someone. It squeaked and squawked loudly in her ear before she heard voices. At first she couldn't make them out, then she heard someone.

'Fuck! Hold her down, will you? I can't—' the voice hissed. *Justin.* It was Justin's voice. Vanessa gasped and paused the recording, not believing her ears. She *was* listening to the attack on Olivia. She was sure of it. Vanessa wasn't sure she could go on. It took her back to a dark place in her own life, the first time that Mark had raped her. The fear and pain she had felt, the sheer terror. She knew what she was going to hear when she pressed play. Olivia, suffering the same fate as she had. She had the proof now. She recognized Justin's voice, but could she bring herself to listen to the rest of it?

She had to. For Olivia. As Wren's mom, she owed her that.

She put her headphones back in, took a deep shaky breath and pressed play.

'*Stop it, Justin! You're hurting her!*' *Wren.* Although she had expected to hear his voice, she was still shocked when she did. She heard the ripping of material, and the sound went scratchy for a period of about five seconds. Wren's voice again, pleading for Justin to get off her. There was silence again, covered by a layer of static, then she heard the sound of flesh striking flesh. It was close to the phone and she heard Wren grunt. Justin or Wade had hit him. She felt incensed. It happened again.

'*Stay down!*' Justin yelled. *Justin hit him, his best friend.*

'*Fuck you, Justin!*' Wren yelled. She heard a grunt from Justin, Wren must have got in a punch or two, then there were sounds of a scuffle and a cry from Wren, followed by a heavy thump. He was on the ground. Vanessa sat forward, listening intently to the sounds of silence. She was crying, tears running freely down her cheeks.

Justin was the one who'd dropped Wren, which meant Wade was with Olivia. Wade, who towered over the rest of them. It must have been terrifying for Olivia. She heard her muffled cry. She knew that cry well. *It had begun.*

There were no more sounds from Wren and with a sick feeling, Vanessa realized that he must have been unconscious and that there was no one to stop Olivia from being attacked. Overlaying her own experiences with Olivia's made her heart ache. She knew the terrifying feeling of wishing you were dead, anything but this. A violation of body and mind. The phone kept recording. It recorded every little detail. Every moan of pain from Olivia, every word uttered by Justin and Wade, when Wade had his turn, grunting when he finished. They laughed.

They laughed.

When it was all over, Justin threatened the silent Olivia that if she told, they'd be back. Then they left. For a long while, there was silence, yet Vanessa kept listening. Eventually there was a noise. Crying. Olivia was crying. Vanessa was crying right along with her. The phone cut out; the battery must have died. The recording was over. She had her proof.

Vanessa was overwhelmed, exhausted, emotional. Wren had tried, tried his best to save her, but he'd been knocked unconscious. The horror Olivia must have felt when she realized that she wasn't going to be saved after all. Vanessa wasn't sure if she could listen to the last recording. She was raw, beaten down, memories from her past swirling inside her head. That recording had been confronting to say the least, but it had also made her remember things that she had worked so hard to forget. She pulled out her water bottle and took a little sip. She felt like she needed a shower, but all she had was a small container of hand sanitizer. It would have to do. She put it on her hands and her arms, trying to scrub away the stain that she and Olivia knew.

Proof. Proof of what they did. Irrefutable proof. She had them now. A big chunk of the puzzle had been caught on Wren's phone. That's what Olivia had meant when she said *Wren knows.* He knew that she'd been raped because he had been there and failed to stop it. No wonder she hadn't gone back to school. She would have had to have seen them, including Wren. The one who'd tried for her and failed her. He would always be the boy who failed in her mind. The young man Vanessa had raised to respect and care for women had tried yet failed.

It was no surprise, given what she had been through, that Olivia had committed suicide. How many times had Vanessa been in that position? But she'd had Wren to make sure she got up every day, giving her something to live for. Olivia didn't have that. She felt too much pain to handle and had swallowed two bottles of tablets to make it stop. Permanently.

Vanessa heard the sound of a lone bird singing above her. It sounded so out of place given what she'd just heard. She wanted to tell it to fuck off. She wanted to find Justin and wring his fucking neck for what he'd done to Wren and Olivia. There'd be no talking his way out of this. Justin was popular and got away with things that average kids didn't. He was the captain of the soccer team and commanded a certain amount of respect, but he didn't respect women. A few times he'd talked down to her and due to her conditioning over the years, she had fallen into old patterns and not called the seventeen-year-old boy out on his behavior.

Finally ready, she steeled herself to play the last recording. Instantly she heard the familiar scratching, followed by a whining noise. Immediately, Vanessa knew that this recording was taken in Justin's car. Someone cleared their throat. More silence. A brief blast of music before it was turned down, then turned off altogether.

'Your taste in music is shit, Wade,' Justin said, Vanessa recognizing his voice easily. Then she heard something else familiar. Wren's laugh. She wondered if he knew that his phone was recording. If he had it open before and forgotten to close it, this could very well be an accidental recording. The timer on the list said that this recording went for almost ten minutes. Maybe there was no great revelation as to why they crashed and Wren died. Maybe she'd been chasing ghosts this whole time and Justin really did swerve for a deer and it really did happen so fast that he didn't have time to react, and maybe Wren's death really was unavoidable.

More static followed her line of thinking. Should she even listen to the last recording? Did she want to hear what was said? Most likely hear the crash? Could she handle that? She was now convinced that Wren didn't know that he'd turned on the recorder. There was a loud rustling noise, Vanessa quickly thumbed down the volume but turned it back up when the noise went away. She was hoping Wren would start talking soon. Not about an English speech, not while being beaten, but just a conversation with his friends.

'Did you see her face? She actually bought it. That was until she saw me smile at you. Fuck. Then she knew. By the way, Justin, you went way too hard on me, I didn't bloody wake up until the next morning. Could've killed me. A few punches, just like last time, that's what I said.' He laughed, a hard, brittle sound.

Oh my God! That was Wren talking.

She quickly stopped the recording, turned to her left-hand side and vomited in the weeds until she was left a heaving mess. The acrid taste in her mouth made her want to vomit again. She wiped her mouth with the back of her hand, spit clinging to it. She wiped it on her jeans. She couldn't even comprehend what she'd just heard, but there was no denying that it was Wren's voice, she knew it as well as she knew her own. He obviously didn't know that his phone was recording, otherwise he would never have admitted to his part in the rape of his girlfriend. She wanted to say that she didn't understand, but she did.

All of those years spent living with Mark had helped shape the man that she heard on that recording. Mark had him at his most impressionable years and he'd learned to hate women. To treat them as dirt beneath his heels. Every time he condemned his dad, he was lying. Every time he said he loved her, he was lying. He had nursed her after beatings that left her with black eyes and broken bones and tended her wounds when she'd been whipped. What kind of monster had she raised? Vanessa was struck with how wrong she had been about Wren: he wasn't her savior, he was his father's son after all.

She needed to listen to the rest. She wanted to be anywhere but here, sitting under this tree where he'd died, but here she was and here she'd stay until she knew every dirty detail of what he'd done.

'She was pretty fun, have to admit that. They never see it coming, do they? Girls are fucking stupid,' Justin weighed in, laughing. She could hear deep laughter in the background and recognized it as Wade's.

'Yeah, they always believe that it'll never happen to them and when it does, they're shocked. Like you didn't play hard to get, you wanted it,' Wren said.

Vanessa retched again, this time down the front of her shirt. She coughed, more bile sliding down her chin. She took her shirt off, sitting there in her singlet, wiping her mouth with the balled-up material.

'Can't believe she killed herself over it, though. It was just a bit of fun, for fuck's sake.' Wren didn't even sound like her baby anymore. She felt such a disconnect that she'd never felt with him before. With each word that he said, she felt a tiny chunk of her heart chip away, falling into the abyss.

His laughed swallowed the car, filling her ears with poison as she listened to their disgusting conversation, led by her sweet boy.

'Yeah but, Wren, while it was fun and everything, we didn't know she was going to kill herself. I mean, no one could have seen that coming,' Justin said.

'I did.' Wren sounded proud of himself. *'She confided in me that she had tried to commit suicide before because she was teased at her old school. I figured she'd try again. One less mess to worry about.'*

Who was this person? Speaking so casually about setting up a young woman to kill herself. Her hands shook so badly that she had to put the phone, Wren's phone, on the ground. She thought she was going into shock. Her head was fuzzy and she was missing some of the words, but then her world snapped back into focus. She was so confused. Where was her empathetic boy who cried when other people cried, who had been the only one there for her when she'd had Ty?

'We need to forget this ever happened, make a pact right here, right now to take this to our graves with us. No one can ever know what we did,' Justin said.

'What you two did,' corrected Wren. Vanessa's blood ran cold.

'What?'

'Did I forget to tell you that I made a recording of you raping Olivia? A recording where I say both your names and am beaten unconscious while you rape my innocent virgin girlfriend?'

Who the fuck was this kid? 'Cos it sure as shit wasn't the boy she had raised.

'You did what?' Wade said.

'You did what?' Wren mocked. *'I recorded you, you bloody idiot. For insurance.'*

'What the hell does that mean?' asked Justin.

'So you'll never bother me again. When I leave this town at the end of the year, I don't want anyone hanging on to me. Not a clingy girl-friend, not two fuck-up friends and not a mom who relies on me for everything.'

Vanessa cried out, startling the birds above. She watched them fly off into the distance. She was a burden that Wren wanted gone?

'I want a clean slate and that was my chance to do it. Don't get me wrong, I had fun with Olivia, but she was a means to an end. Now I have leverage over you two; you won't be bothering me anymore.'

There was more rustling. Vanessa leaned forward, the tension making her muscles rigid and tired. The whine of the engine grew louder. *'What the hell are you doing? Slow down, Justin!'* Wren yelled.

'If you're going to take us down one day, and we'll never know

when, then I might as well do it now – save you the fucking trouble.'
Wren yelled at him again to slow down, but the whining just got
louder as the revs got higher. Justin must have been going well
past the speed limit.

Over the din of the engine, there was a click, just loud enough
for Vanessa to hear. She was about to rewind it, sure that she had
misheard, but with a sinking feeling, she knew she hadn't. She
had just heard one of the other boys unclick Wren's seat belt.

A second later, there was a hoarse yell from Wren, then the
scream of metal on metal, then a huge a crash where they hit the
tree.

Silence.

Vanessa stood, pulling the headphones out of her ears, hands
on hips, shaking as she walked up and down past the tree. She
reached out and touched the gouges which she once touched
with reverence, now wishing she had a knife so she could oblit-
erate them. Coming round to the side of the tree, she saw the
colorful flowers, stuffed teddies and cards, all mourning a
monster. She began kicking them, scattering petals to the wind,
ripping the heads off teddies and tearing up the cards.

'You fucking liar!' she screamed. 'I fucking hate you!' She
began to cry, but she swiped at them angrily. 'I will not cry for
you! You hear me?'

Vanessa stomped back around to the other side, not even
looking at the carnage she'd left, picked up the phone, shoved it
in her bag and stormed back to the car. She probably shouldn't
have been driving because she was sure she was in shock,
running on adrenaline, but she took off anyway, tires spitting
gravel behind her.

She knew exactly where she was going and what she was
going to do. No one was going to stop her today, not even the
memories of Wren that popped randomly into her mind. She

couldn't deal with this, so instead she focused on Justin. She charged up to the front of the bar, ripped the handbrake on and ran down the driveway. She banged on his door, screaming his name. He came to the door, face ashen, crutches angled awkwardly under his arms.

'You alone?' she asked as she barged in.

'I've got some friends over.'

She walked into the lounge room and saw three boys sitting there, staring at her. 'Get the fuck out,' she demanded. They just sat there. 'Fucking go! Now!'

Justin nodded weakly and they picked up their bags and left.

'Stay there,' she said, steel in her voice when he went to move.

'What are you doing here, Mrs Wright? My mom would call the cops if she knew you were here.'

'Oh yeah? What about if I told her you were a rapist and that I had proof?'

His face paled even more, and he looked like he was going to throw up. He put his hand up to his mouth.

'I'm... not...'

'Save it, Justin, I heard the recording that Wren made. It was on his phone and in case you get any ideas, I've already emailed it to myself. You know, insurance. I learned from the best. You raped Olivia.' It was not a question.

'Yes,' he whispered, meeting her eyes.

'There were others.'

'Yes.'

'And Wren took part in all of them?'

'It was his idea. People think I lead, but I follow too, just like Wade.'

Vanessa glared at him. 'Don't try to get out of this, 'cos I heard you. You were laughing. *Laughing.*'

'What do you want?'

'I want to make a deal,' she said, her voice hard, her eyes even harder. 'I'll keep the recording safe, but you have to swear that you'll never reveal Wren's involvement in any of the incidents. If you do, the recording is emailed to the police straight away. Got it?'

'Sure.'

'Three questions.'

'Yeah?'

'Who undid Wren's seatbelt?'

'How—'

'How did I know about that? I heard it, you moron. Who was it?'

'It was me.' He stared at her in defiance. She slapped him across the face so hard he fell onto the couch.

'How did you know the airbag wasn't going to go off?'

Justin looked on the verge of tears. 'It was faulty when I got it – we never got round to having it fixed. Figured it might come in handy one day.'

'Why did you hit the tree? You could have killed yourself and Wade. Don't get me wrong, I wouldn't have mourned you, but how were you to know for sure?'

'I didn't. I thought my life was over so I'd see if I could take Wren with me. I lined up the tree to hit his side, undid his seatbelt knowing that the airbag wouldn't go off. And it worked. He died and we didn't.'

Vanessa strode over to him and he shrank back into the couch, probably thinking that she was going to slap him again. Instead, she kicked his damaged leg. He screamed in pain.

'You don't keep up your end of the bargain, I will ruin you, you and Wade, so fill him in too. Wren's name stays out of it all. Got it?'

He was openly crying now, snot leaking from his nose, holding his leg.

'Are we clear?'

'Yes! Yes!'

Vanessa gave him a brittle smile that felt odd on her lips. Her whole perspective had changed. The world was not as it seemed. Wren was not as he seemed. Had she ever really known him? Had he ever really loved her? So many questions. It was hurting her head. She wanted to cry but found that she was out of tears, just like she was out of fucks. She had solved the mystery, but at what cost? He wasn't depressed, he was worried. Worried that Olivia would tell, that his involvement would come out. Then after she died, he was trying to distance himself from those he considered anchors, her included.

It hurt, Christ did it hurt, but now she knew the truth. But truth or no truth, Wren was still her son and she'd protect his memory till her dying breath. She drove home and sat in the car for a few moments, collecting herself. She looked at herself in the rear-view mirror. Eyes hollow and dry lips set in a thin line, a mask of rage on her face. She tried to calm down, but she was in shock. Her Wren had never existed, or if he did, the goodness had been burned out of him long ago.

She walked through the back door through the kitchen and into the lounge room. Billy and Ty were sitting on the couch watching TV.

Billy looked up at her, seeing the weird look in her eyes, the paleness of her face. 'Ness, you OK?'

Ty looked up too.

'Billy, I'm sorry.'

'What for?' he asked tentatively.

'For the way I've acted. You've been nothing but patient with me. Please don't leave me.'

He stood up and hugged her to him, crushed her to him really. 'I'm not going anywhere. Right, Ty?'

'Right.' Ty came over to hug her, but she stopped him. Vanessa got on her knees in front of him and gently grasped his arms. 'I owe you the biggest apology of all. I haven't been there for you when you needed me. You lost Wren too.' She swallowed hard at the mention of his name. 'I want you to know that I will always protect you, no matter what you do.' She gently hugged him and felt the tears well up within her, spilling down her cheeks. She sobbed; her head bent. Billy grasped her under her arms, lifted her up and wrapped his strong arms around the two of them.

It was finally over.

ACKNOWLEDGMENTS

I'd like to thank my mum, for always supporting me no matter what, for showing me how to be a strong female and for teaching me the lessons of compassion and empathy.

To my family and friends who have supported not only my writing career but me in general. I know I can be an intense handful at times, your love means so much to me. I don't know where I'd be without it.

To my wonderful betas, I appreciate you more than you know, you are an awesome bunch.

I'd also like to thank the team at Boldwood Books for taking a chance on me and my book, Amanda, Nia, Sarah, thank you so much. As well as Rebecca and Candida, thank you for polishing my baby. You've all played an important role in getting me to where I am today, and I appreciate the heck out of you.

And finally, to you, my readers. Thank you from the bottom of my heart for reading Never Ever Tell. I have many more books in me, so stick with me and I'll take you to the dark places that you'd normally fear to tread. Don't worry, I'll hold your hand.

Kirsty x

MORE FROM KIRSTY FERGUSON

We hope you enjoyed reading *Never Ever Tell*. If you did, please leave a review.

If you'd like to gift a copy, this book is also available as an ebook, digital audio download and audiobook CD.

Sign up to Kirsty Ferguson's mailing list for news, competitions and updates on future books.

https://bit.ly/KirstyFergusonNewsletter

ABOUT THE AUTHOR

Kirsty Ferguson is an Australian crime writer whose domestic noir stories centre around strong women and dark topical themes. Kirsty enjoys photography, visiting haunted buildings and spending time with her son.

Visit Kirsty's website: https://www.kirstyferguson.com

Follow Kirsty on social media:

- twitter.com/kfergusonauthor
- instagram.com/kirstyfergusonauthor
- facebook.com/authorkirstyferguson
- bookbub.com/authors/kirsty-ferguson

ABOUT BOLDWOOD BOOKS

Boldwood Books is a fiction publishing company seeking out the best stories from around the world.

Find out more at www.boldwoodbooks.com

Sign up to the Book and Tonic newsletter for news, offers and competitions from Boldwood Books!

http://www.bit.ly/bookandtonic

We'd love to hear from you, follow us on social media:

facebook.com/BookandTonic

twitter.com/BoldwoodBooks

instagram.com/BookandTonic

Lightning Source UK Ltd.
Milton Keynes UK
UKHW021021210820
368606UK00016B/1193

9 781800 481527